Sunshine and Rain

a *City Limits* Novel

MJ
Embrace the panther.

m. mabie

Editing by Lori Sabin
Book formatting by Stacey Blake, Champagne Formats

ISBN-13: 978-1539653097
ISBN-10: 1539653099

Other Books
by m. mabie

Fade In

The Wake Series
Bait
Sail
Anchor

The Wake Family
Knot

The City Limits Series
Roots and Wings

Coming Soon
The Very Second Time
Tide

For the timeless Gretchen Mabie, our matriarch.

Chapter One

Sunny

"Do you think you'll see him again?" my mom asked over the phone.

Her voice was a gentle nudge indicating she hoped I would. I'd been out on a third pseudo-date with a guy named Mike the week before. As far as dates went, they'd been *okay*, but I wasn't feeling it.

Again.

"I don't know, Mom. He's nice, but there's no spark. No chemistry." I was a dating veteran and probably jaded in my ripe old age of twenty-eight.

Was it too much to want that telltale gut feeling like you'd been startled by fate? Was it too much to expect a special something to come to life when you were around a guy?

Lately, it seemed so.

"Honey, I don't mean to be the bearer of bad news, but

you're knocking on thirty. I love you, but you're the pickiest girl I've ever known. When are you going to realize sometimes love takes a while? You never give anyone a chance."

Watching the timer tick down the seconds on the last song I had programmed before I'd be back on the air, I had a sinking feeling.

Maybe she was right.

I'd been out with dozens of guys in the past few years, and each time I found something wrong with them. It wasn't that they weren't great guys. Most of them—aside from the few bad apples—were good men. Regardless of whether it lasted one date or a few months, either the guy or I would break things off. I think it was about split down the middle, though.

Half the time, I'd give him my *I think you're a really nice guy, but I'm just not looking for a serious relationship right now* talk, which was always a lie, and we'd part as friends. I *was* looking for a serious relationship—actively—but, coupled with that, I was looking for someone who I'd actually *enjoy* growing old with. Someone who pushed my buttons and, frankly, really turned me on. None of those things were happening.

On the flip side, sometimes they just kind of lost interest in me, which never hurt my feelings, and the calls would simply stop. Then, I'd move on.

Nothing dramatic, but sadly, my relationship status was predictable and not looking like it was going to change anytime soon. Especially if I continued on the way I had been.

I was single—or I wasn't too far off from it, considering I still had Mike on the line. *Technically*. Seriously though, he wasn't busting down doors to see me either. There was no urgency, which made it feel so boring.

The facts were: I was getting older, and most of my friends were either already paired off, married, having babies, or at least settled down.

I wanted that for myself, but life in a small town is already pretty predictable. I wanted to feel that rush of excitement when I met *The One*. The One who'd make me forget there were only 3,400 people in my life because I was the most important one—*to him*. I wanted my love life to be something extraordinary. It didn't have to look that way to anyone else, just me.

Maybe I was a hopeless romantic. Emphasis on the pathetically *hopeless*.

As months tore off the calendar and I attended weddings and showers, everyone's lives changed. Except mine. I was still single.

Was my mother right? Had I set the love and romance in a small town bar too high? Maybe what I was looking for wasn't really out there, aside from sappy love songs and chick flicks.

"I don't know. I *might* keep seeing him," I relented knowing she was partially right, but she wasn't seeing my point of view at all. She'd married my dad when she was twenty-one. What did she know about dating *or* being single for any real stretch of time?

In the instance of time, there wasn't enough for me to get into it with her that morning. She'd bring it up again, sooner than later, and I had work to do.

I needed to focus on my programming for the rest of the weekend, and it was already almost noon on Saturday. If I wanted to get out of the radio station, I had to get my ass in gear. To ease out of the subject, and ultimately off the phone, I acquiesced. "If I don't hear from him first, I'll probably call in a few days and see if he wants to do something."

"That's my girl. Give it a chance." My mom's voice had changed into encouragement mode, which was better than listen-to-your-mother mode. Besides, she didn't have to bring up my age. I wasn't knocking on thirty. I was only twenty-eight, dammit.

God, that *sounded* a lot like knocking though.

"Okay, I've gotta get back to work. I'll talk to you tomorrow."

"All right, Sunny. Be careful if you go out tonight."

"I will. Love you."

"Love you," she replied and hung up. I had seconds to go and I slipped my headphones back over my ears, clicked on a few songs to add to the next block of music, and came in right on time.

"Good morning, Wynne-ers. It's Saturday, and I feel like getting my dancing shoes on. One of your local favorites is performing at Sally's Tap tonight. Boots and Barflies will play from eight to midnight.

"I wasn't able to make it to the field last night—I noticed the rain stopped, which was a pleasant surprise—but I want to say a big congratulations to all of our Wynne High School graduates. While the skies were clear last night of rain—*which has sadly returned with a vengeance today*—I heard from a reliable source that Coach Fry's yard got a Charmin Extra-Soft kind of visit in the wee hours. My source also said she saw which cars pulled away about three this morning. So y'all better head over to her neighbor's and start cleaning up. God, it's going to be a mess, but I'd do it quickly if I were you. That old bird has a big beak and likes to squawk to anyone who'll listen—*Hi, Mom*."

I clicked my mouse to add a few more songs and rubbed my foot over the hairy dog lying at my feet, then continued. "And before I roll you into another sixty-minute block of your favorite country here on WDKR, I'd like to pass on a Baby Renfro update. I know a lot of us here in town are thinking about them. Hannah and Vaughn are doing just fine and baby Sawyer is getting bigger every day. They might get to come home Monday, and we all hope they do. The Renfros wanted me to pass along how much they've appreciated everyone's love and prayers since Sawyer came a little earlier than expected, but asked me to remind everyone that she's still really small and working on getting stronger. They'd like to keep visits to a minimum when they first get home—at least for a few weeks until they get settled. They can't wait for everyone to meet her." I finished with the next block, adding some old standards and local favorites. Then, as cued, the first song began to play as I sent out my familiar call.

"Now how about a little music? As always, keep that dial right here on FM 98.5, like you have a choice."

They didn't. WDKR was the only thing you could pick up between here and Browning.

I swiveled on my seat, switching feet to rub my dog, Andy, and pulled up the new playlist I'd built the night before while I ate a bowl of cereal for dinner. Then I programmed some of my new favorites into the weekend mix that I'd already partially planned for later.

It wouldn't take me long to line out the next day or so,

then I could head over to Hannah and Vaughn's. Her dad and our friend, Dean, were putting the last of their furniture together for them, and I'd told the guys I'd stop by with my woman's touch when I finished work for the weekend.

The last thing my best friend and her husband needed to worry about was putting furniture together, considering they'd spent the better part of the last month at the hospital with a very tiny baby girl. All they needed to concentrate on was getting some sleep, *in their own bed*, with their first child under their roof for the first time—as one complete family.

I finished and made sure everything was loaded on my computer, then shut down the overhead lights in the four-room radio station where my grandparents worked together for over forty years, and locked up.

I didn't usually *lock* up, but this year's class of graduates were pranksters. I didn't need to leave myself wide open for trouble, especially after I all but ousted them by name on the air that morning. They were good kids. I wasn't sure if they'd retaliate or not, but I was prepared. Just in case.

After letting Andy back into my house, which sat behind the station, I ran to my red Honda Civic. The sprinkles from earlier had turned into an all-out downpour. I was sick of the rain and pretty sure everyone else was, too.

I drove the few miles into town and pulled up under the awning at the truck stop so I wouldn't get drenched, then ran in.

"Hey, Sunny," called Donnie from the other side, mopping up the wet floor by the other door nearest the diesel pumps. "It's raining buckets."

I headed for the cooler and answered, "I know and it's

only supposed to get worse. If up north gets as much as they're predicting, we'll probably flood." It wasn't a new thing for Wynne—every ten years or so we had a serious flood. The town wasn't in danger too much, but many houses and farms sat in the flood plain. They would be in harm's way if a levee failed. I, along with the entire town, prayed major flooding wouldn't happen, but it looked like it might anyway.

"That's what Dub said at the coffee shop this morning. What a shame. Let's just pray it doesn't come to that. So, that baby's finally coming home then?" He looked up and propped his hands on top of the mop.

Sawyer Renfro had been born about eight weeks early. She was in much better shape than she had been, but still a preemie. Wynne was a small town and not afraid to pull together for one of its own—no matter how little or new the resident. Nearly everyone I ran into asked about her since I'd been her mother's friend for a long, long time.

"I think so. Hannah said since she was gaining weight like they'd hoped, they're thinking they might get to come home on Monday."

"Well, good. If that Sawyer is anything like her momma, she's tough as nails. She'll probably be ornery as all hell, too."

I laughed. He was probably right. "You can count on that, Donnie," I said.

Pulling a case of beer from the cooler, I packed it to the counter. The bell rang over the door, and I looked over my shoulder to see who it was.

Tall.

Jeans.

Ball cap pulled low.

Wet t-shirt, tight across a muscular chest.

Whoa. I swallowed.

He nodded, but I couldn't see his face. I wasn't much for dating Wynne guys—I'd exhausted the available age appropriate population years ago—but I knew everything there was to know about the crop of men in the area, and this stud wasn't registering.

Donnie rounded the counter and stood at the register as I looked in the big, round security mirror hanging in the corner, trying to be sneaky, and watching for a quick glimpse of the man who was taking his time at the cooler in back.

The ass in those jeans was squeezable. *Hell, biteable.*

He was probably just passing through. Dammit.

I'd never get lucky like my best friend, Hannah. New, hot men in Wynne were like Halley's Comet: they only came around once in a lifetime. At least one of us caught the last one.

Donnie rang up the beer and said, "Nineteen thirty."

I opened my wallet to fish out money as he looked over my shoulder to talk to the man who was then standing behind me.

"Rhett, are you old enough to be buying that?"

My stomach dropped. *Rhett?* Like *little* Rhett Caraway?

Little. Rhett. Caraway.

I spun on my heel; the notion was just too crazy to believe.

I looked up his long torso, then side to side over his broad shoulders. My jaw hung open. There was no fucking way in small town hell *that* was Rhett Caraway, the young boy who used to follow me around like a little lost puppy.

"Sunshine." His voice was low and completely different from when we were younger, yet something about it was still the same. He didn't make eye contact with me, and tucked his head. *Sunshine.*

I quickly turned around when Donnie coughed, and I took the change he was holding out for me. The old pot-bellied gas station attendant's smart-ass grin teetered from mocking to teasing.

Son of a bitch.

I'd lost my fucking mind. There was no damn way. It wasn't possible.

I grabbed the case of bottles off the counter and damn near toppled over the rack of maps and postcards.

The guy's—*Rhett Caraway's*—large arm came up to steady me but stopped just short of actually touching my side, and I successfully dodged him like the round plastic balls we'd averted in gym class.

Yuck. I felt like such a pervert.

That couldn't be him. He was just a kid.

I raced to my car, throwing the beer in the back seat. Then I got in and drove off, heading down the hill to town.

What the hell?

I was twenty-eight.

Twenty-*fucking*-eight. *Knocking on thirty,* as my sweet mother had reminded me earlier.

My mind was running like a striped-ass ape.

Get your shit together, Sunny. You just perved out on a damn seventh grader.

But, he didn't look like a seventh grader anymore. That was for damn sure.

My heart was pounding like I'd just missed hitting a deer by a thread. Guiltily, I looked into the rearview mirror as if he could see me or hear my thoughts.

If seventh graders looked like *that*, then what the hell did I look like? *Ew.*

I tried to force myself to do the quick math, but my head hurt and I couldn't focus on anything except his body. Then, I almost gagged thinking about how gross I was. I could be on *To Catch a Predator* with that Chris Hansen guy.

When I got to the stop sign across from the town square, I tried to calm down. Placing both of my hands on my forehead, I took a deep breath.

"Get your shit together, Sunny. He was buying beer, too. That couldn't have been the same Rhett. It's impossible. You're ridiculous." But, I knew it was him.

I didn't even care about the rain when I pulled up behind Darrell's truck, which was parked in his daughter's driveway. I got out and walked, totally zoned out. When I reached the porch, I sat down on the stoop and opened the case. Pulling out a cold bottle, I took a long drink and downed about half the beer.

Little kids are old now? I wanted to cry.

Up until recently, I'd still felt like I was twenty-one. Fuck. Most of the time, I still acted like I was twenty-one. Proven more by the fact—it wasn't even three o'clock and I was already drinking my first Saturday beer.

Sunny, grow up.

I was on my best friend's porch, a girl who I never saw getting married and starting a family. Well—as bitchy as it sounded—at least not *before* me.

God. What in the actual fuck was going on? It was all hitting me at once, like when I finally figured out the twist in *Fight Club*. I'd been tricked, sucker punched by time.

"Hey, Sunny." I heard Darrell behind me through the screen door. "Whatcha doin' out there, dummy?"

What *was* I doing? Fuck, everyone else's life was moving forward, and I was still the same old Sunny Wilbanks. Single. Working at my family's radio station. *Knocking the hell out of a thirty-year-old door.*

"I'm old as fuck, Darrell, and I'm having a beer about it," I droned.

He chuckled, then answered in time with the door squeaking as he stepped out to join me. "I'm a long-time member of that club. Pass me one of those." He took a seat next to me on the wet stoop, then yelled, "Dean, get your ass out here. We're having a front porch pity party for Sunny. She just realized she's as old as shit."

Even through the dust knocked up by my epic freak out, I laughed. Darrell O'Fallon was like an uncle to me and the biggest jackass I knew, but he somehow always had a way of making me feel better.

I whined, "Stop. This is serious." I'm sure I wasn't the first twenty-eight-year-old single female who felt like I did. It was just a first *for me.*

I had just creeped on a seventh grader for fuck's sake.

Dean came out and took a seat on the wooden porch swing behind us, and Darrell handed him a brew. He took a long swig of it and asked, "So who told you you were old?"

Were there assholes who actually did that?

"No one."

He gave me a skeptical head nod, his bullshit sensing

eyebrow cocked.

"No one *had* to tell me. I got smacked in the face by it at the truck stop." I finished my beer and grabbed another. My current reality check was no doubt going to get me shitfaced.

He leaned back in the swing, waiting for me to elaborate. I flicked my bottle cap at him, then admitted, "I just saw Rhett Caraway up there."

He choked on his drink and a howl came from him, causing his leg to fly up and meet his open palm as he proceeded to laugh his ass off—*at me.* "Oh my God. That's perfect. Think he'll tag the water tower with Rhett loves Sunny again?"

That wasn't funny. He'd gotten in trouble for it.

"Shut up. I doubt he'll be doing that again." I'm sure he was well over his schoolboy crush on me. The way he looked, I was sure he had plenty of girls to chase who didn't turn him down like I did all through my high school years.

We'd been too far apart in age back then. *Way* too far.

What Dean said jogged the memory for Darrell too because then he was snickering as well.

The old jerk teased, "I forgot about that. He had it bad for you, girl. Poor boy. You wouldn't even give him a sniff."

"Gross! He was in seventh grade. *I was a senior.* Come on, dude. That's not cool." I kicked his leg. "Be nice."

He raised his hands in the air defensively, but the whole situation brought back a couple of memories for me, too.

Chapter Two

Rhett

"Hurry up, Caraway. You're going to get in so much trouble, man," Lucas, my best friend, yelled up at me from where he stood on the ground.

I was probably going to get in a hell of a lot of trouble, but I didn't care. She'd see it, and then she'd get it. I wasn't going to quit until she was mine.

I shook the can of yellow spray paint and finished what I'd climbed all the way up the Wynne water tower to do, which—by the way—had nothing to do with chickening out.

This time she'd know I was serious.

I'd tried to make her see over and over, but nothing got her attention. Not candy. Not letters. Not words. But, this … she couldn't ignore this.

Nobody could.

Just as I finished with the Y on her name, I heard the whoop-whoop of the squad car.

The lane was muddy as all hell, and I had to drive through the grass in the middle to make sure I didn't get stuck in a rut. I stopped at the shed near my cabin to make sure the doors were closed. The whole drive was a mess, and it just kept raining.

As I'd expected, the lake-sized puddle was growing closer and closer to creeping inside the building. Around back, I left my truck running while I jumped out and ran over to pull the door securely shut.

The weather sucked, but it would be a good night to sit on the back porch, listen to the rain and the radio, drink, and try to pretend Sunny Wilbanks didn't look as good as she ever did.

I knew I'd run into her sometime or another, but I hadn't expected her to look that surprised to see me. Almost like she didn't recognize who I was.

She probably still saw me as that little punk kid who was always bugging her. Always embarrassing her.

I couldn't really blame her, but she wouldn't have to worry about that any longer. I wasn't a twelve-year-old with a crush anymore.

I was a man, just back home from college, who had no desire to get turned down by that girl—not even one more time. Turned down by anyone, for that matter. I had a much different approach to women than I'd had in those days.

I couldn't help but feel a little pride, though, as her eyes gave me a thorough once over at the truck stop. She might have still looked the same, but I didn't. Years of conditioning and strength training had transformed me. Yeah, I'd been a farm kid, so I'd always been strong, but I was in the best shape of my life and I knew I'd changed a lot since the last time she saw me.

Running made sure of that.

It was something I started when I was a young boy, one who was still years away from a driver's license, and needed to get a letter—or whatever it was on that particular day—to a girl. So, I'd run it to her house. That same running turned me into a high school state champion runner, then a collegiate track career that paid for damn near all of my education.

Before returning to Wynne for planting season, I actually placed in both marathons I competed in. All of that juvenile girl chasing led this small town boy to places all over the nation and a few other countries, but I still always knew I'd find my way right back to my hometown.

The last time she saw me I was a lovesick kid. Regardless, I was an adult, and not so damn lovesick anymore.

She was right all those years ago—after I got caught, paint in hand, her senior year—to tell me what she had. I could still remember the way she looked when Officer Long called her down to talk to me as I waited for my mom and dad to pick me up.

"Rhett Caraway, you have to stop this. I'm about to go off to college, and you're not even in high school yet. I think you're sweet—*I really do*—but you need to get over this crush."

Fearlessly and unshaken by the trouble I was in, I'd confessed, "But I love you, Sunny."

Her blond hair fell off her shoulder as she turned to

look at me with the prettiest blue eyes I'd ever looked into.

"I know you do, but I can't love you back. And you deserve to give all of that love to someone who can. You wait until some girl starts chasing *you*, Rhett. Let her send *you* love notes, leave *you* gifts, and call *you* on the phone. Then, hold her hand. Let her call the station and request songs for *you*. Then, kiss her. Hell, let her spray paint the hell out of the water tower with your name and hers. Then, marry her. When the right one comes along, she won't tell you no like I do. She'll love all of your sweetness and your gifts. She'll appreciate you, just the way you are."

Damn if she wasn't right all those years ago—I didn't have to chase girls anymore. Especially one who didn't want chased.

I told myself all of this, but I still turned the old radio to WDKR and listened to her electric voice that evening. It did the same thing to me as it did all those years ago. Made my heart pound faster. Made me feel queasy and reckless at the same time, but maturity helped me keep those things to myself. As a man, I had restraint, control … qualities I hadn't possessed as a boy.

I wouldn't ever be that crazy kid chasing the high school cheerleader again, but I couldn't help but wonder if she still looked as good in her game skirt as she did a decade ago.

Sure she did, and I bet she looked even better out of it.

Back then, she'd been taller than me, but I towered over her now.

Her perfect ass probably fit in the palm of my hands.

Back then, I wouldn't have had a clue what to do with a girl like her if I'd actually gotten her, but time changed many things. Because I sure as hell would know now.

It wasn't the healthiest thing to do, but I let my mind wander all over the place in the privacy of my back porch. Thinking about a gorgeous blond and the dumbfounded expression on her face when she laid eyes on *me*.

It was quite a bit later when I looked at my phone, hearing a door shut out front. It was just past seven thirty and getting dark early because of the overcast. My younger sister Haley yelled, "Rhett, you here?"

"Yeah. Back porch."

The cabin didn't have a water view, although the river wasn't far, but if it kept raining it would get much closer. However, it did have a view of one of the fields I'd planted that year. My dad before me. My grandpa before him.

I was a runner and an athlete, but I had dirt under my skin. A farmer. One day all of that land, and hopefully more, would be mine, and I'd run Caraway Farms like my family had for generations.

"I brought you some spaghetti leftovers. Mom made too much. God, it is weird being back in that house." Haley was only a few years younger than me, and a freshman at State back home for her first summer break. At nineteen going on twenty, coming back to Wynne for the summer wasn't nearly as exciting after being in the city.

"Want a beer?" I offered. I was twenty-three, and that's what big brothers did. Especially one who wasn't having the best time drinking alone, but probably wasn't very good company for anyone else.

"I'll have *one*, but I'm going to Smiths' for a while."

Luke Smith had been my best friend since I was born, and his younger sister was Haley's best friend, too. It wasn't that uncommon for there to be a party on their property.

It used to be us high school kids, then it was on weekends when we'd be back from school, and now it was mostly our younger siblings and their friends. Until the bars closed, then everyone and their dog would be there.

Literally. It wasn't uncommon for people to *actually* bring their dogs.

"So, what are you doing back here? You look like Dad pouting at the rain. He's on the back porch at the farm doing the same thing."

That didn't surprise me, but I was grateful for some space. Thank God, I was staying at the small hunting lodge my family owned a few miles away from them, instead of up at the farm house.

It was probably just the rain that had my dad in a mood. He was stressed about the weather, but he'd come out of it. We all knew there was nothing we could do about it.

My attitude had been pretty bleak lately, too. Working ground on a shitty year was stressful for men like us.

"It's just quiet back here," I said, just as the music stopped and we heard a familiar voice come through the speaker.

"Keep that dial right there, Wynne. We've got another sixty minutes of non-stop country. Just how you like it … all night long … on WDKR." Her voice tickled my chest and made me smile when I heard her say "all night long."

That voice could call me for dinner any night of the week. To hell with it, I'd eat six times, then ask for sevenths.

And I wasn't on my own—the whole town loved her. She was *their* Sunny Wilbanks, small town celebrity. I'd only been back for a few weeks, but I'd already picked up on a few things regarding her.

Not that I'd asked anyone anything about Sunny, but her name just happened to come up everywhere I went. I'd heard it all.

"Have you seen Sunny?"

"She's doing real good, Rhett. Looks real good."

"She's single, you know."

Then the ladies would get dreamy, and the men would punch me in the shoulder and give me a look that made me almost deck a lot of them on her behalf. They'd been partly joking, and partly: "I'd love a swing at that Sunny Wilbanks myself."

There was no one to blame for their behavior but me. I'd been an obnoxious kid. A pain in the ass, always going on and on, never knowing when to shut up about her.

When people would mention her, I'd nod and keep to myself. Honestly, I didn't want to talk about Sunny Wilbanks anymore. I'd embarrassed her enough when I was a child.

The dust would eventually settle and it would go away on its own. That's how things worked in a small town. I just had to pretend and wait it out.

Listening to the next song, a modern version of an old favorite we'd never heard before, Haley and I silently acknowledged it was pretty kick ass, especially for a small town station.

It was Saturday night and, historically, when Sunny would play *her* favorites. I doubted many people listened to the radio on Saturday nights, but I always liked it. No one would notice if it was country that stretched out of the normal two-stepping favorites.

Being in the city and coming back, I recognized that

she was a damn good deejay. My opinion wasn't biased anymore. It was a fact that she was fun to listen to, and whatever her choices were, she played great songs. Classic country standards Monday through Friday from eight to five. Then she'd mix in edgier, newer music on nights and weekends.

The leather boot I wore tapped along to the beat.

My sister cocked her head to the side and her light-brown braid swung onto her shoulder. Her pursed lips and arched eyebrow told me she had an opinion but wouldn't let me have it until I asked for it—which I didn't *want* to do.

Knowing she wouldn't drop it, I asked, "You gonna chew on that or spit it out?"

She sighed and rolled her eyes. "Listening to the radio, Rhett?"

Was this whole town crazy? Haley had that same dreamy, closed mouth grin the women in Wynne all shared.

It was the *only* radio station, but, by default, it had to mean I was chasing Sunny Wilbanks. Not just listening to the music—*like I was.*

I shook my head and kept my mouth shut, prepared for her to have her fun. For the unrelenting reminders of how I publicly made myself look like an ass as a kid, all because of some silly crush I had on the blond cheerleader.

Soon I had my fill of her giggles and boot kicks, and I snapped back at her.

"Haley. Knock it off."

She shook her head but dropped it. "*Fine.* Why don't you come to Smiths' with me?"

I leaned my head against the wall behind the cheap lawn chair I'd found in the shed. "And hang out with all of your underage friends in a machine shop and drink cheap beer from a warm keg? No, thanks."

A clap of thunder interrupted us, and I noticed the wind had picked up and the rain intensified since my sister arrived.

She urged, "You know it'll be fun."

It might be, but I was perfectly content where I was. Okay, maybe not content *exactly*, but it wouldn't be the same at my best friend's house without him there.

Luke probably wasn't ever coming back to Wynne. And, that weekend, he was on a trip to Cozumel with his girlfriend, Brittany, where he was proposing after three years of dating. He was out of school, had a great job, and was ready to take the next step. I was happy for him.

Although I was glad to be home, where I'd always pictured myself being after college, I wondered if the time for finding a girl of my own had passed.

The pickings in Wynne weren't great. Well, there *were* exceptions—notably one out-of-my-league sexy, blond disc jockey.

I guessed it was as it should be anyway. Not only was I suffering from a condition where everyone I saw acted like my boner was hanging out of my pants and my tongue was dragging the ground trying to get with their golden girl, but it was raining non-stop. Even if the rain took it easy on us over the next week, if up north got much more, we'd be flooding and I'd be busy as hell.

Needless to say, things weren't really going that great for a single farmer with a healthy sex drive in Wynne so far that summer. And, despite the inches of precipitation my land was getting, my options for something physical, in the short term, had all but dried up. It wasn't wise to sleep around in a small town.

The only thing not getting wet in Wynne was my dick.

I shook my head. "You go. Call me if you need a ride, though. Those roads are probably washed out in spots." I didn't want her to drink and drive, *period*, but I especially didn't want her driving through water-worn, back gravel roads—drinking or not.

"Oh, I'll probably just stay there."

Lightning streaked the sky over the field, and I waited for the thunder to roll before I asked, "Wanna take my truck?" It sat higher and had better tires than her little Jeep.

She tipped back her beer, then answered, "That's sweet, but no. I'll be fine. I know the roads pretty well." I supposed she knew them about as well as I did, we'd both grown up on them. Besides, I'd seen her drive machinery worth much more than this little cabin, like a pro.

"Call if you change your mind. I'll be here."

I opened up another beer and took a drink.

She kicked my foot again as the song changed to a slower one from last summer. "Rhett, if you want, I can hang out here."

I swallowed and considered it. She would want to *talk*, though, and there was nothing I wanted to talk about. Sitting alone, listening to the rain, with my thoughts and old fantasies, I'd be just fine.

"No, thanks," I answered.

"Well, that just hurts. You didn't have to be so sure about it." Haley was giving me shit, and I knew she wanted to see her friends.

I fired back. "Don't be butt-hurt, Hay. I don't have enough beer for the both of us." At the rate I was putting them back, that was true.

After flipping me off, she picked up the empty bottles and tossed them in the garbage can. “Don’t be stupid. I have my own cooler and it’s full. I am a Caraway, too, remember?” She was and a damn good baby sister. Standing there in her muck boots and jeans, nails painted, with a hot pink bottle koozie, she was a perfect mix of my dad and mom, the farmer and the beautician.

“I’ll see you tomorrow,” I said and turned up the radio.

She knocked my ball cap off and walked back through the house. As she hit the front door, I heard through the open windows. “Seriously, Rhett. Don’t you have a fucking iPod though?”

I did, but to hell with it. I was content, listening to WDKR and entertaining my imagination with an old friend.

Chapter Three

Sunny

"One more, and I'm done," I hollered at Dean from down the bar. Soon, Sally would be giving us last call.

Dean was getting up early the next day to ride to the hospital with Darrell, but he liked the band. So, he'd told me he wouldn't drink much then drive me home.

"Whatever, you old cow," he shouted back.

There were only a few people in town who treated me like an actual person. Even in a small town, when you're in the public eye—or ear—they seemed to have a little more gumption to say whatever they liked to your face. I was used to it, though. Besides, I *was* an old cow—at least that's what I'd told pretty much everyone I'd seen all night. The *drunk* old cow I was.

I didn't want to be the old chick at the bar, dammit.

I looked around, and I wasn't the oldest by far, but I was

one of only two women around my age who were there *and single.* BethAnne didn't count though because she was a ho.

I'd thought about my earlier conversation with my mother all night. I bet my mom *loved* that I was considering another boring-ass date with Mike. He lived in Gilbert, another small town about twenty minutes away. But, he'd had a graduation party; otherwise, he probably would have come over for the band. Either way, we weren't at that point where you always called to confirm rendezvous points.

That night I felt old and damn near desperate, and that was no fucking good.

I didn't want to be the old chick.

I *wanted* to be the love-drunk twenty-one-year-old who'd danced all night then rode her boyfriend piggyback out of the bar about half an hour earlier. Now *she* was having fun.

God, I craved something like that. A relationship with a thrill. Something spontaneous. With arguments and hot as hell make up sex. I wanted laughing and lounging, staying up and sleeping in with a guy who was my best friend.

Basically, I was drunk, delusional and tiptoeing into a sad place where drunk girls cry for silly reasons. But, seriously, how had I missed the pivotal step that everyone else had seemed to fall right into?

Quickly, I realized I didn't need any more beer.

"Wait. I'll take a Coke for the road," I told Sally.

She looked at me funny. There was a party out at Smiths' farm, not far from my station and house, which I would typically hit. Yet, I just didn't feel up to it.

"Dollar," she said and slid it over to me. "Dean driving you home?"

I loved that old gal. She'd driven me home a few times. Not that I was a drunk or anything, but when you're single in a small town, there's just not a lot to do on the weekends. I wasn't about to wreck or get a ticket. I always returned the favor on her few and far between weekends off.

"Yep, we're heading out now."

She looked down at Dean and he shrugged when he caught her eye.

Dean was such an old soul. I may have considered him as dating material at one time, but he'd been hung up on Hannah since we were kids. At our current ages, it would have been like kissing my dad. He mostly hung out with the old guys in town, and although he was a great guy, he didn't do it for me. *Surprise, surprise.*

I didn't do it for him either. Earlier that night, he'd told me my dancing looked like a frog on a hot sidewalk. Then he'd told me he was running home to poop—but he'd be back.

We were definitely *just* friends. To hell with it, we got along and were in the same damn boat. Up until that day I'd thought of us as the "loners," but I'd been wrong. We were the *old* "loners."

"Let's go, Dean-O," I said and we left.

He drove slowly to miss the places where the water was standing on the road.

"Is it ever going to stop raining?" I asked.

"God, I hope so. We went down this morning and pulled out Hannah's boat and dock. They say the river is going up, but they have no idea about a true crest yet."

Living in a river town, we were all used to it. There was a minor flood about every few years, but this had already changed from minor to something more serious. The ARMY Corps of Engineers had already checked levees and hauled in the first of many truckloads of sand for bagging into the bank's parking lot.

"You need your car in the morning?" Dean asked.

"I'll probably go to Mom's for lunch. She can pick me up. I'll get it then."

"Okay, that works," he said as he pulled into my long drive, past the station, and up to my little brick ranch house. "Oh shit, Sunny. Looks like you lost a pretty good limb over there." I looked out his side of the Cherokee and saw what he was talking about. It was hard to tell, but there was definitely a lot of brush. "Damn. There's another one up there on the station roof, too," he added.

It was difficult to see through the rain, but the security light showed there was some damage. I turned the volume up on his radio and nothing came out over the airwaves.

"*Fuck*." I was really winning.

"Do you want me to check it out?" he asked, but it was still coming down like a cow pissing on a flat rock out there.

If we'd lost power, the security light would have been out. It had to be an antenna issue, and I didn't have a clue what I was going to do about it. Good thing the town electrician had been working on our old radio station as long as we'd been on the air.

"Nah, nothing we can do tonight. I'll get on it in the morning."

I mentally added it to a long shitty list. I was old as fuck. The town kids weren't kids anymore. There was basically a whole tree laying over in my yard, from what I could tell. I was probably going to keep seeing Mike, the *just* okay guy. And my radio station was fucked.

Not a good day for Sunny Wilbanks.

"Text me pictures of Sawyer tomorrow," I reminded him for the third time before I got out.

He groaned, my repetition annoying him, and replied, "I will. Let me know if you need anything. Help cleaning up or whatever."

"Oh, I'll have my dad do it," I said as I hopped straight into a mud puddle, soaking straight through my shoe. *Perfect.* "Night, Dean."

"Later," he said as he put the SUV in reverse and backed out of my driveway, slowly studying my mess.

After washing my face and brushing my teeth, I hopped into a tank top and shorts. Then, I crawled into my bed with Andy and flipped the TV onto the music channel.

Tomorrow would be a better day … although, I didn't really believe it.

"Mom, it's freaking huge. I need to get it cleaned up so Eddie can come look at the antenna," I explained to her over the phone the next morning.

I wasn't the only one who had damage. There were a few trees down in town, too. The ground was so saturated, and the wind gusts we'd had the night before were just enough to uproot a big tree between my parents' and the Frys' houses.

"He'll be out there when he can, hon. It's a mess here, too. A lot of the tree is in the driveway, Sunny. He can't leave until he gets that moved out of the way first."

She'd sent me pictures. I knew there was nothing they could do for me at the moment. They couldn't even come get me to help them with their garage blocked by the tree. And I couldn't drive into town because I'd left my car at the bar.

It was what it was.

I gave Andy a scratch behind his ear and told her, "Okay, I'll go do what I can and just wait."

Eddie, the electrician, told me he'd be out when he could get to it, but a few people in town were without power and he was going to try to get them back on before he headed my way. It wouldn't be until later anyway.

Andy and I had already done a walk around to see what was damaged. Luckily, it was just a smaller limb that had fallen on the station. I was thankful no windows had been broken out and that there wasn't much visible damage. From the ground, nothing on the roof of the station looked too smashed up, just knocked over a bit.

Most of the mess was from a much, much bigger limb that had fallen in my yard. That sucker alone was the size of a full freaking tree.

I put on sunglasses—happy to need them for once—and headed back out. There wasn't a lot I could do, aside from cleaning up some of the smaller pieces, but even that was a chore on the two acres my house and the station shared.

I was relieved when I heard a vehicle coming down the gravel. Maybe my dad had gotten a ride out to help me. Andy was sleeping on the cement just inside my garage, but looked up to see who was coming.

I looked in the vehicle's direction, but it wasn't my dad.

It was Kent Caraway and—*oh my God*—Rhett creeping up my drive. They stopped, and I walked over to Mr. Caraway on the driver's side.

"Good morning," I chimed, unable to hide the distress in my voice.

He looked at me sympathetically. "Morning, Sunny. You got a mess out here, too," he stated, rubbing his whiskery chin.

"I know. My dad is supposed to be out, but they have a tree down there, too. What are the odds?"

Lately, I'd been carrying my luck around in a bucket riddled with holes. So the odds were actually pretty good.

He nodded and his eyes backed up his agreement. "Yeah, we saw that. But your dad said you had some damage, and, since he's tied up, he asked if we could give you a hand."

Rhett sat ramrod straight, arm hanging out the passenger window, adjusting the side mirror. He wore an old t-shirt with the arms cut off, leaving big gaping holes on the sides, showing off his body underneath.

Stop it, Perverella. He's a kid.

"You don't have to. I'm sure you're busy. I can wait for Dad," I said, looking down at my sneakers, avoiding nice Mr. Caraway's son.

Before I could protest any more, I heard Rhett's door open and close. Then he swiftly lifted a chainsaw out of the back and headed for the limb.

I looked at the man behind the wheel; he winked then turned off the ignition. I backed up a step so he could open the blue Ford's door.

"Looks like we're staying," he said.

I hadn't talked to Rhett since we were kids, but even more than his crazy physical transformation from boy to man, his personality had changed, too. When I was in high school, there wasn't a time when he *wasn't* trying to get my attention. Now in the snap of just two days, he had all but ignored me twice.

It was confirmed: I was an old maid who'd lost her allure.

A green penny left out in the rain for too long.

Washed up.

I was in a funk.

Andy and I stayed out of the way while the Caraways worked. Rhett cut down the huge limb, piece by piece, as his dad carried brush to the back and put it in a pile.

"Sunny, whatcha got planned for all this wood?" Mr. Caraway asked a few hours later.

I hadn't thought about it, but I really didn't need it. My house didn't have a fireplace, and, even though I loved a good bonfire, I'd probably never have one—especially not by myself.

"No clue. Do you want it?" I asked him as I handed him a cold bottle of water from the refrigerator in my garage. Giving them the firewood was the least I could do for the help.

"Yeah, we'll take it off your hands, if you don't want it." He wiped the sweat from his forehead with a handkerchief before he opened the bottle and took a long drink.

"Help yourself."

I watched Rhett, now shirtless, standing on the thickest part of the limb, gliding his chainsaw through it. There was no way he'd be able to hear us talking—let alone hear the wicked things I was thinking in my head.

Mindlessly as I stood by Kent, I opened the extra bottle of water I'd brought out for the hot, young man cleaning up my yard and cooled myself down with a chug from it.

Mr. Caraway patted me on the back, startling me out of my thoughts. Water spilled out of my mouth about the time Rhett made eye contact with me for the first time that day. Not that I was gawking, but I totally was.

He was so handsome. And strong. And sweaty. And that backwards hat. And those boots. And the way he effortlessly tossed the wood like it weighed nothing. And the way his white t-shirt hung loosely out the back of his jeans like a white flag of surrender.

I lost my mind and asked, "How old is he?"

Mr. Caraway chuckled and took a few steps away. "Oh, I'd say you two are about the same age now. Aren't ya?"

He'd lost his mind too, and I shot him a look that told him so, but he just laughed and went back to work.

For a while, I poked around in my garage. Watching. Okay, pretending like I wasn't watching.

The more I looked at the radio station, which was in the same direction as Rhett, the more I thought I could reach the part of the limb that hung over the side—if only I had a little height. I grabbed a stepstool and hauled it across the yard and set it up about a foot away from the brick. I climbed to the top, only gaining a few feet, but it was just about enough to reach some of the leaves that lobbed over the edge of the roof. On my tiptoes, the stool rocked atop of the soft ground, but I was close so I leaned forward.

"Don't do that," I heard coming up behind me. "Get down."

I looked over my shoulder at a very determined looking Rhett Caraway.

"I just thought…" I began as I started to back down off the stool. I stepped aside and he didn't even stop as he took the stepladder in one stride. He braced himself with a hand on the wall, and with ease, yanked down the limb I'd been struggling to reach. It fell in the opposite direction of where I stood.

"Thanks," I said.

He didn't say anything, but he gave me a slight nod and turned to head back where they'd been working since they'd arrived.

"Hey, I said *thanks*," I called as I followed him. He didn't have to be so short with me.

Still, he didn't stop or turn around. His dad continued cutting and kicking away the manageable chunks.

"Hey," I yelled, growing more frustrated.

He turned around and adjusted his cap, then looked at me to say something, but didn't.

"Aren't you going to talk to me?" I asked.

Something familiar clicked, and I saw a hint of the look he used to give me.

"Yeah," he answered, but that was it. *Yeah*.

"Well, *say* something then."

He bent down and picked up the biggest piece at his feet and tossed it into the back of his dad's pickup. His jaw tightened, but his eyes laughed. Then Rhett said, "Thanks for the wood." He laughed under his breath and got back to work.

I'd walked right into that one, and it made me laugh, too. His wit was sharp and I couldn't resist myself when I countered, "Well, you can *only* have it if you stop ignoring me."

His dad stepped around him into the bed of the truck and made room for more pieces. They exchanged a look I couldn't read as Rhett said, "All right then."

I marched back to the house feeling disappointed and reminding myself that I was old and he was not.

Chapter Four

Rhett

Yeah, she'd given us a truckload of wood, but what I was really talking about was the chub I worked up watching her ass reach for that limb on the roof of the radio station. A distraction like that wasn't what you needed while working with a chainsaw, and I was lucky my dad took it from me when he did.

After handing him the Stihl, I automatically went in her direction. I was halfway there when I realized she was damn near tipping the flimsy stool over. I didn't like seeing her in harm's way, which remedied the tightness in my jeans.

I was probably imagining it. If not though, she'd been staring at me all day. I didn't mind, but my dad was there, and I didn't feel like hearing shit about it until the end of time.

I'd known something must have happened at her station

the night before when the music went silent in the middle of a song, but thought it was probably a power thing. So when I was on my morning run—past her place, on my new and purely coincidental morning route—I'd seen the mess.

When Dad picked me up to head over to Coach Fry's, and we'd seen that they had all the help they needed, I was relieved when Mr. Wilbanks asked us to stop by Sunny's to help her. I was going to do it anyway, after we helped Coach, but at least it wouldn't have seemed like my idea.

Sunny helped where she could and stayed out of the way when she couldn't.

We were about finished, and she was in the house, when Eddie pulled up.

"Hey fellas," he called, as he hopped out of his old-ass work van, flicking his cigarette into the gravel drive.

"Eddie," my dad hollered back. "Busy day, huh?"

"Oh, yeah. Wasn't nearly as bad as I reckoned it was gonna be. She's my last stop." He pulled his ladder off the top of the van and walked it over to the wall of the station.

I leaned against the truck bed, and my dad followed Eddie to give him a hand.

We'd cut up the massive limb, but her yard was pretty wrecked. Leaves and sawdust everywhere. I felt bad leaving it the way we were about to, but I reminded myself it wasn't my place.

Feet crunching across the gravel behind me caught my ear, but I didn't turn to look at her like I was compelled to do. I was doing well with not looking like a fool so far, and therefore challenged my cool streak to continue.

"I really appreciate y'all coming over to give me a hand.

Dad said they're almost cleaned up, too. Now, if Eddie can get me up and running, I should be good to go." I noticed how different her voice was when she spoke to me—as opposed to when we were younger. The difference between speaking to a child and a man.

She stood at my side, and just like in the truck stop, I was reminded of how little she was compared to me. Her head barely topped my shoulders.

"Glad we could help," I replied, looking at the sky to avoid looking in her blue eyes. We weren't supposed to get any more rain that day. The forecast said we might get a shower or two that night, but the weather could only distract me so much.

"Can I pay you?" she asked, kicking the rocks at her feet.

"No," I retorted automatically. We didn't help for money. "Just get that station back up. It sucks working without anything to listen to."

That made her smile and sway. "Oh, nobody really listens to it that much anymore." Her eyes caught mine and I noticed how blue they were. Like a cloud-free, blue sky.

"Some of us do."

Eddie waved at her and she waved back, but still devoted most of her attention to me. "I don't think the power went out, so I might not have to do a full reboot. *Fingers crossed*. I should be back up in a few hours."

Since it wasn't raining, I'd probably get some mowing done before dark, but I'd be listening.

A few moments went by after I tore my eyes off her and focused on Eddie and Dad, but I didn't say anything.

"You sure are different than you used to be, Rhett."

I didn't reply, wondering if *different* was good or bad.

A decade ago, I would have been talking her ear off. Trying to get *her* to talk to *me*. Notice *me*. I'd changed, but she had, too.

"You living at home now?" she asked, her voice a little quieter.

I lived on our property, but not under my parents' roof. "I'm staying in the cabin on the south eighty."

She viciously slapped at her tan leg. "*Damn blood-sucking mosquitos*. Farming with your dad?"

I laughed inwardly at how her expression changed in a blink from furious back to fine and dandy. I replied, "When it's not raining."

"Well, it's good to see you back in Wynne." She shuffled a few feet away, heading for the station, giving her legs a few more swats and swearing at the bugs under her breath.

I couldn't take my eyes off her.

After a few slow steps, she turned around and smiled at me in a way she never had before. "You look good." She leaned forward on her toes and added quietly, looking straight into my eyes, "*Really* good." Then she jogged off toward the station and said thanks to my dad as she passed him.

Dad was grinning from ear to ear as he walked up, but I didn't want to hear it so I jumped into the driver's side of the pickup and cranked it to life. He waved from the passenger seat to Sunny and Eddie, and then to her parents as they pulled in when we turned onto the lane.

"Guess you can keep this load of wood down at the shack, if you want. Drop me off at the house." He looked at his watch. "It's still early and your mom's got a list for me.

Damn weather."

I flipped the visor down to shield my eyes from the elusive afternoon sun. "I'll split it and stack it around back."

"Coming down for dinner?"

I wanted to say no, but I was starving and it was Sunday. My mom probably had something already started to feed her family. Besides, it would be a hell of a lot better than whatever leftovers I might warm up for myself.

"Yeah, I'll be down. I have to get my truck anyway."

"Reckon." He pulled his hat off and smacked it off the dashboard. "Sunny was glad to see us. You know, I think if I was her, I'd probably cut the rest of that damn tree down and trim up those two apple trees in front of the station."

He was probably the only man I knew who got excited about finding *more* work to do. Growing up, there was one word you didn't say around my old man. *Bored*.

He'd mock, "Well, I love ya, son. So, I'm gonna help you out and cure that boredom for ya." Then he'd put my bored-ass to work.

My father was a sun-up-to-sun-down guy. He kicked back on Sundays and loved a good vacation when they happened, but he didn't sit still much.

Answering him about the trees he was hinting at, I said, "They're hers. She'll do what she wants with them."

"Well, next time you talk to her … maybe tell her." He played with the radio, looking for an alternative station, fidgeting, and being an all-around terrible passenger. "I'd see if she has a weed eater, too. Someone ain't doing a very good job trimming. Maybe she needs some help."

He wasn't very coy. I could read through his bullshit.

"She's the one who's gotta live there. If she doesn't mind,

why should you?"

His face bunched and he pitched his mouth to the side, shaking his head. "You telling me you wouldn't *love* a reason to talk to her?"

"Dad," I warned. I wasn't getting into it.

Was I the only person in this town who remembered anything? Maybe they didn't get it because they weren't the one getting rejected.

He scoffed. "What? All I'm saying is I think she'd listen to you."

We turned into the farm's driveway, and I swerved to miss the big puddle that nearly covered the entire width of the road.

"I'm not stupid, Dad. *Leave it alone.* I'll be back for dinner. What's Mom making?"

He looked disappointed as he hopped out in front of the wraparound front porch, but he accepted my change of topic. "Pot roast," he answered. He clapped, then rubbed his hands together. "Wash up and be down by five."

I let off the brake just when he reached out for the window frame to say something else. "Just a second, Rhett." He looked behind himself to check our privacy. "You're a free man. She's a single woman. If you don't *want* to talk to that pretty girl, then you are stupid, son."

I left the auxiliary power on in my dad's old farm truck, door open, so I could hear if and when the station came back to life.

I'd been cutting wood nearly all my life. Stand. Split.

Stack. Repeat. I could do it in my sleep, and it didn't take me very long to work through the truckload from Sunny's.

I leaned across the seat to turn off the ignition just as I heard WDKR come alive.

"Are you out there, Wynne? I'm back and ready to get the music rolling. We had a little nature knock at our door here at the station last night, but we're up and running now. Thanks to Eddie, the best electrician in the world. Make sure you give him a call if you need anything. Also, thanks to the Caraways and the other good Samaritans who helped me and others around town. Now, how about some tunes?"

She went straight into a classic Dwight Yoakam song, and I switched it off feeling proud.

I pulled off my boots and socks at the back door and put them on the floor beside the old washer and dryer we used to have at the farm. Either my mom didn't want to do my laundry, which I really wouldn't expect her to do anymore, or she wanted a new washer and dryer and used me living in the cabin as a good reason to get them for the farm that spring. My guess was the latter.

I stripped down to my boxer briefs and strolled to the refrigerator for a swig—orange juice straight from the jug and a slice of cheese to hold me over until dinner. Then I hopped in the shower and took a minute to let the thrill of Sunny talking to me wash away the day's sweat.

I wasn't about to look like a fool again, but damn, if her attention didn't feel like getting my best time in a race. There was no way she was truly into me—it wasn't possible—but privately it sure was fun to think about.

Maybe I *would* look at those trees my dad was talking about. I wouldn't want the station to go out again.

We made it through the meal with my dad only bringing her up twice. The last time my mom kicked him under the table. At least someone was on my side.

"*Kent*. Stop it," she scolded. Then, she scolded my sister, too. "Haley, put that phone down. And, Rhett, you need a haircut. Want me to do it after dinner?"

It was getting too long, so I answered, "Yes, ma'am."

After we ate, and Haley cleaned up the kitchen, I met my mom for my cut. She used to work uptown with Sunny's mom, Penny. When we were about seven or eight, my parents built a mini-salon on the side of the house so she could work from home. She wasn't nearly as busy as if she'd stayed in Wynne, but she had quite a few regulars.

I sat in the chair and she draped the smock around my shoulders then sprayed my head with her squirt bottle.

"Don't let your dad or anybody else tease you about Sunny Wilbanks. She's a pretty girl, Rhett, but there are *lots* of pretty girls." That statement made me curious. She was the only person saying anything like that. Almost everyone who'd brought her up acted like I was still thirteen.

"What's wrong with Sunny?" I asked as she ran a comb through my hair to find my part. "Leave it a little longer on the top and shorter on the sides."

"There's nothing wrong with her, honey. But *you* don't want her." She stepped around my legs and started finger cutting the front.

"Oh, I don't?" I asked, taking the bait as I looked up at her.

She firmly grabbed my chin and moved it so that I was looking forward, but first said, "You must not. Otherwise, you'd have her. Now keep your head straight."

She trimmed me up and ran the clippers through the back before dusting me off and letting me stand.

Before I left, she loaded me down with groceries and a pile of old towels for the cabin, having replaced them with new ones for herself. It dawned on me that maybe she liked me living out there because she finally had somewhere to send her hand-me-downs when she wanted new things. I couldn't complain—I was benefiting from her recent shopping sprees.

It was sprinkling again by the time I got back to my place, and as I walked up to the door, I saw a case of beer with a note taped to it.

Rhett,

Thanks for helping me today. Have a few beers on me. If you'd like me to pay for your time, just call.
402-822-0825
Sunny

I wasn't sure what to think, but maybe it was time I started taking the advice I'd gotten from a pretty girl a long time ago.

Chapter Five

Sunny

"Dean told me about it," Hannah admitted. "So what did he look like?"

"He's handsome. Like crazy, *crazy* hot. I'm so damn gross. He's like a kid compared to us." I didn't want to burden my best friend with my May-December problems, but she called *me*. It was her fault.

"Shut up. So you went to his house?" she asked, followed by a shushing sound like she was holding Sawyer.

"Well, first I went to his mom and dad's, and his mom met me on the porch, and *then* she said he lived out at their hunting cabin. Of course, that's when I remembered he'd already told me that, but, on the rare occasion he actually talks to me, I can't even fucking concentrate or listen. I'm so dumb. Anyway, besides, I haven't even been down that dead-end road in forever. So I chickened out and came home and had a beer myself. Okay, it was two."

She laughed as she listened to me go on and on.

"So I drove down to his place with beer and left my number because he wasn't there. Or maybe he was but didn't want to see me." I paced my kitchen as I droned on. "No. There weren't any vehicles, so I'm pretty sure he was gone. Ugh. Doesn't matter though, Hannah. I don't think he wants to talk to me."

"Oh, I doubt that. Maybe he's shy now. He hasn't lived in Wynne for years."

I sat on my couch and played with the condensation rolling off my glass of iced tea. I was conflicted. It was odd being a few years older, but I was so drawn to him.

"Hannah, he's not shy. He used to call my station twice a night and request songs. He'd damn near talk my ear off."

Her voice rose as she reasoned, "Shit changes. Look at me."

She was right, I supposed. People could change, and she was a testament to that. Just a year ago she was a single tomboy, and now she was a new mommy and married to a great guy.

But, if things *had* changed, then that only proved my theory: Rhett Caraway didn't give a shit about me anymore. For the first time in my life, that kind of sucked.

"So, you're home then?" I asked, not wanting to argue myself into a corner.

Hannah didn't have the time to listen to me go on about being a panther—which is what I decided I was since I wasn't twice his age, but only five or so years. Plus, I thought panthers were classier for some reason. I would have liked to have thought my display of recent morals—*like not jumping his bones in front of his father*—gave more scruples in return.

Yes. I'd held back like a saintly panther, which wasn't good in all situations of my life. I still hadn't called Mike, but he hadn't called me either.

After giving it some thought, I could admit that my mom wasn't stupid, and I was starting to agree with her. I needed to give a relationship a fair shot at going somewhere. So, even if it wasn't the guy from the next town, I had to be hopeful that maybe it would be the *next* guy.

I could compromise. Give myself a shot at finding someone special, someone I could invest in and see myself with for a while with my future in mind. In turn, I still really wanted to find the one who I hopefully couldn't live without. Someone who really did it for me.

A few seconds later, Hannah spoke. "No, tomorrow. Her temperature spiked a little last night, nothing major. They just want to be safe. One. More. Night," she chanted.

"I have some packages for you. Text me when you get home."

I unlatched the screen door to the garage when I heard Andy scratching. He'd run in there since it started raining again.

"I will. You text me if the Fuck-hot Farmer calls." I wasn't going to comment on that. I was still feeling saintly. "I've got to go. I'll talk to you tomorrow," she said.

"Okay, bye."

He was totally fuck-hot though. It wasn't fair to other men how attractive he was.

An image of him shirtless, mowing my yard, came to mind. I chalked it up to early onset panther syndrome and bent over at the hip to catch a breath that rushed through me, the image having left me winded.

The vantage revealed I needed new tile. I'd ask my dad if there was anyone in town who did that, which I knew was a tightly loaded question. Because, if he didn't know anyone, he'd consider *being* the one.

He was my dad and he rocked. A complete nerd, but he was cool.

The radio station gene skipped a generation, right over his skinny, nearly bald head. He hated country music, and my Grandpa Sonny knew a station with my dad's preference in music—think Simon and Garfunkel, Joni Mitchell, and James Taylor—would fail in our town.

Dad had been a great student though, and my grandpa was really proud of him. So in place of his natural predecessor, Grandpa Sonny taught me. Which was kind of perfect since I'd been named after him.

He was Sonny with an O, and I was Sunny with a U. *Close enough.*

I loved the shit out of our time together, too. He'd let me talk on the radio when I was a kid, and my mom would record it for me so I could listen to us talking over the air later.

I didn't do sports in high school—except cheerleading, although we didn't do any competing around here. No, I was too busy for stuff like that. I was at that station next to my grandpa every free moment I had.

Everyone loved him. He was "Sonny Wilbanks on WDKR-Radio in the Heartland," and the coolest guy I knew. A career military man who came back home after basic training, married his high school sweetheart, and took her along for the journey.

As children, my dad and my uncle traveled all over the world with them. Then he retired young from the military and bought the run down station in Wynne.

The rest was history.

After catching my breath, I shuffled through the mail on the counter from the past week, which wasn't all that exciting.

Although my grandfather had passed away, my grandma Bette was still energetic and outgoing. Sharp as a tack, too. She still did a lot of the bookkeeping and ad selling, but it was mostly an excuse to keep calling her friends who spent money with the station and find out the local gossip.

She liked doing the clerical work; I liked running the station. We had a good thing.

Grandma Bette didn't need the money. Grandpa had left her with full benefits—the kind you couldn't buy anymore. So, out of the station's modest profits, she gave herself a small cut—which she claimed was just enough to get her hair and nails done uptown—gave a piece to the station for upkeep and upgrades, and paid me the rest.

Most of the mail went to her. Usually I only got sale ads and personal bills, but one envelope caught my attention. An orange one. *Wildcat orange.*

My stomach sunk a little as I slid my thumb through it.

Congratulations Class of 2006!

You're invited to the Wynne Wildcat 10 Year Class Reunion.

The old cow in me cringed from the validation of it all.

The invite was full of things, including a weekend long schedule with the family, welcome barbeque, and other events.

Also, folded inside the envelope were a few pages formatted to look like our old school newspaper. It had cute headlines like: *Guess What Wildcat Couple Just Bought a House?* And *Second Generation Best Friends*, featuring BJ and Mandy, best friends from our class and their daughters who were—you guessed it—best friends.

I was cynical and pouting about being old as I twisted off the top of a beer and sat at my kitchen table to read the damn newsletter.

I finally got over myself by the time I was on the last page where a few fun games were making me laugh. Whoever took the time to put all of it together did a pretty cool job. A nickname crossmatch game, a teacher word find, and an alumni crossword. I grabbed a pen out of my purse and played as I drank my beer.

When I got to nine down and the clue was: *Single, no kids.* Noticing it was a five letter word—last letter Y—I decided I'd had enough fun.

Then I drank two more beers, and Andy and I decided I needed to get my act together. *For real.* I might just be single, no kids Sunny now, but by the next reunion I wanted to be happily married, with some kids *maybe* Sunny.

The sun had set on my time to just play around and see. Things needed to start happening.

But first, after three beers, I got curious if I could still fit into my old high school clothes. I knew just where they were.

A few hours later, I was jamming out in my bedroom to the playlist I'd made for afterhours weeknights, and wearing my old cheer skirt zipped up only halfway—the only half that would connect.

Even though my relationship status hadn't changed much after ten years, my ass sure had.

Chapter Six

Rhett

"It's Thirsty Thursday here at WDKR, and I tell you what, I could use a cold one. But, until I sign off, how about some drinking songs to wet your pallet? If all this rain hasn't drowned you yet, I've got a long block of rain songs for Fun Friday here at the station."

Then, Sunny played "Friends in Low Places" followed by about six other drinking songs.

She was funny like that. She had a day for everything, a song to fit every occasion. She knew country music like the back of her hand and always had cool facts to go along with an artist or song. So, even though she was playing to a certain crowd, she did it her way.

It wasn't until late in the evenings when you'd hear newer music that wasn't as mainstream. I listened damn near every night, and many of the records she'd played had found their way to my iPod for when I ran.

Whether it was the music or the sound of her familiar voice through the airwaves, it helped pass the time.

There wasn't a whole lot we could do on the farm, with the weather the way it was, so I was in the big shed changing the oil in the John Deere 4020. My grandfather had been meticulous about keeping his machinery in pristine condition, and it was something that easily passed down from him to my dad, to me. When you don't have the money to buy new every year, or trade, you learned how to maintain what you had. It was second nature to us.

Dad had been in and out that day getting ready for the sand-baggers to come the next day. It was forecasted to be one of the only dry days in the next few weeks, even though it was still going to rain that evening. But, to take advantage, we'd be bagging sand at the shed by the levee the next day. There would easily be a handful of men there to help us.

Workdays like that, as bad as it sounded, were usually kind of fun. You'd see different people come lend a hand and shoot the shit to make a bad situation almost tolerable. We had about six thousand acres, and if the levee failed, we stood to lose about half.

The Corp of Engineers had brought in loads and loads of sand, leaving some at the bank for anyone who needed it to keep water away, mostly people who lived near the swollen creeks. Additionally, they'd brought the lion's share to our property, which ran alongside the river for much of our levee district.

Good years were great, the really dry ones not so much, and wet summer months were a pain in the ass. At least on the scorching years that were about as frequent as the floods, we had irrigation to pump in needed water. We could do something about it.

Flood years were out of our control. Sure, we could tarp and bag the levee, but above that, it was wait and see. And pray. *And drink*.

Since the next day was Friday, I expected to do a lot of both, especially with the water going up another foot this weekend and more rain up north on the way down.

I heard my dad pull up again, and by looking at my watch, I knew what time it was. *Lunch*.

I'd run almost nine miles that morning and only had a couple bowls of cereal. I needed food.

Depending on where we were working, sometimes I'd go home or bring a sandwich. If we were close to the farmhouse, we'd swing in and hang out with Mom for a while. Or sometimes, if it was raining and we couldn't do much of anything that afternoon, we'd hit Diana's Diner for lunch, then have a few beers in the shop.

"I don't know about you, but I could use a big ass cheeseburger," I said to him.

He strutted in with a couple new belts and random parts he'd picked up at the implement for spares to have on hand—like we needed more, but because it was raining, he'd had nothing much to do except dick around in town.

"Yeah?" he asked. "You buying?"

I looked up from the tractor, having finished with my task. "You driving?"

"Yeah, suppose so."

"You got beer in your truck?"

He cocked his head at me. "Are ya writing a book, son? Clean that shit up. Let's go."

He had beer. I knew my dad.

I cleaned up the mess I'd made and closed the side panel on the green machine while he hauled a bucket of ice from the ice maker to cool down his well-used, red Coleman cooler. I hopped in the cab of his truck, which he'd pulled half into the shed to keep from walking through the rain—and that was the official end of my workday.

The road was sloppy and washed out in spots. If we ever had a few days in a row that were dry, one of us would be grading it to smooth out some of the deeper holes and ruts.

"On the way back I'll show you where they think we need to start. There are a few weak spots we should get to first, then head north and work our way down," he said as he drove.

He was justifiably worried, not that we didn't have insurance or that we were inexperienced, but it just sucked seeing something you loved and worked hard for get fucked up right before your eyes.

Beans looked like shit.

Corn looked like shit.

My dad, although he was holding up pretty good, looked like shit, too.

We pulled into the diner and everyone in town was there. That wasn't much of a surprise, though, on a soggy day in a farm community. We parked across the street in O'Fallon's lot and ran to the door.

"Hey, boys," called Roseanne, Diana's only other waitress. "Just find somewhere and I'll be right there." The diner was asshole to elbow, but we found two seats at a table with a few of my dad's buddies.

"Kent. Rhett," the threesome all said in greeting.

"Dub. Norm. Dean," my dad said back. The chair barked across the floor as Dad took a seat with them.

"I'm gonna go wash up real quick. If Roseanne comes back, I'll take a double cheeseburger, everything on it. Fries. Salad with Ranch and water," I told him and walked around the full chairs and tables to get to the bathroom.

I should have scrubbed up back at the shop with the degreaser, but I was led by hunger and climbed into the pickup without doing it first. I lathered up as well as I could with the yellow Dial soap and gave them a decent wash. There was still shit under my nails, but I'd eaten plenty of meals dirtier than that and wasn't dead yet.

"How in the hell are you in here *and* on the radio at the same time, Sunny? I just heard you," Dub shouted as I walked down the hall back to the dining area.

"It's called *a prerecording*, Dub. Hell, I'd have to live there full-time to be on-air all day *and* all night." She smarted off with her hip pushed out, her hand resting on the belt around her small waist. I knew that sassy voice better than my own.

I had to walk around her to get back to my table, but mouthing off to Dub, she didn't hear me walk up. Not thinking much about it, my hand found her hip and gently moved her to the side so I could pass.

"Excuse me," I said and continued to the table. Ready for the hyenas to tear into me.

Quietly, she replied, "Oh, sorry. Excuse me, Rhett."

I'd heard her say my name lots of times, and sadly, it never got old.

Dean called to her, "You heading down the street?"

I took my seat facing the counter and watched as a

big smile broke across her face. Her blue eyes bright and excited.

"Yeah, taking them some lunch. Hannah needed a tenderloin."

I wasn't exactly sure who they were talking about, I didn't know any Hannahs, but whoever she was, Sunny was excited to see her.

My ice water was already at my spot, so I assumed my dad already placed our orders. Not wanting to call attention to myself, or her, I messed with my phone.

It was one thing if they teased me; it was another if they teased her *on account* of me.

"Sunny, didn't Kent clean up that tree for you? You gonna buy your father-in-law's lunch?" Dub said good-naturedly, but I still wanted to knock the shit out of him.

She just laughed and, thank goodness, Diana popped up with her to-go bags. The whole place silently looked at Sunny then at me to see what we would say or do in response. I gave her one glance then went back to my phone, hoping that no reaction would be best.

Old turds like Dub McCallister only keep going if you let them know they're on your nerves. The only thing I could do for myself—or her, for that matter—was let it roll off.

My dad, God bless him, chimed in, "Well Dub, I ran a plow through your yard for the garden you're planting—if this damn rain ever stops. I reckon you owe me lunch first."

"You son of a…" Dub cackled and laughed, throwing his napkin at his empty plate. He took it as well as he dished it out. "I can't feed you and this big boy of yours. I'll need a gosh-damned second mortgage," he said as Roseanne brought out my salad.

"Hey, I thought I heard you say there'd be another band in town this weekend," Dean said to Sunny when she was halfway to the door.

"Yeah, Joey Settles and some other guys are throwing something together for Sally's birthday tomorrow," she answered. Then, bags in hand, she walked back our way looking determined as she stopped by Dub, slapping him on the back. "Kent, you should go. Take out my *mother-in-law*."

"I'll ask her." He laughed, punching Dub in the arm, egging him on.

Then she said, "Rhett, you should go down, too. Dub, you keep your dumbass at home."

I looked up from the weather application I was studying, just in time to see her smile at me.

There it was again. That new smile. Fuck, I liked it.

She was probably just giving it back to the dickhead at our table, but she'd asked me to go to Sally's.

No jokes about my age.

"I don't know," I said.

But, she was already at the door when she turned, holding up a pink-tipped finger, and fired back with a wicked gleam in her eye. "Don't argue with your wife."

Son of a bitch.

I stared at the door, though she didn't wait around.

My dad kicked me under the table, but it barely registered. I was still living in the moment when Sunny said she was my wife.

Fuck. I think I stayed in that haze the whole afternoon.

After a few more than a six-pack with my old man, that feeling followed me home and all the way to bed.

I doubted it would ever happen, but I'll be damned if just hearing her say the words didn't reignite something so deep inside my chest that I lay there and replayed it until I fell asleep.

Her being my wife sounded just fine to me.

I went for my morning run even earlier the next day. Keeping the same route, I worked at improving my time.

We bagged and tarped the worst spots from about sun up until sun down, taking advantage of every second of sunlight. More people than we'd expected showed up, having heard something about a bagging at our farm over the radio. Apparently, Dad had called the station to let anyone who could make it know we'd be having a workday at the levee.

We were far from finished, but we'd covered a lot of ground. The rain had been taken out of the forecast for the weekend, for the most part, and most of the guys said they'd come back on Saturday to help again.

One thing was sure as the day's work came to an end: come hell or high water, I was going to be at the bar. I'd thought about nothing else except seeing her.

Surprisingly, I felt pretty confident as I showered and drove to town. She'd left me beer. Gave me her number. *And* invited me out—even if it had been in jest. Maybe I wasn't just seeing what I wanted to anymore.

Besides, it *was* Sally's birthday, after all.

Chapter Seven

Sunny

I loved the songs that the makeshift band was playing, and they'd covered some of my oldest favorites. They were just a thrown together group of musicians, but they were on a pretty good roll. Even early in the night people were dancing, and the bar was packed.

I wished that Hannah and Vaughn were there, but they were just getting settled at home with baby Sawyer. So, I was riding solo.

Dean was still there and my parents had come down for a few drinks earlier when Sally's brother was frying free fish for her birthday. My mom brought potato salad and they'd had a couple beers before heading out.

That was one of the things I loved about living in the small town—everyone pitched in for a cause. Whether it was to throw a good woman a fun birthday, lend a hand in cleaning up storm damage, or helping protect a neighbor's land from the swelling river.

They didn't always have time, but, when push came to shove, they *made* time. That's how towns like Wynne survive.

The band finished up their first set, and before they headed to the bar to get cold beers, I headed there first to beat the rush.

"Hey, Sunny. How you doing?" asked Aaron, my cousin. He worked for the fire department, so I was surprised to see him there. He didn't get out much.

I shouldered my way up to him at the front of the bar. "I'm good. How've you been?"

He smiled and took a drink. "Busy, but good. Hey, I was on the clock last week and you played some song I hadn't heard before." He squinted in thought. "I think it was last Wednesday. We were coming back from a wreck … someone went off in a ditch south of town. Anyway, I can't remember how it went, but that guitar part was awesome." He chuckled. "I know that's not much to go on, but is there any chance you remember what that song was or who played?"

I pulled my phone out and scrolled through the playlists I'd made on an app I used when I was at home looking for new music.

"Bud Light, Sunny?" Faith asked from behind the bar. Faith didn't work at the bar that often, but it was Sally's birthday, and her sons, who usually helped her, were getting her good and drunk.

"Yeah," I answered then hit play on the modern bluegrass song I happened to love, holding the tiny speaker up to Aaron's ear so he could hear it over the music streaming through the band's PA.

"That's it. Shit," he said. "Who in the hell is that?"

"They're called Wind Through Wichita," I answered and pulled my phone back. "The whole album is so damn good."

"Thanks, Sunny. I'll look them up," Aaron said.

I handed Faith a twenty to pay for my beer when I heard a familiar laugh a few feet away. *Mike.*

I took a deep breath and recommitted to the idea of giving it a shot. Although, if judging by how much enthusiasm I felt were any clue, I'd say I was, at best, only mildly excited.

He hadn't seen me yet, and I noticed he was with a few of his friends. I'd met them once before, and together they were a raucous brood. As Faith got my change down the bar, they gave her some shit and ordered shots.

By that time, Aaron had turned in his stool talking to someone else. I said a prayer for myself and tried to find more than the mere shred of enthusiasm I felt about Mike being there. *Tried* being the most telling part about how I felt. *I was trying to like him.*

After getting my change and tipping, I strode down the bar and bumped into Mike's arm. "You guys out causing trouble?"

His eyes looked down at me and he grinned. Mike wasn't killer handsome—like a Fuck-hot Farmer I knew of—but he was all right. Brown eyes, dark hair graying at the temples. He wasn't fat or fit, but somewhere in the middle. *Average. Yippee.*

I heard my mom's words in my ears and they reminded me. Who was I to be so damn picky? If I was such a great catch, wouldn't I be caught by now?

"Oh, we might be," he answered, then the three of them laughed. He called behind the bar, "Add one more shot. She'll take one, too."

I didn't love shots, but the night was young, so I was still in good shape.

His friend Sam said, "We were just talking about you, Sunny." He was a shorter guy, but a prime example of a good ole boy. Plaid shirt, no sleeves, pack of Marlboros in the pocket. Ball cap, frayed bill.

"Anything good?" I asked.

"We were just giving Mike hell. How many times have you two been out now?" His elbow nudged their other friend. I didn't know his first name, but they called him Graves.

"I don't know." It was hard to say how many times we'd actually been out, like, together. We'd hung out a handful of times, but maybe only two date-dates, which consisted of Diana's once and the ice cream place in Gilbert a different time—both ending at a bar. "Three or four, maybe," I answered and looked up to Mike to confirm.

He didn't look amused like his buddies as he took a long drink from his beer, then set it aside to hand out the plastic shot glasses.

"What is this?" I asked. The dark liquor didn't look kind.

"SoCo," Mike answered.

Gross, but I could do it.

Sam lifted his in the air and toasted: "To Friday night mistakes and strong Saturday morning coffee."

We all lifted and tipped back the Southern Comfort.

As I let it rip down my throat, my eye caught Rhett walking through the door. I'm sure it was just the shot warming my stomach, but the sight of him was timed perfectly with the heat that spread through me.

My panther instincts were getting stronger by the day.

Hell, a few days ago I'd all but humped his leg in the diner. It wasn't my fault, though. He was young and strong and sexy and Jesus needed to take this panther's wheel.

"Who remembers a little band called Alabama?" bellowed Joey Settles from the stage. The band had assembled for their second set. I might have loved new music, but there was something about a three-part harmony that did it for this small town girl. I knew it was only seconds before I'd be out front jamming along.

"I'm going to listen to the band. Thanks for the shot," I said as I handed the empty plastic shooter back to Mike before heading up front.

I was probably only three steps away when I heard Sam tease Mike. "Maybe if you get her good and drunk, then she'll finally fuck ya later." I didn't turn around, but I had to stop to let someone by and heard him answer his friend.

"I guess. If that's what it's gonna take," he said and laughed.

I decided then and there, I wasn't doing any more shots. Furthermore, Mike could do as many as he liked and fuck *himself*. I was single, but I wasn't cheap or desperate.

Rolling my eyes, I made my way to the stage. Joey, the lead singer, was an older guy and a pretty good friend of my grandfather's, so I stood next to his wife and proceeded to get my country on.

By the time the band was on break again, Mike and his friends were out back in the beer garden. I saw Sam standing just outside the door with a cigarette hanging out of his mouth.

A few times I'd turned around while dancing, noticing that Rhett had taken a seat at the end of the bar close to the dance floor.

When Mike would catch my eye, he'd make like he was taking another shot and point at me.

No, thanks, buddy.

If he wanted in these pants he sure as hell wasn't going to get there by getting me drunk. The longer the night went on, the more resolute I was that being with Mike was off the table. I could do better—even back at square one.

Was it a mistake to expect someone who wanted to have sex with me to actually give me some attention? Maybe dance with me? Maybe try to have a conversation or see what I was doing when there wasn't alcohol involved? Someone who appreciated me or acted like they even liked me or found me interesting? Someone who *I* found interesting, for that matter?

It got to the time of night where the bar was hopping and people had wandered outside, the crowd spread wide from the front sidewalk under the awning all the way out to the covered beer garden in back. Sally and a handful of couples still danced, but it was about that time where I needed to decide if I was going to stay and drink more or go home.

The problem was, I liked the view so much.

Rhett was younger than me, and that still felt a little

weird, but he didn't look like a kid anymore. So, maybe I wasn't a panther. Maybe I was just a girl who appreciated a handsome man when I saw one.

I'd seen people walk over to him and shake his hand, and then they'd look my way. A few girls around his age sat next to him, but he turned his stool to watch the band, away from their attention.

My beer was empty, as luck would have it, so I went to get another, hoping if I ventured over to him he'd finally talk to me. I took a shot.

"How did the sand bagging go?" I asked as I approached him. Surprisingly, he didn't look away; instead, he smiled. Damn, he had a nice one.

"Pretty good. Got a lot done." His big hand rubbed over his mouth and he added, "Thanks for the beer the other night."

You could have called and thanked me.

He wore a light gray t-shirt that was tight across his chest and around his biceps. He had a ball cap on and dark jeans. Plus, he smelled *so* fine.

I probably looked like a shit show, sweaty and melted from dancing, but I didn't care. He was chatting with me.

"You're welcome. I appreciated you guys helping me out," I answered and moved around him to set my empty bottle on the bar. When Faith noticed me, she held up a finger to ask if I just wanted one. I noticed he was a little low so I held up two fingers, ordering one for him, too.

It was weird. Rhett Caraway was old enough to drink, which only reminded me that I was bordering ancient. I took a deep breath with that thought and let it out slowly, feeling a little disappointed.

If only he was older, then maybe it wouldn't have been so damn awkward.

Fuck it. If I was wishing, I would've chosen to be younger.

Lost in my thoughts, I heard his voice, but missed what he'd said and reflexively leaned in and asked, "Huh?"

"I said the band sounds great." He spoke quietly, which I didn't mind because it gave me a reason to watch his mouth and stay near him to hear.

"Yeah, those guys don't play that often anymore, but they should. Plus, Sally's having a good time." I threw the money down and leaned over to grab the pair of beers from behind him, again noticing how mouthwatering he smelled. There's just something about the smell of a fine man that caused me to tingle all the way to my toes.

"Did you get finished at the levee?" I asked and handed him my extra beer.

He frowned first, but took my offering. "You didn't have to buy me beer."

"You can get the next one," I acquiesced and shrugged my shoulder. It was just a beer.

He leaned in and said, "Thank you. We got a few of the worst spots in better shape. We'll be heading to the north end and working there next, then follow the levee down." He took another drink and finished what was left in his last bottle.

All of a sudden, I felt a hand wrap around my waist and I stepped out of the way, spinning out of its hold.

"Sunny, we're heading out to a party. Ride out with us?" said get-me-drunk-and-fuck-me Mike. There he was, probably thirty and totally within my appropriate age range, but I wasn't even slightly interested in going *anywhere* with him.

"No, I think I'm gonna stay here a little longer. You guys go and have a good time. I'll see you around." I pressed my hand on his chest to get some room.

"Your car here? I can just ride out with you." He wiggled his eyebrows and added, "Let's get more shots."

I shook my head. "I don't want any more shots, and I think you should go with your friends."

He cocked his head to the side, looking at Rhett and back at me then pulled my hand to follow him, which I allowed, but only a few steps away.

"*Mike*."

I could smell the liquor on his breath, and it put me off even more. He lowered his voice to talk to me. "Sunny, I thought you liked me. I thought we might have something going on here."

He was still holding onto my hand, which I shook off.

That night had been eye opening. In the past, I'd thought he'd been a pretty all right guy, but he seemed a lot more interested in spending time with me *after* the bar, *after* the drinks, than he did otherwise. Add that to the things I heard him and his friends saying about getting me drunk, and I wasn't able to come up with a single reason I had to stoop to that level for company.

"I'm not really looking for anything serious right now." A familiar line I'd used many times. Which wasn't really true anymore, but I wasn't looking for someone *like him*. I was positive of that.

Mike didn't take it hard; in fact, I don't really think he grasped what I was saying or actually paid attention. He held up a finger to his friends to wait for him and said, “Well, I’ll see you at the party later then.”

Whatever.

“You guys have fun.” I didn’t bother standing there anymore, and I sat my bottle on the edge of the bar top next to Rhett before I asked him, “Can you watch this? I’m going to the bathroom.”

He nodded and turned in his seat so that he faced the bar-back again.

I made a beeline for the ladies’ room, hoping that by the time I made my way out, Mike and his two friends would be long gone.

While I stood in line for one of the two stalls, I looked at my face in the mirror. Mascara smudged under my lashes, I pulled a paper towel from the dispenser and cleaned up my raccoon eyes, slapped on a new coat of lip-gloss, and appeared somewhat refreshed.

I read the most current small-town headline news in the stall, indicating that Hannah and I were correct. Rhett Caraway was hot as fuck. There was a lot of truth scratched into the paint in that bathroom.

Luckily, when I came out a few more people had left, probably heading out to the party at Smiths’ farm. People milled around in the beer garden and a few sat at the tables waiting for the last set of music.

I had a good buzz, but it was getting clear that I needed to slow down. The beer I was drinking was probably my last. I leaned against the stool next to Rhett and grabbed my drink as the guys took the stage one last time.

“I think I’m going to go dance a little more. Thanks for watching my beer,” I said. As cute as he was, and as fun as it would be to chase him, I felt more like finishing up the night and going to bed.

Alone.

I wasn't going to throw myself at Rhett Caraway, especially if he wasn't interested anymore.

Chapter Eight

Rhett

I watched her across the bar, dancing like a maniac, and tipped my cold bottle back.

As a kid, I thought she was pretty—and she was. But as a man, seeing the woman she'd become, I realized I'd been wrong all along.

She was gorgeous.

Swaying her hips, completely off time. For a girl who listened to as much music as she did, she sure as hell didn't have any visible rhythm, but it also didn't appear like she cared. Arms raised above her head, she held her hair up to cool her neck from the heat coming off the dance floor. Blithe like a fawn through a field, she was clumsy but kept my attention.

She might have been acting coy, but I noticed how often she looked my way.

My. Way.

I should have known better—I'd been lured into that smile my whole life. There was something different, something new behind it, though. It wasn't only kindness, the kind she'd always shown me. Not anymore.

There was chemistry. Curiosity. Attraction. And it was coming *from* her.

Everything in my body screamed to go out there and wrap her in my arms and dance her around the hardwood. Yet, I wasn't that kid anymore. The boy who dropped everything for a girl years older than me, only to get shot down. If she wanted me to dance with her, she'd have to ask. Even then I'd need to give it a good think.

One thing was for sure, I *wanted* to, but I had a literal lifetime of embarrassing myself trying to catch her attention. It was her move to make.

Before I knew it, I was smiling back at her and shaking my head at how funny she was. Her zeal was contagious. Perfectly wild, she whirled around the bar carefree of anyone's opinion. I'm sure she knew how silly she looked, but she did it anyway which was something I could relate to—at least in my younger years.

Looking like a fool, yet not giving a shit.

Her glassy blue eyes held mine and silently asked, "Aren't you going to come over here?" That would be too novel. Too predictable. And, in my experience, a waste of time.

I lifted my beer in the air, wordlessly asking her if she needed another drink.

She puckered her lips to hide her smile, but nodded that she'd take one. She called, "One more."

I turned on my stool and found Faith right behind me

watching the show, too. "Faith, can I please get two more Bud Lights?"

"Think she's just playing with you, Rhett?" she asked, which caught my attention. There wasn't a single person in town who didn't remember my trivial, boyish history.

I leaned over to pull my wallet out of my back pocket and grabbed another twenty. "Hell, I don't know. She might be." My answer was short and sweet.

"Well, it wouldn't make her a bad girl. Sometimes it just takes the good ones a little while to come around." She patted the bar in front of me before heading to the cooler.

Was that what this was? Sunny Wilbanks finally coming around? I doubted it.

She'd always be just out of my reach, regardless of how I'd always thought I had a chance as a kid. I wasn't naïve like back then. And, to her, I'd always be the kid with the crush.

I looked above Faith's head at the bar clock that read twelve fifteen. "You know what? How about one for her and a twelve pack to go? I'm gonna head out."

She cocked her hip, placed her hand on it, and leered at me disapprovingly as she held the cooler door. I didn't owe anyone an explanation, but beer has a way of opening your mouth for you.

"Faith, I'm not chasing her anymore. She's told me no enough to last a lifetime." I scratched the back of my neck feeling stupid for having said what I did, but it was true. Then added, "My lifetime for sure."

She walked back without the drinks, seeming pretty hell-bent. "So what? Things change, Rhett. They always do. You're both adults these days, and if you're going to be a coward now, you sure as hell picked the wrong time to start."

I wasn't a coward, but I wasn't a fool either.

"It's late," I argued, knowing it was time to call it a night.

"But maybe not *too* late," she said as I looked over my shoulder and saw Sunny walking our way.

Wasn't it too late? She'd told me herself that it wasn't ever going to happen. Sure, it was ten years ago, but rejection is rejection. I wasn't about to head down a dead-end road with the girl of my dreams, only to figure out I was still in it alone. I'd already survived it once, and I doubted I'd be able to do it again.

Faith slid Sunny's drink across the wooden bar top. She packed up the dozen beers I'd asked for in two six-pack carriers and handed them over the bar to me. "Twenty-six dollars."

I opened my wallet again, pulled out another ten, and set the bills on the counter.

"Hey, where are you going?" Sunny asked. Her shoulder bumped into mine, and I turned in the stool.

"Heading out," I said. I could sit there and watch her for another hour, but it was nothing more than torturing myself.

"Are you going out to Smiths'?" She looked down at the floor and bit her bottom lip. That shy thing she did was almost powerful enough to crush my defenses. It was completely opposite from the way she'd behaved around me my whole life.

I hadn't planned on going out there, but … did she want to go? Did she want me to ask her to go? She'd turned that other guy down and I'd heard her say in very plain English she wasn't *looking for anything serious right now.*

I wasn't sure what to say. "I don't know."

"Well, if you are ..." she started, then laughed. "God, this is weird." She looked up at me and swore. "Shit, Rhett."

I still wasn't going to ask her. I knew better.

"Spit it out," I told her.

She looked like a deer in headlights. There were a thousand times in my memory where I asked her to go somewhere, or do something, and there she was waiting for *me* to do it again. Things *had* changed.

"I mean, I left you my phone number, and I bought you some beer. I mean, it's weird as hell, but I just thought that maybe you'd want to ..." She was struggling.

I loved it. Every second of it. The part where she was nervous to say what she wanted, but mostly because she was actually paying attention to *me* for a change.

"To...?" I prompted, desperate to hear her say it.

"I don't know. To hang out? *Do* something. Talk. Ride around." She shrugged and her brow rose hopefully. Her eyes looked past me behind the bar at something that made her smile again, then added, "We could do anything."

I tried to keep that dude inside of me who was bursting to jump and shout out in victory, at bay. Sure, I was older now and she wasn't in any danger of jail time anymore, which I didn't actually realize until she'd already been gone a few years. It wasn't her fault I'd been so much younger than she was. She didn't really have a choice back then.

But, she did now.

"You want to go with me?" I asked, praying I hadn't read her wrong. Praying I wouldn't hear her say no once again.

"Yeah," she said. "I'll go with you." Embarrassment

mixed with excitement on her face and she held her lips shut tightly around a smile causing two sexy dimples to appear on her cheeks.

"All right then," I said. I needed to hold onto my cool with both hands.

"Faith, can you grab my purse from back there?" she asked.

In the reflection of the Miller Lite mirror hanging on the wall across the room, I saw Faith hand Sunny her purse and give her a thumbs up. Sunny flipped her off, and then said, "Let's go, Rhett."

In all my life, I never thought I'd *ever* be leaving a bar with that girl, but I wasn't about to complain. For what it was worth, just hearing her admit she wanted to go with me was enough.

I hadn't noticed earlier, but I'd parked right next to her. As we walked across the street, she walked toward her car. Not my pickup.

I stopped at my truck bed and flipped up my cooler's lid.

"Do you care if I take my car home and let Andy out?" she asked.

Two at a time, I plunged the bottles into the ice water in my cooler. That was fine with me. I could get a grip on the way.

"That's fine. I'll pick you up," I agreed.

"Oh, shoot. You left your passenger window down."

I looked through the back glass to see. I had, but maybe it wasn't too bad.

"Oh well. See you in a few minutes," she said, and hopped into her car.

After she backed up and pulled away and my cooler was restocked, I folded the cardboard six packs and opened the passenger side door to check the seat. It wasn't too damp, just wet on the door where rain had gotten through the few inches where the window was cracked.

Unfortunately, the seat was dry for the most part. *Dammit.*

That would have been a great excuse to slide her over to the middle of the bench seat next to me. Ironically, it was the one time that summer when I was disappointed by the rain *not* fucking something up.

There was no time to dwell on it. I was going to Sunny's to pick her up because she'd asked me to. I didn't think that was really sinking in yet.

I'd fantasized about her in a lot of places. My truck. The tractor. The barn. The meadow by the creek. *My bed.*

As I drove to her place, just outside of town, I reminded myself a few key things. Not to get my hopes up and not to get ahead of myself.

It had stopped raining by the time I pulled in her drive, but I noticed again that it was badly rutted. When I got around to smoothing out our roads, I'd be over there working on hers, too.

Because I was neighborly.

Because I didn't want her hitting one and jacking something up under her car. It was a safety thing.

She was standing on the small concrete porch steps watching her dog run around the yard. I could have been wrong, but, in my memory, Andy used to be a lot smaller. A lot different. In fact, I thought Andy was a Jack Russell something, and this dog was some kind of hound. Part beagle and part something shaggy.

I hopped out of my truck, but left it running, and walked around to lean on the front.

"You said Andy at the bar, right?" I asked, crossing my arms across my chest trying to decipher what was going on. I hadn't paid her dog much attention the day Dad and I had been there helping her.

She leaned on the small white iron rail flanking her steps.

"Yeah," she said, not really following. "Andy, my dog. I don't have some guy named Andy held hostage in my house. Why?" She was backlit from the light on in the house as she stood in front of the storm door.

"How old is Andy these days? He's looking pretty good."

Her head tipped back and she laughed, then pointed at the dog who was making his rounds near my truck and peeing on my tires. "That's a different Andy. He's Andy number two. Andy number one got hit by the school bus a few years ago."

She patted her thighs, a signal, and the hound took off straight for her, leaping the three stairs in one bound. She scratched him behind the ears and crouched down to kiss him on top of the head. "You be a good boy. I'll be back in a while." When she opened the door, he went in.

Sunny walked down the steps, looking at my truck and then at me, and held a finger up. Around to the passenger side of the truck, she opened the door, and I heard her give the seat a few swift pats.

"Yep, it's wet," she said, but I'd checked it and knew better. She shut the door and walked around to the front where I was still standing against the corner of the hood. "I'll get in on your side." Then she walked to the driver's side door and waited for me.

Sweet Jesus. Sunny was getting into my jacked up truck.

I took a deep breath and pinched my arm. Half expecting to wake up, but I didn't.

It was real.

The door creaked as I swung it open for her. The huge tires and lift kit made the step up into my Chevy a stretch for someone her height. First, she tossed her hoodie in, then held onto the seat as she climbed. Her ass bending and heaving into the cab as I stood like a statue trying to keep my hands off of it.

Having something that tempting right in front of me was a true test of my self-control.

She scooted over, about as far as she could, sitting just to the right of center, giving me more than enough room.

I hopped in and put my arm behind her to look behind us as I backed out of her drive. Her leg wasn't touching mine, but I could covertly fix that with a few poorly timed turns.

When I got to the end of her driveway, I caught her looking up at me and saw someone I'd never seen before. Almost a stranger. Her blinking lazily in the dashboard lights, mouth parted. I held her gaze, and she snapped out of it.

"Wait," she said.

There it was. She was changing her mind. She wanted to stay home. She'd made a mistake.

"Don't move," she instructed and leaned up to pull something out of her pocket. "We need a picture."

"Of what?" I asked.

"Of *us*. It's our first road trip," she explained, like it was something monumental. Her voice sounded young and like I was out of my mind for *not* knowing it was such a benchmark moment.

Before I knew it she had her phone held up in front of us. "No. It's too dark," she noted. "Can you turn on the dome light? I hate the flash on my phone. It makes me look like a zombie from *The Walking Dead*."

I laughed because … well, I laughed because of about thirty-seven different things, but mostly because as weird as she'd claimed she felt earlier, now she seemed comfortable. Even relaxed.

Here I'd been infatuated with this girl my whole life, and I was quickly learning that maybe I'd been focusing on all the wrong parts of her.

I turned on the light overhead like she asked me to do.

"That's better." She leaned into the crook of my arm, and I inhaled the sweetest lungful of air. A hint of some kind of perfume that reminded me of flowers and honey.

If she was relaxed, I was the exact opposite. I didn't know what to do with myself. What the hell was happening?

Keep your shit together, dude.

"Hey, you gonna smile?" she teased and my eyes met her eyes reflecting in the reverse view of her camera. "It's not a mugshot, Rhett."

Maybe not. However, I'll be damned if I wasn't held prisoner to the moment. When she smiled at me, I gave in to it and gave her my best.

"There you go," she praised before she pressed the button.

I was a gentleman, so I'd never do it, but I wanted to

throw that truck in park and kiss the hell right out of her. For the first time in my life, I felt she might want that, too.

After she reviewed it, apparently satisfied, she turned it off and slid it into the small compartment in my dash. Sunny's phone was just sitting in my dash. No big deal. Yet, it gave me pause.

Check yourself. Act like a man, dammit.

I moved my arm from around her, back to the steering column and shifted the truck from reverse into drive. Then, we tore down the muddy road.

She turned the radio on and WDKR played a song I'd never heard before. "I like what you play at night," I said.

"Thanks. I don't think many people actually listen to the station after they get home from work, so I don't feel like I'm trying to please anyone. You know? I just play what I like."

I drove with my right arm to keep it from pulling her closer, and I propped my left arm on the rolled down window ledge as the warm night air filled the cab.

Soon we were pulling into Smiths'.

They had a farm like us, although theirs was a smaller operation. However, the second you pulled down their lane you could smell the money. Well, you could smell the hogs. The Smiths had a machine shop at the back of their property and I drove straight for it noticing how many vehicles were out there for a Friday night.

Evidently, everyone who lived in or around Wynne was there. I went past the spot I wanted, then backed in to avoid making her get out in a huge puddle.

I turned off the ignition and turned the key back to the auxiliary so that the radio didn't turn off yet. Her head was swaying off time to a song she obviously liked.

Leaning against the door, I watched her.

She smiled and then started singing quietly, grinning the whole time. She was not good. Not even through my rose tinted glasses could I ever trick myself into thinking she was a singer.

"You like singing?" I asked when the song wrapped up.

"Oh, yeah, but I suck so bad." It caught me off guard and I laughed out loud. "I can't dance either. I'm sure you noticed." Her expression was one part humility and one part confidence.

"So why do you do it then?"

She leaned back and her ass shifted down into the seat as she propped her leg up on the hump in the middle of the floorboard.

"Well, I love music. It's what I know." She thumbed through her phone looking at a playlist. "You know what they say about teachers?" She glanced over at me and waited for me to answer, but I wanted her to keep going so I just nodded. "How those who can't do, teach?" She shrugged and a whisper of a laugh left her before she added, "Well, musicians who can't play, deejay."

I huffed, feeling a laugh grow in my chest, but I didn't want her to think I was laughing at her so I let it stay inside. It was quite the opposite, she was funny.

From the way she looked, she was laughing inside, too. The way she didn't take herself too seriously was refreshing.

"Makes sense," I said.

"What's something you suck at but do anyway?" she asked.

Chasing her was at the top of the list, but I was sure I

didn't want to admit it. Especially, since I was sitting next to her in my truck in the middle of the night. Then again, her sitting there had nothing to do with me chasing her to get her there.

"I don't know. I'll have to think on it. I'm sure there are plenty of things I'm not that great at."

She leaned up and scanned the parking lot, the pole light giving off a brilliant amber cast to the area. Then she sat back with a huff and a growl.

"There are a lot of people here," she muttered and turned my way, her blond hair falling off of her shoulder. "You know if we walk in there, we'll never hear the end of it."

She didn't need to elaborate.

I wasn't worried about what they'd say to me. I'd been used to it damn near all my life, but tonight she was in my truck and smiling and talking to me like I was a man … not a boy. I didn't want them to make her uncomfortable, or change the way she was looking at me for the first time.

It was surreal, and I didn't want it to end.

I suggested, "We don't have to go in. It's getting late anyway. I'll take you home."

Chapter Nine

Sunny

"Okay, we can go," I said, and just that quick he flipped the lights on and cranked the truck to life. About that time I saw Dean walking to his Cherokee—past Mike's Bronco—and he waved at us. Dean wasn't even staying.

I didn't really give a shit about what anyone said. Okay, that wasn't entirely true. Everyone was no doubt drunk, and I didn't want Rhett to get teased for being with me. Especially, not when he'd just started talking. Well, kind of.

Besides that, I didn't feel like being there.

He pulled down the lane and turned back on the gravel country road heading back the way we came. I was disappointed.

"Rhett?" I asked, hoping to get some clue as to whether he really wanted to hang out with me or not. Hell, for all I knew he wanted to drop me off and go find a girl that he wouldn't have to take any guff for being with.

He was lost in his thoughts and didn't hear me, or we were back to where we'd been last week—me talking and him being short.

"Rhett?" I repeated more persistently.

"Yeah," he answered, not taking his eyes off the road, which drove me a little nuts.

"Slow down. Will you look at me, please?"

He was pitched forward hovering over the wheel, but turned his head my direction, slightly.

"Just because I didn't want to stay at Smiths' doesn't mean I want to go home yet."

It was worth the mild embarrassment of letting him know—*again*—that I was at least kind of interested in spending time with him. I wasn't sure if he was getting my hints, though.

I said, "I don't care if we go somewhere else or just ride around, but I want to talk to you more."

Rhett looked at me out of the corner of his eye, but I couldn't read his face. He'd be amazing at poker. He'd probably even beat my mom, and she was the best poker player I knew.

We were all but creeping down the road, then headlights appeared a ways off. When he turned down a different lane, I knew we weren't going back to my place.

Small victory, but I'd take it.

"You still want a few more beers?" he asked about the time I realized we were on his property, down the back road that led to his cabin. A way I hadn't been in a long time.

"Do you?" Answering with a question was a cheap move, but I needed to know what he was thinking. Even if it was something trivial, like if he wanted another beer. He didn't give anything away, and it was severing me from my sanity. It was both nerve-wracking and exciting.

He slowed before his C-shaped drive just off the road.

"Before I pull in here, will you feel comfortable if we stop?" he asked.

I gave him a look like *are you serious*? Of course I felt comfortable.

"Rhett, I've known you since we were kids. I'm fine."

His voice was strong and low as he countered. "You're wrong. We knew each other—marginally—*when* we were kids. Not *since*. We don't know each other now." It was the longest amount of words he'd said all strung together to me since I saw him at the truck stop almost a week earlier.

"Oh," I said. No guy had ever talked to me like that. Like that was what he was truly thinking—but he wasn't entirely wrong.

In fact, he was right.

Rhett didn't know anything about me, and he was damn near a mystery, but I wasn't afraid of him. Honestly, the thing earlier with Mike and his drunk buddies made me feel unnerved, but being alone with Rhett didn't.

I was still wrapping my head around it when he added, his voice gentler than before, "I'm not a kid, Sunny, and you're not just the smoking hot cheerleader anymore. So, when I ask you something, I need to know. I might not say—*out loud*—every single thought I'm having, but I always speak my mind when I do. Not only that, but I'm a lot bigger than you, and from our history, you know I at least have the ability to come on a little strong—innocent as I was back then. You're at my place in the middle of the night, after you've been drinking, and your cell phone keeps beeping because it's about to die. I need to know if you feel okay being here. The last thing I want is to make you uncomfortable."

The truck idled on the road near his cabin. I looked over to it and, just as it had been the other night, the porch light was on and there was a cat sleeping on the step.

I glanced back at Rhett.

He *was* bigger than me. I *had* drunk plenty, and unfortunately, there had been times when I'd drunk more and put myself in similar situations, but my mind didn't usually think like that. If somebody gave me the creeps, I just wouldn't go out with them.

"If you made me uncomfortable I wouldn't have brought you that thank you just so I could give you my phone number. I wouldn't have asked you to go to the bar and then want to hang out after. Rhett, your passenger seat isn't even wet." I shifted farther away, sitting on the part I'd claimed was damp. Moving away from him got his attention and he watched me closely. "No. I'm not uncomfortable." Then I thought, just to be safe, I'd ask. "Should I be?"

"No," he deadpanned and took his foot off the brake, pulling the truck up to the cabin.

Pickup off. Music off. Lights off.

He opened the door and it squeaked as he pushed it to its limits, before hopping out. He took a step back and held out his hand to me. I inched to the edge of the seat, and with the door out of my reach, he steered my palm into his.

I thought about tripping or falling, so he'd catch me. It was wrong, but I blamed it on the damn panther.

All in all, it was a painfully *uneventful* exit, until then he stepped forward.

"Why *did* you do all of those things?" he asked.

There were many reasons that I'd done them, but when it boiled right down to it there was just one answer.

"Because I wanted to."

The light from the porch highlighted the wrinkle in the corner of his hazel eyes as he cocked his head to the side. He didn't say anything, but his face relaxed as he looked at me.

He let my hand fall, since I didn't need the help anymore on my own two feet. At that point, I probably could have faked an ankle injury, but, like those other thoughts, I let it pass. My hand felt lonely and cooler, free from his big grip.

I anxiously waited for him to say something. I'd never been a patient woman. I talk on the radio for crying out loud. I'm like, get it out. Time's wasting.

"Well…" I said after what felt like minutes.

"Sorry. That was just a good answer." He nodded playfully and licked his lips before walking to the back of his truck, then added, "*Really* good." He lifted the cooler out of the truck bed with little effort and waved his hand at me as he passed. "Come on."

I followed close behind as he opened the unlocked front door, flipped on a lamp, and then crossed the room into the kitchen.

I looked around, and although I'd always just thought of the place as a hunting cabin, I quickly realized it was a lot nicer than I'd ever guessed. It was decorated with primitives, but not so many that it would be a full-time job keeping them dust free and tidy. I followed him through the back kitchen door onto a screened-in porch.

He pointed at two chairs, but I pointed to the swing on the end. The chairs were separate. The swing was something we could share. I liked the idea of that more.

He set the cooler off to one side of the wooden bench seat and sat, holding it still for me to get on nearest the screened-in outside wall.

No quicker than the time it took me to sit, I knew. I'd sat in karma. A wet cushion—and I mean saturated enough to squeeze water out of the bottom as it splashed my sandaled feet.

"Oh my god, I'm so wet," I stated while even more water dripped from the cushion to the floor.

I heard a rush of air leave the guy at the other end of the swing, then I realized what I'd said and I fell into a fit of embarrassed laughter.

"I meant the swing is wet."

The stupid thing I'd said, combined with how I'd lied about the truck seat so I could sit near him was all too much. I was such an idiot, but I got what I deserved.

He leaned over, pulled two bottles from the icy water beside him, twisted off the caps, and held them in his hand.

"Well, I'd say scoot over, but it's just as wet down here," he admitted playfully and passed me a beer. His long legs started swinging us.

I laughed more and he joined me. I liked the sound our laughs made in unison. It was a song I'd like to hear on loop.

It might have been the beer. That late, it could have been delirium. It was probably nerves and excitement. The old and new of it all. But, whatever it was, it felt wonderful and I surrendered to the outrageousness of the moment.

Then something he'd said earlier popped into my head, the line finally floating to the surface of my mind. "So I'm not the smoking hot cheerleader anymore?"

He stopped rocking, and after a beat he let his knees hinge and move us forward again.

"No, but I'm not a smoking hot high school cheerleader either. As devastating as it is, you'll get used to it."

Was that a joke?

"You're almost funny," I fired back and fought the urge to giggle.

I drank from the cold bottle and decided I couldn't sit on the wet cushion another minute. Standing, I motioned for him to get up, too. Pulling the Velcro apart in the three places it was attached, I walked it to a small indoor clothesline on the other side of the porch by a washer and dryer. With a few clothespins pinched on it, I hung the wet seat to dry.

While I was up, he went inside and came back quickly with a few towels.

"Here," he said, handing them to me so he could mess with a radio. I unfolded and laid them the width of the seat and sat. He joined me.

"So how is it being back in town?" I asked.

"Being back in town is about how I pictured it. Except for the rain, I wasn't expecting *that* this summer."

The record rain had been a literal dark cloud over the whole town, but everyone helped out and we'd get through it like always.

"Yeah, Wynne hasn't changed much."

He swallowed and countered, "Oh, I don't know. It has and hasn't. I was always coming back anyway. You know what it's like."

The muscles in his legs flexed as he moved us back and forth.

I agreed, "Yeah, I moved away for school, but I was always pretty sure I'd be right back here. I love the people. It's my home."

His shoulder bumped mine. "Exactly, if I really didn't want to be here, then I'd be somewhere else."

I picked at the label on my beer, enjoying the easy conversation. "Where would you be, if not here?" I'd only been as far as a few hours away from our small town my whole life.

As he thought, he took a few drinks. "Maybe Hawaii or some little town near San Diego. Those places are nice, places I'd go back to."

"I've never been anywhere like that," I admitted.

"No? I like traveling."

"When we were kids we'd go up to the lake for a few days or a week, but Dad was the only one in his office, so we couldn't really go too far. We had a lot of fun, though. Both sets of my grandparents used to go, and sometimes I'd bring a friend with me," I explained.

"We took a few vacations when we were younger. We went to Jamaica once when I was a senior in high school. It's hard to plan stuff like that with the weather and the farm. Tough to plan ahead. I traveled a lot with running, though."

"Running track?" How did I not know he was a runner? And a traveling runner?

"Yeah. I was good in high school and got a sports scholarship, then ran in college. I still compete. I couldn't run for school last year—I'd stayed another semester after graduation to take a few extra classes—but I run marathons. My last half I got second in my age, which is pretty good."

"Hell, I can barely jog. Sometimes I take Andy on a long walk and even that wears me out. I can't imagine running in a race." I was feeling winded just talking about it.

"It's not that bad. It's more about endurance than speed. At least, for me."

I heard a growl in the gutter at the back of my mind when he mentioned *endurance*. Something about going all night strutted by and I rolled my eyes at myself and drank my beer in blessed silence as it passed without coming out of my mouth.

If I had to take a drink to keep from saying things like that around him, I'd surely get myself into a Betty Ford situation.

We talked about places we'd been, but mostly him. It was alarming how untraveled I was in comparison. I had to seem like some old maid who was just chilling in Wynne because she didn't know how to leave.

That wasn't it at all, but it didn't look good.

After my third beer, I said, "What time is it? You're not even drinking anymore and I should probably go home."

He looked at his phone and answered, "Pretty late. I'll take you back," he said and stood, causing the swing to pitch and sway. He steadied the chain on my side with one long reach of his arm above my head.

I stood and wanted to kiss him, and it had nothing to do with the wanton black cat in my mind. It had everything to do with the way his shirt was bunched on one side of his belt, and how the tongue of his boot sat just outside the hem of his jean leg. The way, every once in a while, he'd readjust his hat, and I'd get a waft of his clean hair. The way he seemed like someone I was meeting for the first time, yet kind of like a person I already knew.

Also, but probably most notably, the way I could imagine what his lips felt like on mine without even touching them. The way I could predict the way he'd sound moaning into my mouth, and the way I desperately wanted *him* to be the one to kiss me.

Chapter Ten

Rhett

It seemed like it took no time at all from my driveway to hers. It was nearly three thirty in the morning, and I'd be dragging ass the next day, but it had been worth it.

Not because it was Sunny Wilbanks, but because she was funny and silly and easy to talk to and those things made her more beautiful than any faded memory I had of her.

I wasn't sure what was going on. Some part of me thought that maybe it was a pity thing for how everyone ragged on my juvenile behavior all those years ago. I couldn't deny that, for whatever her sudden interest was in me, I liked it.

I really liked that she still climbed into my truck from the driver's side and sat next to me on the way to her house, even after she'd confessed that it was dry on the passenger side.

If she was doing all of those things because she wanted to, then maybe I should do a few things that I wanted to. Like kiss her.

There were a few moments that felt like a good time, but when you've been rejected by one girl that many times … it takes a minute to adjust to the change of heart. The odds of her actually being interested in me were not that great.

Still, there she was, on my right side as we pulled back into her drive.

"What are you doing tomorrow?" she asked quietly when I came to a stop behind her car. Again, it stunned me. She'd done that on many occasions throughout the night. Hell, over the past week.

It took me a minute to get away from the shock of hearing her say something like that before I remembered what I had to do and answered. "We're working on the levee all day again," I said as I pulled the door handle to get out. When my feet were on the ground, I gave her a hand, and like we'd practiced the move more than once, she took it and hopped right out next to me.

"Oh, that's right. You better get to bed then. The sun will be up in a few hours."

I was well aware.

"I'll be fine." I'd skip my run and sleep in a little.

She stood there looking up at me, then stepped away an arm's length, which was good for both of us. I was dangerously close to pinning her up against the side of the truck bed, and the added space helped me dial it in. My chest pounded, knowing this was the drop off portion of the night when normally a guy would kiss a woman he was interested in.

Call me crazy for having fantasized of that moment for so many years, then holding back when I finally got it. But, if she wanted to kiss me, then she knew where to get it.

However, I wanted her to know I was interested, so I said, "I'd like to hang out with you again."

She smiled a little too quickly to be nonchalant, but I loved it.

"You have my number," Sunny reminded me and walked backwards a few steps. Holding her sweatshirt and phone in one hand, she pulled her keys from her pocket.

Then, I saw something that took me back to that boy I was and I straightened. Stunned.

"Good night, Sunny," I said and stepped into the cab of my truck, hearing her say good night before she walked the rest of the way to her door.

As I drove, I thought.

"What is this?" she asked me, leaning down just a little. Then she yelled behind her, "Just a second. I'll be right there," to her friends who were waiting down the hall after school. They always rode around town for a while when classes were over. I'd ride my bike to the park with Lance and watch them go by.

I cleared my throat to make my voice sound as deep as I could. "It's just a little something I saw for you. It's no big deal."

She held the small box in her palm and readjusted her backpack so she could use both hands to open it. Her smile was thank you enough, but I wanted to stick around and see if she liked it.

She handed me the box after emptying it into her hand, and passed the cardboard back to me to hold while she took the paper around it off.

"Rhett, this is really cool," she said, looking at the keychain I'd bought her. It was a sun that had a button in the middle. When you pushed it tiny white and yellow lights lit up.

I pressed the button for her.

"It's a sunshine key chain because you're my sunshine." I'd had something much cooler thought out to say but kind of choked when it came down to it.

"Thank you. I love it." She bent down and I leaned up, hoping this was the moment she was finally going to let me kiss her. Or kiss me.

It was finally happening. I knew she'd like the keychain the second I saw it.

She wrapped her arm around my shoulders and gave me a side hug. In the moment, I kissed her shoulder.

Like a moron.

I kissed her shoulder.

I prayed she didn't notice.

If she had, she didn't say anything.

"I'm glad you like it," I said as she pulled away. She shifted her bag again and looked behind her where her friends were still waiting and watching. "I've gotta go, but this is so nice." She stepped backward down the linoleum hall.

I didn't know what else to say, but as she turned to walk out the door, I noticed she already had her keys out, stringing them together with it.

She hugged me. Okay, half-hugged me. It wasn't a kiss,

but it was something.

Not only did Sunny still have that old sunburst keychain with the flashing white and yellow lights, but she still used it.

I lay in bed, knowing that I needed to go to sleep, but my mind was working overtime. Adding things up. I was almost trying to prove all of the signals she was giving me were like the ones I'd *chosen* to see when I was a kid. When it came to her, I'd always misinterpreted what she really meant.

What I meant to her.

I wasn't about to stop what was happening, but I was going to step with caution.

She was dynamite back then, but she was damn near perfect now. Maybe because I was older, but I noticed different things about her than I used to. The way her collarbone stuck out just enough that I wanted to lick it. The way she was the perfect size to pick up and carry to the nearest wall to kiss her breathless. How it almost felt like she was waiting for me to do those things.

As a boy, I'd jumped the gun so many times. As a man—as a runner—I'd trained myself not to. Not even with the few girls in my past, through high school and college … I'd always let them come to me.

Was that because of her? Maybe.

Regardless, none of my behavior was her fault. She'd never been mean or cruel. Sometimes she probably should have.

I lay on my side and looked out the window, thinking about how different it was to be with her, like we were finally equals. How all of those same old feelings grew in the same familiar spots, just like the crops in the field outside. I wondered if I tended to whatever it was between us if it would grow and thrive like my ground. If I gave it consistent attention when it needed it, and took a step back when the timing wasn't right, if she—like the land—would do the rest.

I flipped on the radio next to my bed and drifted off.

Morning came early, but I wasn't dragging that much. While the eggs fried on the stove, I watched the sun top the trees to the east and it lit the haze over acres of short, but thankfully growing, corn behind the cabin.

I sipped coffee and ate, thinking about the day's work.

I hadn't slept as late as I'd expected, only getting a few hours and waking courtesy of my internal clock, even despite the late night. I didn't have time for a run, but it gave me a little extra time to throw some clothes in the washer and put the few bags of trash I had into the back of my pickup so I could throw it in the dumpster at the farm.

If we got an early start, and had the help we were counting on, there was a really good chance of getting most of the levee covered. That would be one less thing to worry about, although we all knew if the river topped it, time was our biggest enemy. The levee would hold if the rain ebbed, but if the water had time and the river stayed swollen, it would wear away new weak spots. There'd be nothing we could do.

I counted more than half a dozen beers at the bottom of my cooler, and the ice was still good, so I added a few bottles of water and a couple Gatorades, then hauled it outside.

My phone read six o'clock. Folks would be showing up at the shed.

I walked to my bedroom and opened the sock drawer where I kept her note, the one with her phone number on it and programmed it into my phone before I forgot.

After all, she'd mentioned it the night before.

By the time I got to my truck with my refilled coffee mug, I'd talked myself out of sending her a text three times. It was too early. Yet, there I was, sitting in my truck while it ran with a new blank message.

My youthful history aside, I'd spent the night before with a beautiful woman, and if she were someone new—who I'd just met—and I wanted to see her again, etiquette would tempt me to send her a message. A good morning. Something.

That logic moved my fingers over the screen and typed.

ME: Hope you slept well. Let me know if you want to do something later.

I set the phone on my lap and pulled out of my drive, then slowed when I heard it chime a few seconds later.

SUNSHINE: If you'd get to work, we could have fun sooner than later. I'm at the levee shed with the rest of the town. Hurry up.

I hadn't expected a message that quick—if at all. That woman was getting really good at surprising me.

I ran those back country roads about twice as fast as I

had the morning before and cranked the radio the whole way.

Sometimes it's foolish to ask why when good things are happening. Even at my age I knew that. Sunny was about a hundred good things and every minute she spent with me I found more of them, better ones than I'd been blinded by before.

Her smile was the first thing I saw when I pulled in. They'd already bagged up a truckload, and it was heading north up the levee with a few guys sitting on the tailgate.

I waved at them and hopped out. There had to be twenty-five people there. *Before me.*

I looked at my dad and he was grinning ear to ear. The day before we had plenty of help to get a good start. With this crew, we had enough to possibly finish early.

"Morning," she said with a shovel in her hand. She was wearing lime green running shorts and a white tank top that read *I'm Your Huckleberry*. Her long blond hair was swept up in a knot high on her head and she had on white framed sunglasses.

Yet, she looked like a super model. Pin-up worthy.

I'd get to look at her all day. Talk about motivation.

"Good morning to you, too." An image of me saying those words as she was curled around me, under my sheets, appeared to me about the time I heard my dad holler. Then her assembly line started back up, and I left her to it.

"Rhett," he called again. I held up a hand to let him know I heard him and that I'd be right there. I walked back to my truck and found my gloves, then looked at her hands across the gravel lot and saw she didn't have any on. If she planned on shoveling all day, she'd be in serious pain by evening.

My father met up with me as I tucked the leather into my back pocket and pulled out my phone.

"We got a lot of help today, son," he contended. "A lot of *good* help." He winked and nodded at Sunny.

"Not this early, Dad," I warned and pressed send on my screen.

She answered right away. "Good morning, honey. Are you already down at the levee shed?" my mom asked.

"Yeah, just got here."

"Good, tell your dad I'm on my way. I just called up to the store and I'm bringing drinks, coffee and some doughnuts. Need anything?" She'd probably been thrown off by the amount of people there, too.

"Yeah, actually. Do you have an extra pair of leather gloves?"

"Honey, I think you'll fit your dad's better," she said.

"No, for Sunny."

She gasped. "Sunny Wilbanks is there helping?"

"Shoveling her ass off, Mom. Now do you have any gloves she can wear? She needs them." Yes, I would have loved nothing more than to wax poetic about the miracle it was that Sunny was there, and from the sound of her voice and the look on my dad's face, that's *surely* what it was.

More importantly though, I didn't want her to suffer, and I knew she would before long like she was.

"I'll find her some and bring 'em in a while."

That wasn't quite good enough. "Mom, please find them and just bring them first." She might be an hour if she ran into the right person at the store. Coffee could wait. Sunny's hands couldn't.

I watched Sunny look at the spot between her thumb and index finger. She was already starting to feel it. She was shoveling heavy, wet sand into a bag sitting in a five gallon bucket.

I was relieved that I didn't have to argue or leave to get them myself when Mom agreed. "Okay, I'll be right there."

"Thanks, bye." I hung up and shoved my dad's shoulder out of the way. He was grinning like a fool. "Get to work, Dad."

I slipped the leather over my hands as I marched over to Sunny and held my hand out for the shovel.

"What? I'm doing it," she said, almost offended.

I didn't want her confused by my actions. It looked chauvinistic, but that's not what it was. "I know you *can* do it. Just hold the bag for me. Give your hands a rest for a minute." Sunny didn't argue and passed the wooden handle off. She flipped the bucket over and sat on it, grabbing the next bag and holding it wide open for me.

"You're up early," I said, pushing the shovel into the sand pile beside us.

"To tell you the truth, I couldn't sleep. I tried for a while, then I ended up going to the station and working."

I tried to ignore the fact that, with her leaning over like she was, I could see down her shirt.

Tried. I guess that's one of those things I'm just not very good at, and, coincidentally, another I wouldn't mention.

Work after no sleep? That couldn't be very productive. "Did you get much done?"

"I lined out the whole day and tomorrow, then I got bored." She looked up at me when the bag was filled just past half-full, like it should be.

Holding the shovel between my legs, I pulled the drawstrings and lifted it into the air. "*Bored?* That's one word you don't say around here. You'll get put to work. Spin it," I said.

She gave it a twirl. After a round or two, I set it back down and tied it shut, then handed it off to Dub. He was taking the finished bags and handing them off to the person stacking them in the back of the next truck to head up the levee.

"Well, I am here to work for you. So I suppose I came to the right place." I could think of about a dozen other things to keep her occupied, but shoved all twelve of them into the same place I sent the image of her in my bed.

After a few more bags, my mom pulled up and I handed the shovel back to Sunny. "I'll be right back." It was good timing, there's only so much baseball and oil changing I could concentrate on to keep my dick down with her chest in view like it was.

I ran over, fetched the gloves, and gave my mom a kiss on the cheek. Happy she'd hurried. I knew what she was thinking. Even though she didn't say a word, it was all over her face. I'd seen it on everyone's there.

Surprisingly, nobody was making a show of it or saying anything. I had that to be thankful for. *So far.*

Turned out that five foot three blond was a worker, and even with no sleep she pulled her weight. All day. In the sun.

We alternated between bagging and making runs on the trucks to the levee. But where I went, she followed, talking and joking like we were old friends. Around lunch we tarped and bagged most of the way back to the shed and were heading south next.

I sat on my tailgate and she sat on my cooler, and we ate the turkey sandwiches and chips my mom brought everyone. Drinking our weight in water.

I'd had much worse workdays.

Chapter Eleven

Sunny

I was expecting to feel like death warmed over by noon, but, since I'd kept busy, I was fine.

The night before, I'd lain there in bed, my head swimming and replaying all of it. Over and over. Not tired in the least.

I wanted to see him again, another time where there wasn't really any pressure. He'd said he wanted to see me again, which gave me a thrill. But, Wynne was such a small town; people would talk. They probably already were.

I was the old chick chasing the young guy who was just back from college. When I thought about it like that, it felt a little pathetic.

When I was with him, though, it totally *didn't* feel like that. He didn't seem younger than me—at all. If anything. he was way more mature. Rhett was a man who spoke soft' when needed and spoke up when there was a reason to.

I’d heard him shout a few times throughout the day. To a truck heading out as he smacked the side of it when it passed him. To his dad across the property when we ran out of bags, asking where more were.

I loved how he spoke to me, but hearing him yell reminded me how strong he was. How he tempered his voice in our conversations.

Right before we started again, after eating the sack lunches his mom brought us, Haley, his sister showed up.

“’Bout time you show your face,” he teased her. As I cleaned up my trash, pitching it in the dumpster beside the shed, I listened and pretended to be busy.

“*Your* mother had me making an ass load of sandwiches,” she replied. “You’re lucky I had an extra pair of gloves. When was the last time you saw *Mom* wearing gloves? Come on.”

I’d been truly grateful for the gloves. When I’d put them on I could already feel the wear on my hands in a few places that were raw. I could have kissed him on the spot for being so thoughtful. Then again, he’d always been thoughtful, and I’d never kissed him for it before.

I walked back and waved the leather in my hands and said, “Thank you, Haley. I didn’t even think to grab gloves this morning.”

She shot a friendly smile my way. “No problem. Do …y fit?”

…hey’re perfect. Do you need them back?”

…have more.” She waved me off and tied a red ban-

…er forehead. One of those would have been

…weating like a junkie all day.

…idea to wear a white t-shirt to play

in the sand and dirt. I was a mess, but it was just the first thing I grabbed when I'd decided to help the Caraways that morning.

"We've got enough sand for a few more truckloads, and Dad called for more. Said they should show up in an hour or so. They're hauling it from the quarry." He re-tied one of his bootlaces, and when he squatted I noticed how big and defined the muscles in his legs were.

I'd drunk a lot of water that day, sweating like I was, but watching him made my mouth bone dry all over again.

"Cool. Where do you need me?" she asked.

After standing and stretching his arms above his head, he answered, "Up to you. You can bag up here or ride down the levee on the next truck." He looked at me and added, "We've been going back and forth. Take your pick."

His younger sister gave him a curious look and asked, "Oh, you two"—she pointed between us—"you've been going back and forth, huh?" Her face remained a semblance of seriousness, but her sarcasm was as clear as the welcomed blue sky.

He stood taller and shifted his weight, putting his hands on his slender hips, then shot her a warning with his eyes. That was enough for her.

If he looked at me like that, it would have been enough for me, too.

I wouldn't want to get on his bad side. Well, then again, it was fierce and sexy. Maybe a little of his bad side wouldn't be that awful.

I shook the thought away. Lack of sleep was causing my imagination to do all sorts of crazy things. Like daydreaming about what he could do with those big arms and that strong back.

I was tired, but the panther was wide awake.

As we filled bags, I saw my dad's SUV pull in, and it made me chuckle. He sold insurance and was far from a farmer. I stopped what I was doing and a few seconds later Rhett, beside me, did, too.

My father had on a pair of cargo shorts, an old polo shirt, and the sneakers he wore to mow the yard. It made me laugh that *those* were his work clothes.

"What are you doing here, Sunny? I thought you'd be at the station." He looked at his watch, keenly aware of my normal schedule. I was usually there until early afternoon on Saturdays, but I'd finished my work before the sun even came up.

"Oh, I got done early. What are you doing here?"

"I came to help. They swung by and offered to lend a hand with my tree, and they cleaned up yours. It's the least I can do. At work yesterday, I heard you on the radio talking about the levee. So thought I'd drive over today and see if I can pitch in." He looked to my left and nodded at Rhett.

"What can I do for you?" he asked and stretched out a hand to shake.

Rhett stood tall, pulled his glove off with his underarm and shook with my dad. "Thank you, Mr. Wilbanks. Do you mind taking these full bags and stacking them in that truck bed over there?"

My dad looked behind us to where Rhett was talking about, then started packing off the bags we'd filled.

I didn't know what to say, but I was really happy. Really tired. Really sweaty. Really sandy. And completely happy.

With my head tucked down shoveling, both of us using

my bucket method now, I caught a glimpse of Rhett's face and he looked pretty damn happy, too.

The sand truck came and dropped off another load, but came along with another truck full of bags that were already filled—which was awesome.

I saw my dad and Kent talking a little later, looking our way and laughing at something. Rhett saw it too, but didn't say anything as he shook his head and smacked my shovel to get me back to work.

He was a sexy foreman, so I got right to it.

All but one more track of field was left when they decided to call it for the day.

It was awesome how many people showed up to help them. Obviously, more than the Caraways expected.

Aaron, and the other firemen who had come by to bag during their shift, went back to the station. Even with all of them gone, there were still quite a number of folks milling around, having a few brews, courtesy of Mr. and Mrs. Caraway. Talking to each other across truck beds and leaning on hoods, they shot the shit and gave each other hell after a long day's work.

I hadn't done that much manual labor in my life—well, ever—and I could feel it in my muscles.

Hopefully, I'd sweated a few pounds off and that damn skirt would zip all the way up. It was doubtful, but a girl could wish.

By the time the sun started to fall behind the tree line and the goddamn biting-ass mosquitos started humming around my ankles, the only people left were Rhett, his dad, Mr. Smith, Haley, and me.

"I don't think I can go to Nashville with you, Rhett," his

younger sister said.

I didn't think she was twenty-one yet because every time she'd pull another beer from the cooler her dad would tell her, "One more." That had been three beers ago.

"That's fine," he said to her. "What are you doing?"

"They're letting RAs move in early. So, I'll be heading back to get my hall ready." She smiled as wide as humanly possible. Then she lifted her head to the sky and exclaimed, "I'm going back to school." She seemed supremely eager about it. "Mom and Dad are driving me nuts."

"Better you than me," he said.

She chuckled. "My friend Carrie got the floor under mine, so we're both going back early."

I filed Nashville away in my head and thought about how fun it would be to go. I'd always dreamed of walking Broadway and listening to the music I grew up on. Drinking and laughing and taking it all in.

Maybe someday.

The beer wasn't doing anything for me. Other than being cold and wet, it just didn't taste all that great. I heard a roll of thunder, and, although I hated to go home, I knew my shower and my couch were calling my name.

Rhett had been a lot more talkative with me, in his own way, but he hadn't asked me to do anything later. That was just as well. It was going to be a pretty lazy night for old Sunny.

By the second clap of thunder, everyone was loading up their things. Ready to head out. Haley stood in the back of her Jeep, sorting out the soft top to put back on, and I tried to hand the gloves back to her, but she waved me off again. "We appreciate the help, Sunny. Keep 'em."

"Thanks," I said. "See you later."

Rhett had pulled their old farm truck into the shed and was helping his dad put a tarp over the pile of sand they still had left to use.

"I'm going to head out," I shouted their way as I walked to my car. "See you guys later."

As I got in and rolled down the windows, Rhett jogged over and rested his forearms on the roof of my Honda. I got a delicious whiff of whatever deodorant he was wearing.

"Hey, thanks a lot for today," he said and looked down, his hat hiding most of his face.

"You're welcome. It's no big deal." I stared at the steering wheel and traced the emblem on the center of it with my finger.

"I'm sure you're tired, but…" he paused and let out a huff and a nervous *whoo* sound.

Before I knew it, I interrupted and asked, "Do you want to come over?"

He gave me a closed mouth smile and nodded. "Yes."

I blushed and my palms began to sweat. It was embarrassing how obvious I was, but the pleased look on his face soothed my humility. "All right."

There'd been a flirty tension between us the entire day, but we were working, and there were people around us the whole time. So it was all very casual, but damn if I wasn't dying to know if he was feeling it, too.

It started to sprinkle, so I said, "I'm going to take a shower. Wash this sand off. I'll leave the garage open. Pull in there, if you want." If it was raining, there was no use in him getting drenched. I'd park to one side so there would be enough room for both of us to pull in.

I looked at his face, but all I saw was his fucking lips. God, I wanted to touch them. When my eyes finally lifted to his, he was looking at *my* mouth, and I bit my bottom lip under his attention.

"I'll text you when I'm on my way," he said and stood up quickly, then gave the roof of my car a pat and walked off.

I didn't know how much more of that I could take before I planted one on him. I was becoming obsessed with thinking about it. How he would taste. If he was a good kisser. How it would feel.

Part of the time, I was fantasizing how amazing it might be, and the other part was spent trying to convince myself it would be awful so I could leave the poor guy alone. Maybe he'd suck and I could just sweep it all under the rug. I'd dropped guys before for trying to swallow my face. I could surely do it again.

The flip side of that theory was the terrifying possibility he might think I sucked instead. It was a risk I was willing to take.

When I got home, I let poor Andy out and decided that maybe I should put up a fence and add a doggy door for the little fella.

It was mentally added to my *Hey, Dad* list.

I showered and washed my hair, then put on a flowy tank top and jean shorts. I didn't bother blow drying. My arms were so tired from shoveling and lifting bags all day that I could barely lift them to shampoo. Regardless of my exhaustion, I still applied a swipe or two of mascara. I didn't feel like wearing much makeup, and the sun had given me a nice color, but my eyelashes were damn near clear and I looked weird without it.

It wasn't like me to be such a mess, but he'd seen me look like shit all day. At least I was clean. Delirious, but clean.

I wandered down the hall into the kitchen where my phone was, having forgotten he was going to text before he drove over. I flipped it over and swiped it open to see if I'd missed anything, and I hadn't.

Soon, I was standing in front of the open refrigerator, eating grapes as I browsed my options. I was hungry but didn't have the energy to cook.

It was about a quarter to seven and I thought about calling the diner for something to pick up. Then thought *fuck it* when I remembered I had a few frozen pizzas in the freezer in the garage.

I didn't even bother with shoes, not caring that my clean feet were about to get dirty again as I walked through the garage barefoot. I walked down the wooden stairs, around my car, and then I saw headlights shining on the wall.

Was he here already? He didn't text.

I hoped he liked pizza or had already eaten because I was going to haul ass on one right in front of him.

His truck was loud and I stood with the Tony's box in hand as he turned off the headlights and came to a stop on the concrete in front of me.

Startling me, he honked the horn and laughed as I jumped. Grandpa used to do that shit to me all the time. *Jackasses.*

He was careful not to ding the door of my car as he climbed out, bringing with him a clear plastic bag that looked like it was full of containers. I could already smell something good inside of them.

"What's that?"

He looked down then back at me. "Meatloaf, green beans, mashed potatoes and gravy?" He said it like a question, probably unsure if I'd like it.

But, I did. *I loved it.*

"Oh, shit. I could kiss you right now." Yeah, I knew what I'd said, but for so many reasons it was the honest-to-God truth.

He stood taller then set the bag on the hood of my car, not breaking eye contact with me. "Then come here and do it," he said, earnestly.

It made me laugh, but he didn't crack a smile so I let mine slide off my face.

No. He wasn't just serious … he was waiting.

I was nervous, and even though it was kind of sudden, kissing had been my idea after all. It was about to happen and I had no fucking idea what to do. I took a few steps closer and watched his chest rise and fall.

When my feet were next to his, I tentatively pressed my hand against his stomach to steady myself as I went up on my tiptoes. I felt his muscles tighten and twitch under my palm and I swallowed my apprehension.

"I'm going to kiss you," I said more to myself than him, like I was reminding myself it was actually—*finally*—about to happen.

"I wish you would," he replied, not angling his head down much, but his eyes were cast low to mine.

"I was wishing you'd kiss me first tonight," I said a breath's distance from his lips. Holding myself up on the balls of my feet had my already sore calves screaming.

I heard something hit metal just out of my vision and turned to see his five fingers spread across the front fender of his truck as if to brace himself.

Did he need support for this, too? The thought warmed me.

Just as I blinked and worked up the gumption to do it, he said, "Fuck it," and lifted me up with his free arm. His mouth yet to touch mine, we were eye to eye.

Hazel to blue.

"You can kiss me first tomorrow, Sunny. I cannot wait any damn longer."

My eyes closed and my arms wrapped around his neck, feeling how solid he was. His lips met mine. Closed, but firm and warm. I felt a low rumble vibrate through his chest.

When his mouth parted, a vulnerable sound left my throat and he came at me for more, catching my bottom lip between his and angling his head to deepen the kiss.

If there was a feeling I'd been chasing through my adult dating life, it was that one.

Breathless. The chest-stretching need I'd always craved was there in his kiss.

I moved my hands to his cheeks so I could hold him there with me. My feet off the floor, he held me in his arms and leaned his back against his truck. My leg itched to climb him, hike up his thigh to latch on, but what focus I had left was poured in the kiss.

Our mouths only parted for air, and he kissed me like every girl, in all of history, ever dreamed of a man kissing her. With the passion of a lover. The power of a man who could protect her. And a tenderness that begged for her to return it.

The Fuck-hot Farmer, who borrowed gloves to spare my hands and brought me meatloaf, could kiss like a motherfucker.

Soon the fevered urgency ebbed and turned languid as I slid down his body. My legs straddled the outside of his, which were pitched out in front of him making him a height I could reach with ease.

His warm hand stroked my cheek, and he pulled away.

"Let's eat before it gets cold," he whispered in a husky timbre against my mouth as his lips paired with mine over and over.

More kissing was what I needed. To hell with food. *Let me starve.*

I kissed him back, my tongue sweeping out to swipe his lip. "I'm not hungry anymore."

Rhett's pliant mouth tightened into a smile and a chuckle shook his broad chest. He paired his forehead with mine and exhaled.

In the safety of his arms, I was bold and I admitted, "I wanted to kiss you last night and all day today."

He ran his fingers over my hair as I pulled back to look at him, my confession making my cheeks flush hot.

"I've wanted to kiss you my whole damn life. I win."

Chapter Twelve

Rhett

I was showing her my hand, which I hadn't planned on doing, but the truth was always easier to say and harder to keep to myself. From the time I began thinking about kissing girls, I'd imagined kissing Sunny.

Turns out I didn't have a very good imagination, because the real thing was far superior to any wet dream I'd ever had. And, sweet mother above, I never dreamed the way she'd feel in my arms would make me feel so strong and weak at the same time. Or how the little sounds she made when I kissed her harder would affect my vital bodily functions the way they did. My heart rate felt like I'd run miles, and my breathing was deep and full to provide me with much needed oxygen, exclusively for the purpose of living long enough to kiss her again.

She must really like meatloaf, and I wouldn't soon forget it. I'd always been a little vague about my feelings on the dish, but it was *easily* my new favorite.

The way she was looking at me was reassurance that it wasn't the worst thing I could have said, although it reminded me this wasn't just some kiss. Not for me.

Her blue eyes lazily blinked up into mine, her pupils large but adjusting to the light after having been closed while we made out against my truck … a truck which, by the way, I also had a new appreciation for. She wasn't wearing any makeup. Her hair was damp from a shower, but much messier than it had been when I pulled into her garage because I couldn't keep my hands out of it—and it showed.

She'd never looked better.

Then again, hadn't I just thought that earlier in the day?

Her lips were red from tangling with mine. Seeing how I'd rubbed them made me regret not taking the extra time to shave that evening.

I ran my thumb over them and her eyes fell closed as I smoothed left to right. "You can kiss me whenever you want, Sunshine. From here on out, you go ahead and do that anytime."

She smiled and hummed.

I stood slowly, growing surer by the minute that our night would be a short one. We'd worked hard and slept little in the past twenty-four hours. That might have been why I didn't want to waste much time getting here, but if there was going to be any time for me to put that look on her face again that night, she'd need to eat first.

Sunny followed my cue, stepped to the side, and snatched the bag of food off her car.

"This better be some damn good meatloaf," Sunny

teased as she walked up the wooden steps to the garage entrance into the house. I followed her and stepped into the laundry room.

She had some very delicate looking undergarments hanging above the washer and dryer, and I averted my eyes. Dear God, I wouldn't be able to do *anything* if I couldn't stop thinking about what she looked like in them. Eating included. Fuck, just walking without tripping of my feet was a challenge.

Her kitchen was a smaller room and she had a retro looking, four-person table in the center. It was tidy, but very lived in. She began unpacking the to-go meals that my mother insisted I stop and get for us.

Mom's face was priceless when I told her why I couldn't stay and eat. She was all too excited to make my takeout dinner for two.

I didn't know what to do with myself, so I studied her refrigerator, which was covered almost completely with magnets, cards, photographs, and a calendar. There was a post-it with Mike's number on it. Immediately, the impulse to rip it down and throw it in the trash burst through me, but it was too early to start pissing on her furniture and marking my territory.

We'd shared one kiss and a few hours together. That was it, and it would do me well to keep my ass in check. She wasn't exactly mine to lay claim to.

Yet.

"It's not too cold. I'll just pop the plates in the microwave. That okay with you?"

Whatever she wanted was fine with me. I would have been happy eating it cold in the garage with my hands if I got to be there with her.

"That's perfect. What can I do?" I asked, as I looked at a picture of her with her best friend Mutt in a wedding dress. "Did Mutt get *married*?"

She chortled. "You mean Hannah? Nobody calls her Mutt anymore. Vaughn, her husband—the new dentist—made sure of that. But, yeah. Hannah got married." Her voice was telling at the end, like she was jealous or something. "I've got sweet tea in the fridge, and there are glasses in the cabinet to the left. Can you get us some ice? I drink a lot of tea when I eat. You can leave the pitcher on the table."

"Sure." She actually had two pitchers of tea. I chose the least full one and placed it on the table behind me, then found the glasses where she told me they'd be. She didn't have an ice maker in the door like we had at the farm and like I had at the cabin, so I went to the sink to wash my hands before digging around in her ice bin.

It wasn't awkward or uncomfortable, but a tension grew in the air. While the microwave warmed the first plate and I filled our glasses, we looked at each other. She kept taking long, deep breaths and shaking her head.

"So should we talk about the elephant in the room?" I asked. I wasn't usually one to bring up things—to want to talk about feelings and stuff like that—but dammit, this was kind of important. It was obvious she was thinking about something, and if I knew what was going on in her head, then maybe I could sort out what was in mine.

"Which one?" she asked as she swapped the hot plate for the cold one and got silverware out of the drawer.

"How many elephants do we have in here?"

She huffed. "Two. The old one and the young one."

That was one way to think about it.

After the microwave beeped and we had two hot plates of food ready, she sat down next to me, took a long drink and said, "Who goes first?"

I wanted to think up some excuse to get out of being the one to go, but that was childish and that was the last thing I wanted her to think of me.

"I'll go. I had it bad for you when I was a kid, then I went to school and came home. We ran into each other and…"

I'm getting it bad again? No. That wasn't good.

She didn't try to interrupt while I looked for the right thing to say, but ate and stared at her plate.

"—And now I want to get to know *you* better. To me, it's like you stopped aging and I just caught up. That's how I see it."

Kind of.

Who was I kidding? I still had it so fucking bad.

She nodded and swallowed, then emptied her glass of tea. She could really put it down, just like she'd said.

"Okay, but even though you don't *feel* like we're much different in age *now*…" She began and poured herself another glass, then topped off mine while she was at it. "Wait. How old are you, by the way?"

"Twenty-three."

"And I'm twenty-eight. So five years. That doesn't seem that big of a difference, but when you were thirteen and I was eighteen, *that* difference was huge."

Honestly, it didn't feel that way to me back then either. If it had, I probably wouldn't have trailed her everywhere she went.

She continued, "But you're right, it doesn't seem that different now. I don't see you like that anymore."

I ran a forkful of meatloaf through my mashed potatoes and took a bite. I prayed she didn't still see me as that kid. I was glad to hear we were at least on the same page, but I was still curious about something.

"How *do* you see me now?"

"I don't know. I mean, in one way we kind of just met. In another, I've known you for as long as I can remember. So, that's kind of weird. But, really, we don't know each other *as adults*. You know? It wasn't like I was some full-grown woman back then either. I was still really young, too."

That wasn't quite what I was after. "You didn't answer my question. How do you see me now?"

She leaned back in her chair and propped her foot up on the edge of the seat. Took a few breaths and said, "I see an educated guy. A hard worker. Someone thoughtful. Quiet, sometimes. Funny, sometimes." She blinked and held her eyes shut, like it hurt to admit. "Really attractive." She opened them, one lid at a time. Peeking at me.

Then she took another bite of potatoes and added, "And I like spending time with you so far. These are really freaking good. Did your mom make them?"

I'd never tackled a woman to the ground and fucked her until she screamed my name before, but I was thinking about it.

It was all kind of too much. She'd said what I wanted to hear. That coupled with being there with her. Talking with her like that. How honest she was. It was so unexpected, but I wasn't going to look a gift horse in the mouth. Especially since I'd rather kiss the horse.

I should have said something back. I should have complimented her or told her what I liked, but I didn't, which was selfish.

Regardless, she'd been the one to change the conversation, so I let it go.

"She's a great cook. My dad almost fought me for these two pieces. It's his favorite."

"Do you eat there a lot?"

Did she mean did my mom still cook all of my meals? "No," I said a little defensively and tried to backtrack. "I like to cook. I eat *a lot*."

She didn't take offense to what I'd said, at least outwardly, and said, "I eat at my mom's all the time. I'm a shitty cook, but if my mom cooked like yours, I'd be as big as a barn. My mom is always on some health food fad diet. So, at the moment it's a lot of quinoa."

I laughed.

"It's cool you're staying out at the cabin though," she said.

When she was saying these things all I heard was *you can't take care of yourself*, but I knew that's not what she was trying to say. It was me. My issue.

"Yeah, I love it out there."

"I know. I was lucky when I got back from school that my family let me move in here." Sunny was so relaxed as she spoke. If she was picking up on any of the stupid things I was thinking, she didn't let it affect her.

I told myself to chill out.

"There aren't a lot of places in town anyway," I said.

She chugged her tea and answered with a wet lip. "I know."

"I'm just staying at the cabin until I can start ground work on my house."

Her eyes widened. "*Your* house?"

"My farm." I hadn't told anyone my plans, not even my parents yet. I was waiting until after I talked to the bank next week.

"It's not my business, but don't you have an ass load of student loans? I could buy something now, but not for a long time after I got out of school."

"I have some, but mostly just from the few classes I stayed to take last year. I had a full ride from track, as long as I kept my grades strong, so I didn't have to pay for much." And the little bit of debt I had, I could have paid off from savings, but I was waiting for harvest.

"Wow. Do you already have land to build on?"

I had *plenty* of land.

Most, and I mean the vast majority, of the ground we worked was my father's, but when my grandpa passed the farm down the line, he made sure that Haley and I owned property of our own, too. Caraway Farms still occupied and farmed it, but I got paid a lease every year and a wage from working when I was home. It wasn't anything uncommon for a farm kid.

I wanted to buy more land around Wynne, preferably more tracts near ours, but that was a waiting game. Farm ground around us rarely became available, and when it did it went fast and high.

"I do. I'll take you out there sometime."

Maybe you'll want to stay out there with me.

She yawned and took the last bite on her plate. "I'm so stuffed."

"It's all that tea. You drank half a gallon."

"Shut up. I love it." She got up and picked up my empty plate with hers. "Thank you for bringing that over."

"Thank you for helping us today." I'd been shocked to see her when I pulled in, but to have her there the entire day—technically, working longer than I had—it spoke a lot about her character. Regardless of her motivation, she'd helped.

As she cleaned up the dishes and stuck my mom's coveted Tupperware in the dishwasher, I took the dishcloth she'd set aside and wiped down the counters and table.

She yawned and said, "I know it's Saturday night, but I don't really feel like doing much. If you'd rather go out and do something, I get it."

That was a relief. I didn't want to go into town either. I didn't even feel like drinking. All I wanted to do was sit next to her and maybe kiss her again. It was a short list, but I felt pretty optimistic.

"What did you have in mind?" I asked.

She leaned against the counter and crossed her tan legs. "I think watching a movie sounds good. Although, I'll be honest. I probably won't make it very long. I'm worn out." Of course she was. No sleep last night followed by a long day of manual labor? I was surprised she wasn't asleep already.

"Movie sounds good," I admitted.

"You can pick. I have a bunch in the cabinet over there." She wadded her hair up on her head and held it there, then shuffled down her hall.

Crouching to read the titles she had in her movie collection, I saw one of my favorites and the choice was easy.

I found the remote on the coffee table and tried to work my way through her television and DVD player to get it cued up. Trying to navigate someone else's TV is never easy, but I'd finally gotten there by the time she came into the room.

"What are we watching?" she asked and I held up the case to *The Shawshank Redemption.*

Sunny looked sleepy, but a lazy smile cracked her face. Her head tipped to one side, looking at me like I'd made the right choice as she climbed onto the couch.

Andy was on the other end of the sofa, where he'd been sleeping since I got there, which didn't leave much room for me. The way he looked at me, I knew taking his spot wasn't a good move. I sat in the recliner, then Sunny kicked poor Andy off and patted the cushion for me to move closer to her.

From the opposite end, her legs stretched over to me, while I sunk down into the couch and pressed play.

I'd seen the film dozens of times, maybe more, but it was all relative.

Soon her foot wandered onto my lap, and as if we'd sat that way many times before, I held it in my hand and eventually began rubbing her sole. Little pink toenails. Smooth, warm skin under my hands. When that foot had as much attention as she desired, she stirred and added the other to my lap. So I gave it the same treatment.

It was about halfway through the movie when I chanced a look to the far end of the couch, and her eyes had fallen shut. Lips parted and her face lay peacefully.

I wasn't sure how I was going to get up without waking her, and the position she had her head pitched to the side didn't look like it would be comfortable for long.

I moved her foot to see if she would stir easily. She didn't. Gently, I stood from under her legs and she didn't wake. I walked down the hall to see where I'd be going, looking in all of the doors as I went. A full hall bathroom. Two smaller bedrooms, one with a bed and the other with a treadmill where winter coats hung.

Her bedroom was at the very end of the hall, and I flipped the light on, mostly to make sure I could make it with her in my arms without any tripping hazards. It was pretty clean, but the closet doors were wide open. Additionally, there was an extra standing rack with clothes hanging on it to the point where it was full, too. Shoes spilled out from the floor of the closet and the doors were used to hold belts and scarves and purses.

She liked clothes.

Out of curiosity, I crossed the room, around the bed, and flipped on the switch to her bathroom. Again I found it basically clean, but very lived in.

She was different than the person I'd imagined in my young mind. Hardly the girl I'd put up on a pedestal.

The woman wasn't perfect. No. Instead though, she was real. Tea chugging. Half-full laundry baskets in the corner. Toothpaste on the mirror. She was *normal.*

The more time I spent with her—the more I got to know her—I realized I liked the real version much better. She was easy to fixate on superficially, but underneath the clothes, hair and radio voice, was a woman who was worth a good man's time. If the age thing was something we had to get used to, then it was worth it to get to know her more.

I flipped the bedside lamp on, turned off the overhead

light, pulled down her blankets, and then found her exactly how I'd left her on the couch. Her mouth parted just a little, her lashes fanned over her sun-pinked cheeks.

Yeah. She was definitely worth all the hell I might hear from everyone. She was worth the uncomfortable looks from my family. The talk and chatter, when people didn't think I could hear, didn't really matter that much. Because, at the end of the day, Sunny had kissed me and wanted to spend time with me—even if she had to bag sand just to do it.

I'd take the teasing if I got to touch her. If I got to be with her.

My hands slid under her arms and knees. She fell easily against my chest as I lifted and walked her down the hall to her bed. When I docked her into her bed, she peacefully rolled to her side. Pulling the blankets over her feet then up to her shoulders, I folded them beneath her chin.

The urge to reach out for her once more before I left was too powerful. My fingers ran over her cheek, over her messy blond hair.

I hadn't been in many relationships, so I hoped there was a learning curve that wasn't too noticeable from her end, but seeing her in her bed, sleeping, I had a potent desire to either be the man she deserved or *become* him. She deserved someone who respected her, who *really* thought about her, and took the time to realize she wasn't only a beautiful face.

Bent over, my lips met her temple and my eyes shut to absorb her warmth and scent. A lovely hum exited her with her next breath.

"I couldn't name the things I like about you earlier,

Sunshine. There are just too many. That list gets longer by the minute. Some things never change."

The thought of crawling into bed behind her, and putting my hands all over her body simply to find out if she fit around me like I knew she would, was tempting. There'd be time for that another night, I prayed.

Besides, I liked when she came to me better. There wasn't anything like watching her step up and put her hands on me.

"Good night," I whispered and twisted the knob on the lamp until the room went dark.

I was a patient man. Hell, I'd already waited my whole life. What was a little more?

After I let Andy out for a stroll through the yard, I watched him march down the hall to sleep with our girl. He was the second luckiest dog I ever met.

Before I left, I stood in front of her refrigerator staring at Mike's phone number. On one hand, it wasn't my place to remove it. But, on the other hand, it totally fucking was, and that hand was stronger. It landed in the trash on my way out.

Chapter Thirteen

Sunny

We were about halfway down the hall when I realized he was carrying me to bed. I was so tired, but I desperately tried to cling to the way he felt. How firm his chest was under my head. How strong his arms felt holding my body to his. But, I was in that place between sleep and awake, and I couldn't move.

I felt the cool sheets on my legs as he covered me.

Lucid and partly dreaming, I let myself fall back into a dream where he climbed into my bed and took my clothes off. I could almost feel his hands on my body, and I felt a vibration leave me as I sunk down further into the sensation of him.

In my dream he told me he liked so many things about me he couldn't name them all and told me some things never change. But, I think all he really said was, "Good night."

That was the last thing I could remember the next

morning as I ate a yogurt and waited for Andy to come back in from making his morning lap around the yard.

Usually, I wasn't much for ballads. I'd play the popular ones, but that morning at my kitchen table I noticed myself flipping through online playlists and flagging lots of slower songs for future use.

That day's music on WDKR was already programed, and mostly the standards I relied on, but for fun I ran over to the station and threw in some songs about kissing. I hoped Rhett was listening and that they'd subliminally make him want to make out with me again.

That guy knew his way around a kiss. *Wow.*

It was all I could focus on that morning and all the way into town on the way to my mom's.

"Mom," I called as I walked through the back door into the kitchen. My dad wasn't there, his car missing from the driveway. Both of them worked the occasional Saturday, but they never worked on Sundays. We had lunch together almost every week.

She had the griddle out, the butter, cheese and bread. My mom's grilled cheese was worth driving into town for. It was one of the only things she didn't try to make healthier. I guessed she was deep into a project and knew it would be the fastest thing. I didn't mind.

"Hey, Sunny," she answered from somewhere upstairs. "I'll be right down." I followed the sound of her voice all the way up to my old room.

"What are you doing?" I'd left some of my things when I moved out for college, and even though they'd repurposed the room, some of my stuff still hung on the wall. There were a few boxes on the day bed, and when I stepped in she was reaching up into the closet for something.

"I was looking for a box of pictures. BJ, from your class, called and wanted to know if I had any pictures of you cheerleading from high school. She said they're doing some slide show for your reunion. When she was in the salon last week, I told her I'd look. I thought you still had some in here."

On her tiptoes, she pulled an old shoebox off the top shelf and I immediately remembered what was inside.

"That box should have some. I wonder why she didn't just call me?" I hadn't been asked to help with the reunion at all and would have helped, but I assumed they'd let me know if they needed anything.

Taking the box from her hands, I sat down on the ottoman by the window where I used to do my homework. The Nike box was full and there were notes and programs from our senior year.

The first picture was one of Hannah and me. My mom babysat Hannah in the summers before she went back to the salon full-time. We were so little. I had braces, knobby knees, and an NSYNC shirt on.

"Oh my God, not this one," I laughed and showed it to her.

"Bring that with you. We'll look at the table."

In the kitchen, she busied herself with buttering the bread and making sandwiches. I heard my dad pull in the drive as she said, "Hey, your dad said you were at the Caraways' yesterday."

I had been there, but with the mention of *Caraway*, my mind went back to the kiss and my cheeks felt hot remembering his tongue sweeping over mine.

When my dad walked in, she met and kissed him like always, still holding the spatula.

"The Caraways needed help," I explained, then started to work my way through the box again, pulling a few pictures out to let Mom give B.J.

At the bottom, I found an envelope with the flap tucked inside itself. I opened it and a flutter of something swam through my belly. They were the cards I'd saved from the flowers I'd received. The top one was from my mom and dad on my sixteenth birthday and under it was the first of many from Rhett. I smiled thinking about how many times he'd sent me roses or daisies. For a young man, he sure had game.

At the time, they were sweet and a little embarrassing, but they always made me smile. I didn't care. Getting flowers—from anyone—is usually pretty nice. And, now that things had been turned upside down, I felt something completely different, and the thought of him sending me flowers inflated a warm sensation in my chest.

"*Yeah*, they needed help," my dad teased.

"What?" I shot back, pretty much knowing where he was going.

"You and Rhett seemed to work well together," he said, pretending to be more interested in the cheese my mom was slapping on the bread.

She bumped into his shoulder to either get him away or to quit being a smart ass to me, probably a little of both.

"Don't listen to him, Sunny," my mom argued over her shoulder. "He just said it didn't look like you *minded* Rhett paying attention to you anymore. Your dad is being a shit."

Well, he was a shit who was totally freaking right. I

liked when he paid me attention. In fact, I was hoping he'd have texted or called me by then, but he hadn't.

It was nice out and he was probably busy as hell finishing up the last few spots on the levee. That or maybe it was just Sunday and he was relaxing.

Sure, I'd fallen asleep by nine the night before—I wondered how late he'd stayed.

I wanted to talk to him, but I didn't want to seem like a crazy girl all up in his space either. I'd decided I was going to wait for him to call me. Let him make the next move.

Yeah. That would be best.

Then, if and when he did, I was going to kiss him again. It was nearly noon, and I was hoping to get the chance that day.

"Hey, Rhett isn't a kid anymore," my dad said. "I seriously doubt he's chasing the girls like he used to. Bet they're all chasing *him*. Right, Sunny?" He poked my side as he sat down next to me.

I gave him a warning look, then waited until he filled up his glass with tea and went to take a drink. When the time was right, I bumped the bottom of his glass, causing him to spill.

"Shut up," I told him. I didn't want to talk about it with my parents, but my dad was on to me, and he no doubt had already fed my mother his findings.

My mom handed us each a paper plate with a grilled cheese—split in half corner to corner like always. She grabbed her plate and took a seat with us and said, "He *is* handsome though."

I cocked my head to the side. I thought she'd be on my side, but they were double-teaming me.

"Both of you stop. *Yes*, he's handsome. *Yes*, I was there yesterday helping."

"*Yes*, he's single," my prying mother added.

"I'd hope so," I remarked then tried to smooth over. "I mean he just got back and everything."

They both laughed at me, my dad covering his full mouth with a fist not to choke.

"Whatever you say, Sunny," my mom teased, but luckily that was the end of it.

It was Sunday, but the town was busy. People were in the park and walking along the streets taking advantage of the sun.

I'd hung out with my folks for a while and gave a few things to my mom for the slide show, then went to the truck stop to get a Coke and decided I'd just drive around a while. See who was out and about.

Besides, he still hadn't called, and I was still constantly thinking about the kiss. I was merely wasting time until the next one. But, I didn't want to call him.

It was weird—usually I didn't give a shit to talk to a guy so soon after I'd just seen him the night before. With Rhett, I just wanted to know what he was doing, what he was thinking about, and if he was thinking about me.

I'm sure it wasn't healthy or sane, but there wasn't much I could do about it.

That damn kiss.

After about thirty minutes of driving around aimlessly with nothing to do, I gave in and picked up my phone. Stopped at a four-way on some back road, I let it ring three times and then chickened out and sat it down in the passenger seat.

He was probably busy. Or sleeping. Or doing something and didn't want to be bothered. Why couldn't I just wait for him to call me?

God, I was a loser.

Then my phone rang and it was his name on the screen. *Shit.*

I slid my finger across the screen and answered the call.

"Why'd you hang up?" he asked, and the sound of his voice made me smile like a fool in my car on the gravel road.

"I don't know," I confessed.

"What are you doing?"

I looked around. Telling him that I was going stir-crazy waiting for him to call wasn't smart. "Not much. Just riding around bored."

"*Bored?* What did I tell you about that?"

I laughed. "I don't think I remember. What are you doing?"

"We got done with the levee pretty early, so I took the tractor down a few roads that were getting a little rough. Almost to the shed down from my place."

Ask me to come over.

Ask me to do something.

Cure my boredom with your mouth.

"I'll be back there in about ten minutes. Wanna meet me? We can't have you bored."

I pulled my foot off the brake and turned toward his place, the phone still to my ear.

"Okay. Sorry I fell asleep on you last night," I admitted.

"Did you just get up?"

"No. Actually, I was up around seven. I got a lot of rest

going to bed that early. And on a Saturday night, too. I'm sure you're *so* impressed with my party skills."

"Oh, your skills are impressive." I heard the loud roar of whatever kind of machinery he was on. "Hey, I'll see you in a minute. This thing is loud."

"All right," I said.

"Just pull in behind my truck. It's pretty muddy down there."

"Okay, bye." I threw my phone into the seat again and flew down the road.

When I turned into the shed, he was already off the tractor and had it pulled into the stall behind a big overhead door. Jeans and muddy boots, sleeveless t-shirt and ball cap.

He met me in the drive beside a four-wheeler. "We're gonna move a couple head of cows over tomorrow, and I need to go check a few fences. Wanna go?" he asked and unscrewed the cap on the gas tank of the four-wheeler, then rocked it side to side to see how full it was.

If going meant getting on that thing with him, then yes. I definitely wanted to go.

Chapter Fourteen

Rhett

She was becoming my favorite lucky penny, showing up around every corner.

"I'll go," she answered.

"Good. Get on up there, I'm going to grab a few things." If I could fix anything minor, I'd want to do it while I was there and save time. My dad and I had planned on working on it the next day, but I couldn't pass up an opportunity to take her for a ride.

Luckily it was a beautiful afternoon, and it wasn't supposed to rain for the next few days. Although the river was still high and climbing, forecasts predicted it wouldn't crest later that week.

I didn't wait to see her get on the four-wheeler, knowing I'd only be testing my limits if I stuck around to watch her straddle the seat. I'd already spent most of the night before hard, and it wasn't much better that day.

With a sledgehammer and a few tools I could use if I saw anything that needed a mend, I'd have what I needed. I left the overhead door open, then set the tools on the wire rack behind her and strapped them down with a bungee cord.

Her hands were out to the sides already holding onto the rack. That would be the first thing I fixed. She'd be holding onto me.

Sunny watched my every move, and before I climbed on, I turned my ball cap around.

Her tongue peeked out and wet her lips. She had *kiss me* all over her face, and I fucking loved it.

"I would have called you this morning, but I knew you were tired."

She leaned in and her blue eyes locked on mine.

"That's okay. I didn't want to bother you. Or…" I didn't let her finish. I'd thought of little else than her mouth, and she could talk in a minute. I needed to taste her so I could focus on driving.

A short, sweet kiss wasn't going to be enough, but it would satisfy me for the time being. Holding back from deepening the kiss, I pulled away before she could even open her eyes. Her pretty neck reached out and her lips puckered for more.

God, she always looked so good to me.

I planted another quick kiss to her lips and climbed on, started the four-wheeler, and popped it into gear before I sat down in front of her. We moved forward, but her hands didn't wrap around me like I wanted them to. Like I thought they would naturally.

So, I stopped.

"I want you to hold on to me, Sunny." I pried her hands off the rack on her sides and brought them around my stomach. I turned my head to the side so I could hear her over the rumble of the machine. "Okay?"

Her fingers latched and I felt her chest press against my back as she slid a little closer to me on the seat.

"Okay," she said. "I will."

The field behind my cabin met up with a creek that butted up against a meadow where we let our cows graze sometimes. I rode along the field a little slower than I would have, had I been alone, watching for muddy spots and careful to go around the bigger ones. Nice and slow.

Besides, I was doing the next day's work with the girl of my dreams holding on to me like we were flying down the path.

There was no rush at all.

When the fence line met us it looked to be in pretty good shape. Yet, as we got closer to where it ran through the creek, I could see where the water had repeatedly battered it, but it was too steep in that spot to get down there to fix it. The other side looked like easier access, so I made the tough call to go the long way around to get to it.

More riding. What a shame.

"It's so pretty out here," she said in my ear. Her chin perched on my shoulder as she leaned up to see around me. The back of the seat was somewhat higher and a hell of a lot less worn than where I sat.

"It is." Although I loved our land and was committed to it, I knew the best view on my property was right behind me. *Her.*

"How good are your shoes?" I asked, knowing we were

about to go through some nasty spots.

She kicked her leg out to the side and inspected it. “They’re just tennis shoes. Nothing special.”

I pressed forward on the throttle to get us up the ridge that led to a clear spot on the creek where we’d cross over at a gate.

“You can swing your legs up on my lap if you don’t want to get them messed up.” Topping the hill, I slowed to let her readjust. Like I’d said, she wrapped her legs around my waist and her feet met between my legs over the tank. “Ready?” I asked.

“Yeah,” she said, and I felt her head nod at the same time.

I took it slow going down the grassy side of the hill on the way down, and my free hand held tight to her feet to keep her from sliding around. The steep decline pushed her middle even closer to me, and while going down I instinctively arched back into her chest as I inched down to the water line.

It was clear enough to see the rock pass we’d built up. A lot of it had washed out, but there was enough to get through, even though the water was much higher than usual. I kicked my feet up on the front fender and watched where I was going for loose rock, making my way slowly across the creek.

“Is it usually this deep? You could probably swim in that hole.”

“We did when we were kids,” I said, then felt weird about it. “When my dad rocked up this crossing it made that side deeper. The water is up pretty high, even in this creek. These rocks are usually dry right here.” At the moment, they were under about a foot of water, making the creek up about two feet.

We crossed just fine and headed through the pasture, back up to the spot that needed mending. Even if I wasn't able to repair it myself with what I'd brought, at least I'd need to know what to bring the next day.

The pasture wasn't too large and it ran right up to the back of the farm. We had two fields we used for winter wheat and grazing, and the other one was in much better shape to plant. This one, with the creek, was a bigger mess and had a lot more soft spots, but the cows wouldn't care. There was plenty to eat aside from the hay we'd have for them up at the barn.

I turned off the ignition and hopped off, then pulled my rubber boots out of the rack and slipped them on to wade into the creek. The fence wasn't in terrible shape. A large branch had fallen off upstream and washed against it, causing the posts to lean over from the weight of the rushing water. I had what I needed.

I pulled the limb away and threw it on the bank, thankful the water wasn't higher than my knee-high boots. Wet feet sucked and full boots were a bitch to walk with.

"Do you need any help?" Sunny called from the four-wheeler.

"Nah," I said, repositioning the post in the soft ground. If I could get it upright it would hold the fence tight and high enough that the cows wouldn't try to cross it.

Up the embankment I went and grabbed the sledgehammer. She watched my every move.

On my way to her, I thought about how I'd wanted to take her on a ride, but my priorities were changing. The closer she'd sat, the tighter she'd held on, the more I wished we *weren't* on a damn four-wheeler but somewhere a lot more comfortable. Hell, at least somewhere I could reach her mouth.

"Is it bad?" she asked, probably seeing the concentration I wore on my face, but it wasn't for the fence. It was all about her.

"No. If I get those two posts upright it'll be fine." I grabbed the handle of the tool I needed and headed back down.

The weight of the four-wheeler had made it across the crossing fine earlier, but I didn't want to push it a second time. It had been pretty washed out. We'd have to go up by the farm and ride the road back to the shed near my place to get back. It was a longer ride, and the sooner I was done, the better.

I propped the posts up with a few big rocks to hold them where I needed them, and with a few swift hits they were planted deep enough to do the job. We'd do a better repair when the water went down and we could get back to fix the crossing. Until then, it'd be fine.

Her face was slack and her mouth hung open as I climbed the grassy hill back to her.

"What?" I asked. Had she seen something? A snake? I was a farm kid, but I still didn't like those fuckers. I pulled my boots off over my shoes and stuck them back into the rungs of the wire rack.

"Nothing. You're just so strong," she said with a laugh in her voice.

My whole life I'd wanted her to see me as someone stronger or older or more capable, even as a kid I'd wished

I was taller so she'd look at me differently. Over the past few weeks, I'd seen her do just that and it was doing something to my ego. Not in a shitty, arrogant way, it was more like validation. An evening of the playing field.

At the same time, I was seeing her in a different light, too. I supposed that was only natural. We were both adults now.

When I climbed on the front of the ATV, I could have sworn she placed a kiss on my shoulder just before I started it. God, she did things to me that weren't typical.

As I navigated that side of the property, I tried to remember any other girl, or woman for that matter, who had such an effect on me.

I'd had girlfriends, a few casual flings. The one legitimate high school girlfriend I'd had moved away my senior year. We didn't even try to pretend like some long distance thing was going to work. She broke up with me, if I remembered right. Anyway, I survived.

It wasn't anything nearly as painful as when I watched, from my bike hiding behind a bush across the street from her house, the day Sunny drove off to college. The day I thought I'd never see her again. Convinced she'd never come back. That day had royally sucked, but I got used to it and things moved on. I'd had no choice.

Yet, there we were. Together. Riding over the tall grass. Even though she didn't need to, her legs were wrapped around me and her hands held different places on my chest. I glanced down and one of her thumbs was rubbing up and down over my shirt, though I couldn't feel it much as softly as she was doing it.

There hadn't been any other spots along the fence that

looked bad, and, frankly, I didn't have it in me to wait until we got back to touch her again. Really touch her.

I looked up to the farmhouse, the back of it was just in view in front of the barns and sheds at the back of the lot. No one would be looking back there. Not that I cared, but maybe she would.

My thumb eased off the throttle, and we slowed to a stop. Then I put on the e-brake and killed the engine. I climbed off and took a few steps back, crooking a finger for her to do the same, which she did.

She tried to hide her smile, but failed beautifully as she leaned against the seat, teasing and pleasing me at the same time. When I couldn't keep the cool on my face and grinned at her, she shyly looked around the meadow and something behind me caught her eye.

I reached out for her hand and gave it a slight tug so she'd come closer. Willingly, she did. Oh shit, what it did to me.

"I want to take you out." From that moment on, I decided I wasn't going to squander whatever was happening.

She was interested, for whatever reason. I'd been cautious, treading lightly, but I wanted her to know I wasn't just some guy who wanted to kiss her when we were alone, then go our separate ways. I wanted more than that.

I wanted to take her to dinner, wanted to go out and ride through town, and for her to always sit in the middle. Wanted the beginning of something, not just some novel thing.

"You do?" she asked, but whatever had her attention wasn't letting go of it. "What is that?"

I turned my head and could barely make it out on

account of how badly it had been neglected, but it was still standing.

"Is it a tree house?" she asked.

Tree house didn't sound as silly as *my fort* did, so I answered, "Yeah. It's old."

The look in her eyes was almost enchanted, and they shined a deeper blue. "I want to go check it out. I always wanted a tree house when I was a kid."

The thing was, I knew what was in there. I didn't want to go up.

Maybe my dad had cleaned it out, but I seriously doubted he'd been in there. I hadn't been inside the fort for nearly seven years. Probably early high school. Still, I knew it wasn't smart letting her see inside.

A diversion was needed.

I grabbed her other hand and tried to steer her focus to me. It was all I had.

"Come here. Let me kiss on you."

Her eyes parted with the fort, and she stepped between my legs. "Let's go check out that tree house. Maybe I'll let you kiss on me up there."

She was tough.

"I also want to talk to you about letting me take you out." I leaned forward and pressed a kiss to her neck, which I'd dreamed of doing nothing short of a million times.

She tipped her head to the side and allowed me more, but insisted, "Rhett, let's go up there."

"I don't want to. It's old and there are probably snakes in there. Plus, it's most likely rotted out." I didn't believe half of that, but I'd rather lie—if it would work—than let her up into that tree.

It didn't work.

"I'll let you take me out if you take me over there first."

She left off a part. An important one.

"And the kissing?" I asked, hoping she'd come back to that.

Sunny grinned and leaned into me, throwing her arms around my neck. "I'll let you kiss me either way. Rhett, you can kiss me whenever you like, but if you want to take me on a date anytime soon, I suggest you get up that ladder and let me in your tree house. *Please.*" Her eyelashes batted up at me.

She wasn't shy about what she wanted. Dammit.

"All right, but give me those lips first." Just in case she changed her mind after, at least I had one more chance to feel her mouth on mine.

"Deal," she said with a wide smile. She turned my cap around for me so it wouldn't hit her in the face then pressed her lips to mine. I didn't think I'd ever get over the way it felt.

Or the way every time she kissed me I wanted to strip her naked and show her all the things I wanted to do with her. Now that she was about to see my fort, I worried *that* might not happen, so I concentrated on giving her everything I had in that kiss.

I held on to her, tipping her back a little. She moaned into my mouth, and my dick twitched and throbbed behind the denim of my old work jeans.

My mouth found her neck and I lost myself a little.

"I think you're trying to distract me," she said, her words shaky and low.

My mouth near her ear, I asked, "How am I doing?"

"Pretty damn good, but I *really* want in that tree house."

I paired our lips again and prayed it wasn't for the last time.

Chapter Fifteen

Sunny

It was clear he was trying damn hard to get me to let the idea of going into the tree house slip away, but it looked so cool.

The tree that held the structure was a short walk across the meadow, along a hill line. After he planted another knee-buckling kiss on my lips, I pulled away and tugged his hand in the direction of the big oak tree.

"Just remember I was young when I hung out in there, okay?" he said, readjusting his hat as we walked through the grass. I didn't want him to be embarrassed, but curiosity was driving me forward.

When I was a kid, the neighbors had a great tree house, but I didn't. We didn't have any trees that one would work in, and let's face it, my dad wasn't all that confident in his handiwork.

This one was incredible. It almost looked like it had

two stories from the outside, but maybe it was just tall on the inside. I couldn't tell yet.

"I wanted one when I was a little girl. I wanted to have my friends over and sleep in it. Did you ever sleep out here?" I asked as we got to the tree.

He stepped up to the ladder, which was more like small foot shelves built into the massive tree trunk, to make sure it was solid and could hold his weight.

"No. I had to be back up at the farm by dark, but I spent a lot of time here." He took a few steps up, bouncing and satisfied that it was sturdy enough. "Let me go up and make sure it's not full of spiders and stuff. I haven't been up here in years."

Yeah, I wasn't that afraid of snakes. So when he tried to change my mind with that threat, I didn't give it much thought. Actually, I probably just hadn't had any bad experiences with snake. But spiders? Yeah, me and those sumbitches were never going to cohabitate.

"Okay, but no lying. If it's fine I'm coming up." I expected him to make some kind of excuse to not let me in. I wasn't sure what he had up there, but he did his damnedest to keep me out.

When he got to the top of the ladder, he unlatched the toggle and pushed the door open above his head, then stepped up to peek around.

"What's it look like?" I hollered up. "Is it gross?"

He laughed, looked down the tree at me and said, "No. It's not *gross*. You can come up, if you *really* want to. Do you need help?"

I'd watched how he did it. I could manage.

"Nope."

One foot above the other, I climbed the eight or nine feet up until my head was rising through the floor like his had done. He was standing inside and held a hand out for me to take as I took the last few steps up.

It was awesome.

When my feet were on the floor inside the tree house, he stepped away to open the windows. They were on hinges at the tops and when pushed open, they were held there with a propped up board in the center.

"Did your dad build this?" I asked, looking around the room in the tree, amazed.

Rhett scratched his head and the back of his neck. "A little. Mostly he helped me with a material list and cuts for the frame. Then I did the rest. Well, Lance helped sometimes, too."

It creaked a little, but didn't sag under my weight when I walked around.

He opened a few more windows, and the light that poured in was all you'd need for a cool hangout.

"What about Haley, did she play up here?"

"No. She wasn't allowed," he said quietly as he looked through a pile of magazines he had on a makeshift table in the center. There were two upturned milk crates for chairs.

Then I saw a wall that had writing on it, and he stepped in front of it as I got closer to read it.

"Now, just a second. I was eight or nine when I built this. And I had it pretty bad for this one blond, high school cheerleader." His face was stoic and sincere, his hazel eyes showing a hint of vulnerability. "I never thought you'd come up here. *Ever*, Sunny."

Did he think I'd make fun of him? It saddened me that

he might. I never made fun of him when we were younger, why would I do it now?

"I think it's cool up here," I said, then I leaned up to give him a quick kiss. It was a far cry from the physical persuasion he'd tried to use on me to forget the tree house. My kiss was more of a *thanks* and *don't worry* kiss. When I left his lips, he moved to the side so I could check out what was so important and top secret.

FORT RULES:
No girls, except Sunny Wilbanks.
Only radio station is WDKR.
Cussing is okay.
No telling on what happens in the fort.
No smoking. It's wood.
Take your trash when you leave. Raccoons live in this tree.

Below the rules there were scribbles of my name and proclamations of Rhett Caraway's love for me. *4-Ever.* There were drawings of the sun and in one spot there was a place that said *I'm going to marry Sunny Wilbanks*, then it went on to say *Rhett and Sunny Wilbanks.*

I tried not to laugh at young Rhett for thinking he'd take my name. It was so sweet. My hand covered my heart as I looked over all of the precious things he'd written about me.

When every inch of the wall had been examined and absorbed, I turned to see him sitting on a milk crate, which again made me almost lose my laugh. His big body was crouched down on the red plastic makeshift chair. He'd opened the back of a battery-operated radio and was messing with the corroded springs that years out in the weather had claimed.

Taking a seat on the blue milk crate, I waited for him to look at me. I was positive he was embarrassed, but there was no reason for it. It wasn't funny or stupid to me. It was endearing and it made me feel really special—even if it wasn't a timely representation of our situation.

He'd been a kid when he wrote it. Now we were adults, and it felt like we were the same age. He was a man and I was a woman, and there was not a damn thing wrong with that.

"Hey," I said and kicked his foot off to the side of the tiny table. "Look at me."

He crooked his neck up, his expression almost defensive.

"Stop it. We aren't breaking any rules, Rhett." Then I smiled and pointed to the first rule. "See? I'm allowed up here."

"It was dumb, Sunny." His words, although trying to make light of something he'd done as a child, kind of pissed me off, and I stood.

"It is *not* dumb. It's really nice, Rhett."

He challenged, "Nice if you're a kid."

"Who cares?"

"I care. I know what everyone is saying. What this looks like. Rhett Caraway *still* chasing Sunny Wilbanks."

"That's not what it feels like to me." I stepped forward.

He was a man, and that was only proven further by this pride, but he had to know a few things.

I sat on his lap, praying first that the milk crates would

hold us, and second that the floor would. Then I took the radio away from him and put it on the table, wrapping his arms around my waist.

"I don't see you as that little boy, Rhett. But *don't* be ashamed of him. Hell, there's never been anyone else who treated me as sweetly as he did. No one who ever paid me that much attention. No one who ever tried to make me smile every day. Even as an adult, no one ever worked that hard to make me like them.

"And maybe that's why I never did. No one ever made me feel as special as I did when I was in high school and this younger boy was chasing me. You're the only guy who has ever bought me flowers. The only one who ever left me my favorite candy bars in my car every morning before school, which I'm still not sure how you did. The only one who ever brought me thoughtful gifts. The only one who never asked for anything but a smile from me."

My hands met the light stubble on his relaxing face, and I held his gaze there. "It doesn't matter *when* you did all of those things. You did them, and they count. If anyone had ever treated me better than Rhett Caraway, then I'd probably be with them, but I'm not. I'm here *with you.* Maybe it wasn't the right time back then, but who knows? Maybe it's my turn to chase you a little. Because no matter how old you are, it feels pretty damn good."

My eager lips were an inch from his and his arms around me only grew tighter. I felt small sitting on his huge thighs, his strong hands creeping up my back as I turned a little more and threw my leg over to the other side.

I opened my mouth like I was going to kiss him and he leaned into it as I pulled away holding his face in place.

Halting his approach.

"Now, let's talk about this date you want to take me on," I said quietly against his chin before placing a kiss there.

"Wherever you want to go. Whatever you want to do," he said, his breathing coming deeper and rushed as I dodged another kiss on the lips from him. "Dammit, Sunny. Just fucking kiss me." His big hands found my ass and pulled me tighter against the stiffness in his jeans. I rocked, gaining only a fraction of the pressure I really wanted.

"Friday night. Pick me up at six."

His brow bunched together as I rubbed against him even more. It was sexy as hell seeing the effect I had on him. The way his handsome face looked frustrated waiting on me to couple our lips. The bob of his Adam's apple as he swallowed his patience. The muscular tick in his jaw.

"Don't move," I whispered against his mouth as I licked across his bottom lip. Teasing him. Tasting him and loving the thumping I felt pound through his chest into mine.

As far as tempting him went, my time was up. He'd hit a breaking point and couldn't wait any longer. One of his hands found the back of my neck. He pressed my mouth to his, and I let him because I was confident he knew what he was doing.

Chapter Sixteen

Rhett

The way she was grinding against me in my old fort, feet above the ground, hidden away from everyone, made me consider ripping her clothes off and giving her everything.

How lame would that have been? Waiting my whole life to get the girl I'd had my eye on, only to have my first fucking time with her in a dirty old tree house. That wasn't good enough for me.

Regardless, my hand slipped up her shirt despite my brain screaming at me to slow down. A sweet sound came from her throat as I ran my hand over the fabric of her bra, and another when I pulled her breast from the cup and ran my thumb over her nipple.

Christ, she was better that I'd ever dreamed.

As I shared my attention between her mouth and her chest, I felt her hand wander between us and grip me through my jeans.

"*Rhett*, where did you learn to kiss like this?" she asked breathlessly.

It was hot in that fort to begin with in mid-June, but add to that the most beautiful girl I'd ever known saying my name into my mouth—well, it was all around record setting.

I'd shifted my focus to her neck and broke away long enough to answer. "I had a lot of time to kill waiting on you."

She sighed and leaned her shoulder into me as she tried to work my button fly with one hand. "Time well spent," she appreciatively noted.

It was *time* for me to cool us down before we set fire to the pile of old wood in that tree. She deserved better than some back pasture fuck in broad daylight, but hell if it didn't feel good. Her hands on me, even through my clothes, almost annihilated my damn near crippled resolve.

"Hey, we should head back," I said, but my mouth was a complete hypocrite and it kept washing over her hot skin. The way her neck smelled alone could have changed my mind, but I needed to be strong.

A *boy* would fuck a girl in a tree house. Rushed and out of control.

A *man* would take his time and make sure she was comfortable and taken care of completely. I was a man and looked forward to the latter, even if it wasn't in the cards for that night.

"No," she protested. "I like it up here." Her voice was slow and there was a hum pulsing through us when she spoke.

"We can come back sometime, Sunshine. But if I don't stop I'm going to make a mistake and it's not worth the risk."

She put up a good argument pressing against me like she was. Her hand moving over my cock, moving her mouth to my ear. "But, I want you."

Unmerciful words, if I'd ever heard any.

I screwed my eyes shut tightly and reminded myself I hadn't even taken her out on a date yet. If I wanted her to respect me, to see me as a man worth changing her mind about *looking for anything serious* with, then I needed to behave like I deserved it.

The truth was, later that night I'd relive our trip to the tree house in my mind and I'd envision the panting and pawing I knew we were going to miss out on that day.

"I want you too, but not here—*like this*. Not today. Not this time." I leaned back as far as I could to gain much needed space. Otherwise, she was likely to change my mind. Very likely.

She released a disappointed breath and her kiss-swollen bottom lip pouted, but she relented. "All right." She re-adjusted her bra and stepped off my lap.

It sucked, but sometimes the right thing sucks. I learned that lesson a long time ago. It was just ironic that I was the one slowing things down now, when she'd always been the one to gently remind me that we couldn't be together back in the day.

I closed a window and she closed the others, making it much darker in the tree house. Then she got on her knees and stepped down to the first step on her way to the ground, not saying much.

I hoped I hadn't upset her, but she'd given me a lot to think about with what she'd said. I found it very hard to believe no one else had ever sent her flowers or fought for her attention. Honestly, I was shocked there wasn't more than one guy vying for her smiles.

Fools. They were all fools.

I'd show her what it was like to be treated the right way by a man who respected her body, her mind, and her heart.

It wasn't easy climbing down a tree packing that much wood, but I managed. When my feet were on the ground after locking up the fort, I found her waiting by the tree still looking sort of put off.

My hand reached out to hers for our walk across the meadow and she took it, offering me a half smile.

I had to admit, I was at least mildly pleased that she was disappointed, but with that new power came responsibility. I didn't want anyone to take advantage of her, especially not me. It wasn't honorable to do what we almost did.

If things went well, and I prayed they did, I'd want to be able to look her father in the eye. Not that I wasn't prepared to make her lose her mind with desire, but I wanted better for our first time.

Then, maybe some other time I'd bring her back and finish what we started in my fort, for old times' sake. Besides, she'd be right—it wasn't breaking any of the rules.

When we were almost to the ATV and she was still quiet, I knew I had to explain. I knew what rejection felt like, and that was in no way what I was aiming for.

"I'm not sure what's going on in your head right now, but I want you to know why I stopped us." My feet quit moving and when I paused, her eyes met mine.

The sun was starting to sink behind the trees and her blond hair looked like wavy golden silk. I stepped closer to her and brushed it off her sun-kissed, freckled shoulder.

"Sunny, I don't want some fling. I don't want a taste of something only to have it gone before I had a chance to hang on to it with both hands. The first time I have you underneath me, I don't want to be thinking about anything but you. Shit, I don't know if that old fort could handle what I want to do to you."

That made her blush and her pretty smile returned to her face where it belonged.

"I don't know how guys in your past treated you—not well enough, if you're here with me, though. I don't think they knew what they had, but I do and I'm not in any hurry. I'm not going anywhere. I don't want to rush this." I pressed a kiss to her forehead. "Any of it."

Her posture relaxed and we started walking again. She swung our hands as we made it the last few yards to the four-wheeler.

"Are you a virgin?" she asked, making sure to keep her voice measured. The way she said it was sensitive, but I about lost my shit choking with laughter.

"No," I answered and waited as she mounted the back of the ATV. "Not even a little, but thanks for asking."

"I didn't think you were or anything. I mean, you certainly seem to know what you're doing. I was just curious."

"Are you?" I asked.

She laughed outright and it echoed off the hill. "Not even a little." She laughed more, then added, "I mean I'm not a slut or anything, but when you date for as long as I have…"

I shook my head and held up a hand to stop her right there. I wasn't nearly as interested in her sexual history as I was about who she'd *dated* and why it hadn't worked out. She was far from an old maid, but where we came from most people paired off in their early twenties.

I wasn't naive; she hadn't been waiting around for me—no matter how cool that notion was.

It had to be something else. Right? Was it the relationship thing? Maybe she liked being single.

As we took off across the tall grass I went slowly so we could still talk. "Any serious boyfriends? Any jealous exes I should know about?" I asked to test the waters.

"No. Nothing like that. There were a few guys I dated for a couple months, but nothing serious. My mom says I'm too picky. What about you?"

She was picky? That was interesting because so far we'd hung out on my porch, where she sat in an ass-full of wet cushion. She'd shown up to do manual labor—*for free*. Ate my mother's meatloaf like it was her last supper. Then called *me*. We hadn't exactly had a typical start, at least not compared to relationships in my past.

"No jealous exes for me either. I had a few girlfriends in college, but I didn't have enough time between school, work, and running. It was hard to juggle a girlfriend into the mix. Most of the ones I met just wanted to stay out late and drink, which wasn't really my thing. I dated another runner, a girl on the ladies' track team, for a little while, which was less stressful, but she was just as busy as I was. So it didn't work out." I turned my head to the other side so I could see better as we rounded a bank of trees. She followed me to listen.

"Besides, when I told her I was coming back home after school to farm, you could almost see the color drain from her face." I laughed thinking about how Natalie reacted. She couldn't understand that I loved living out in the middle of nowhere. No Wal-Mart. No mall. No Applebee's—which was funny because that's where the conversation, and ultimately our breakup, took place.

I loved traveling and seeing the world, but my home was in Wynne. That's just the way it was for me. Being close to my family was important. I'd dreamed of running our farm all my life. Maybe if I'd met someone who was worth changing my plans for, then I would have. But, as fun as my college years were, and as many girls as I'd had purely *just* fun with, there had been no game changers come along.

I supposed if I was questioning why she was still single, I'd have to reexamine my own relationship status. Sometimes, in those days, I just liked being single and that was okay, too. Like what she'd said to that guy at the bar—*she wasn't looking for anything serious.*

However, the more time I spent with her—the more I learned about the real Sunny—the more I wanted her all to myself, and that feeling was no joking matter.

It *was* serious.

Every touch only stoked my need for the next. At the end of every kiss, I was already mapping out my way to the following one. Every smile became a challenge. I wanted more. Better. Sooner.

"I totally get that. Wynne—good or bad—is my home, too." That was comforting to hear.

I drove around the side of the big barn as we approached my parents' farm. Driving through the gravel, my mom came out waving, so I drove closer to the house than I'd planned.

Sunny's hold on me weakened.

"Where've you been? I called you," she said, relieved.

"We went out checking fences," I answered as my mother noticed who was on the back of my four-wheeler. I saw the curiosity in her casual expression, but she smiled.

"Hi, Sunny. How are you, sweetie?"

"I'm fine. Thanks for the dinner last night. It was delicious."

She stood on the stoop to the back door of the big old farmhouse and waved the dish rag she'd carried out with her. "No trouble. Glad you liked it. Anyway, Rhett, the Smiths have some hogs out. Your dad's down there, but you might want to hightail it and see if you can help."

"Shit," I said. "How long ago did they get out?"

"Just about an hour ago?"

Hogs. Sometimes it was easy to get them back in, other times it could take hours. It was a messy job, but they were our closest neighbors and that's just what you did.

You helped.

Sunny wouldn't want to slop around in pig shit, and I wouldn't expect her to. "Can you drive Sunny down to the cabin shed? That's where her car is." I knew my mom wouldn't mind.

"Yeah, just a minute."

Got off the ATV and Sunny followed me as my mom ran in for her keys or whatever she went back in for. Didn't matter. I was glad to have a quick second before I needed to head down the road.

"This might take a while, or I'd take you back myself. If

the weather holds out for this week, I'll be pretty busy, but I'll try to call. Message me whenever you want. I'll see you Friday?"

The look in her eyes mirrored how I was feeling. It was Sunday, and Friday was a long way off, but it would be worth it. I'd work my ass off this week to make sure I was caught up for the weekend.

I kissed her like it wasn't new, like I'd kissed her good-bye a hundred times. She kissed me back much the same, but it felt so normal that it pushed a thrill right through me.

My mom came out as our lips parted. "I'll call you later," I said and started the four-wheeler again.

"Okay, be careful," Sunny said. Only my mom told me to be careful. That only added to the high I was already feeling.

I revved the engine like I hadn't all day and tore out of my parents' drive. The four-wheeler fishtailed as I pulled out on the road before I kicked it in the ass and made my way to the Smiths'.

Chapter Seventeen

Sunny

Rhett spun out and got the ATV sideways. I wasn't sure if he was showing off or just in a hurry, but I was kind of impressed with how well he handled it. He was good at handling things, including me.

Nevertheless, he'd been really careful when I'd been on the four-wheeler with him the whole day. I couldn't deny it was sexy watching him rip through the gears and tear down the gravel road. His ass didn't even touch the seat as he flew down the dusty lane.

"You're parked at the west shed by the cabin then?" Marcia, his mom, asked breaking my line of thought.

"Yeah, I appreciate the ride."

"It's no trouble, Sunny. I'm glad we'll get a few minutes. I haven't talked to you in a long time." She spoke as she walked to her Explorer. Mrs. Caraway was a beautician, just like my mom, but she worked out of her house. She had always been sweet to me, so I knew better than to be worried, but I was still sort of nervous.

Things were changing.

"How's your grandma? The radio station?" she asked as she pulled around and out of the drive.

"She's good. The station is fine, too. Same as always."

As we rode over the hills, it felt like the few miles' drive was taking forever, and I didn't know what to say so I just looked out the window.

When we came to a stop next to my car, she turned off the ignition and turned a little in her seat to talk to me. My instincts said, "Get the fuck out of here," but I didn't, knowing it would only look rude.

"So you and Rhett seem to be hitting it off," she said.

I wasn't going to lie to her, there was no point in it, but I was damn near thirty and her son was a college graduate living on his own. So even if it wasn't exactly her business, I wanted to be on her good side. It was all very new so there wasn't much to say anyway.

"We've been having a good time," I said.

"That's what I'm worried about, Sunny." She folded her hands on her lap. "Everyone knows how much he cared about you when y'all were younger."

"I remember," I said, hoping to lead her to her point.

"Well, it's just he might have stronger feelings for you than you do for him, is all. I know you two are having a good time, but he already catches so much hell from everyone."

I hated when people teased him. Always had, but there wasn't much I could do about it. Besides, I didn't give two shits what they said about me.

However, I could appreciate a mother looking out for

her son. I really could. And she wasn't being mean or shitty with me, but she was wandering into a place where she was overthinking things.

Right? We hadn't even been on our first date yet, and that still wasn't for another five damn days.

God, I hated that Sunday and Friday were so far apart.

"I think it's sweet you're thinking about him, but you don't know what he's thinking—and honestly, neither do I," I cautiously admitted, not wanting to offend her.

Of course, from what he'd told me I knew he was interested in seeing me again. He had a way of making me feel special, but I didn't want to get ahead of myself. Rhett was a good guy, I'm sure he treated all women respectfully. Even though that was kind of frustrating when I'd wanted him to get a little disrespectful with me earlier.

"Oh, I know. I *do* know that," she repeated, appearing to tread lightly. "But, well, Sunny, you just haven't been one to have a boyfriend or anything."

I took a long breath. Did she assume I'd flirt the pants off her boy then drop him for the next guy? That wasn't really the image I wanted around town.

"Listen, Mrs. Caraway..."

She smiled and interrupted. "Marcia."

I returned her genuine grin with one of my own. "... Marcia, I'm not sure what's going on. I don't think he is either. But he's not thirteen, and I'm not eighteen anymore. We're just getting to know each other. So far, I like him *a lot*. I think he's starting to like me too. *Me*. Not just the cheerleader on the radio he *thought* he liked so much when we were kids. *Me*."

I'd kept my voice tamed, although I felt defensive

inside. I wasn't sure if it was for Rhett, who was a grown-ass man and could take care of himself, or for me, a grown-ass woman who had never had some gossipy, dramatic love affair that the whole town had to whisper about.

Either way, I continued since I had her attention. "But we're both single and not rushing into anything. We haven't even been out on a date yet."

She patted my leg. "Okay, Sunny. I know it's not my place to say anything, but he's just a good boy—*man*—and I'd hate to see him get hurt or have to deal with more guff around town. That's all. I'm glad y'all are having a good time. *Truly.* He's had eyes for you for as long as I remember. And as a mom, there's nothing I want more than to see my kids get what they want. You know?"

"Yes, ma'am." There was no use in arguing. She wasn't saying I'd hurt him, but it was clear she wasn't so sure I wouldn't either. "I need to go let Andy out. Thank you for the ride."

"You're welcome, sweetie." She started the SUV and rolled the passenger window down to add after I got out, "Sunny, I know you're a good woman, too. You might not see him as that little boy anymore, but I'm his momma. I *always* will. Just be good to him, and I hope you know what you want."

She didn't give me a chance to say anything else. The Explorer backed out into the road, but she still waited until I was in my car before she drove off.

What did I want?

As I took my time on the back roads to my house, I thought about that question. All answers went back to his mouth on mine, but I knew the true answer had to be something much deeper than that.

A few weeks ago, I would have said a nice guy who treated me well enough. That's what my mom was telling me I should want. A mature relationship, one that could grow and last.

I wasn't sure he'd want something so serious with all that he had going on. The farm. He still liked to compete and run competitively. Additionally, he'd mentioned a house he planned to build, and that his past relationships hadn't worked out mostly because he had other priorities.

Would the kind of relationship I was getting interested in only get in his way?

I was pretty damn sure I wasn't going to break Rhett's heart, there was just no way I could do it. But, after all of this time being picky and not getting too attached, searching for that one guy who gave me butterflies and hijacked nearly all of my thoughts—now that I'd found him, would he want the same thing?

When I pulled into my driveway, I immediately noticed someone had smoothed out the ruts. The potholes that had been there earlier were gone. I smiled, knowing it must have been him.

He didn't call and I fell asleep watching a *Real Housewives* re-run, but the next morning I woke up to a text message that he'd sent late the night before.

RHETT: It's late, so I hope I don't wake you up. Just wanted you to know I had a great time, and I'm looking forward to Friday.

I fixed a big cup of coffee and headed over to the station with Andy right behind me.

Again, I noticed how many love songs I was playing,

but I didn't give a shit. Who was going to stop me? I finished up pretty early, and as I waited for everything to upload and process in my old program before I left for the day, I swiped my phone open to reply to his message.

ME: Is it only Monday? I hope the week flies by.

"He's a *great* kisser," I confessed to Hannah while she fed Sawyer on her couch.

It was Monday night, and I already wanted to call or see him or text him every five minutes. So I dropped by to see my friend and ensure I didn't act like the crazy person I felt inside.

She said with a faraway look, "I can't imagine what he'd look like all grown up. Last I remember seeing him was a few years back. I remember him being tall, but that's about it."

Lucky for her, I had a few photos. A couple I'd taken *with* him Friday night and a handful from sandbagging on Saturday. But, there were others I'd taken when I couldn't help myself.

I opened my phone to the gallery, brought up the last one, and started there.

"This was yesterday." I held the phone in front of her and quickly yanked my hand closer.

"*Holy shit*, Sunny." She stole it away from me and stared at it with her mouth open. He wasn't shirtless—in that one. "He's a *real* man! Wow."

"Who's a *real* man?" asked Vaughn, my best friend's husband, as he walked into their living room with two beers and a bottle of water for Hannah. He handed one to me and sat on a close by chair.

"Sunny's new flame." She made a face like that wasn't exactly right. "Old flame?" Her tongue hung out as she thought and readjusted Sawyer. "Anyway, Sunny's guy. When we were in high school, he was younger than us, and he had a huge—*I mean huge*—crush on her. He moved back to town, and now he's like super-hot and Sunny is perving on him."

That sounded mostly true, but I wasn't perving. He was an adult.

Vaughn gave me a clever smile and asked, "Are you dating him?"

I didn't feel weird or like there was anything wrong with it, but I didn't want Rhett to get more shit from people than he already did.

"I don't know."

Hannah kicked my foot. "You don't know? I'll tell you. *You are.*"

She looked at her husband, who was putting his beer down. He put a cloth over his shoulder, and they silently made some sort of transaction where they exchanged the baby. Then he reclined into the chair and began patting her on the back.

Hannah still had my phone on her lap, and she reached for it again before I could steal it back. She thumbed through the pictures. I presumed she'd found my favorite when she reached for a pillow and hit me in the head with it.

"Okay, we are kind of dating, but we haven't gone out yet or anything. We've just hung out a few times," I explained to Vaughn.

He gave me questioning expression as he nodded. "Well, that's good, Sunny. Why do you look so stressed about it?"

Stressed? Did I look stressed?

Hannah said, "Wow." Then she caught herself being the pervert she'd accused me of and quickly laughed it off, passing back the phone as she smiled brightly at her husband. "You're pretty wow, too, Astro. Don't you worry." She turned to me and added, "But he's right. Why are you so freaked out? This is the fun part."

I wanted to smack her and remind her of the way she flipped before she went out with Vaughn, but that wouldn't do anything except prove them right.

"Because people already tease him about me *and* he's a little younger…" I listed.

"But…" Hannah prompted.

"*But* I can't stop thinking about him, and—you're right—it's freaking me out. This isn't how I date. I don't just try to run into guys on a daily basis, and I've done that a few times in the past few weeks. And working—like *working* working—*sandbagging*? What the hell?"

They both smiled. Vaughn moved Sawyer to his lap and held her with one hand as he patted her back, still working on that burp.

"That's what it's like, Sunny." Hannah got on the floor and scooted closer to where her little family sat. She kissed her daughter's cheek, where she was perched on Vaughn's leg.

"But guys, I'm old, and I don't need to be messing around with fresh-out-of-college guys who aren't ready to do the kinds of things a girl my age should be *thinking about.*" There it was. Blah. I'd puked my emotions out on their floor.

They might have had to work at getting their baby to submit to their tactics, but I was spewing all over the place.

"What are you supposed to be thinking about?" Vaughn asked.

"Oh, I don't know. Date someone who's ready to settle down a little, I guess." I took a long drink of the Newcastle and set it on the floor beside me where I lounged cross-legged. "He's only twenty-three. I'm twenty-eight going on twenty-nine over here."

But it was more than that. I added, "I know what I was doing at his age. This settle down shit just snuck up on me all of a sudden. He's not ready for any of that. Shit, I'm barely ready for that. It's just messes me up because I think I really like him, and he seems to like me *again? … still? Whatever*. What if I'm only attracted to him because I'm trying to delay the inevitable, guys? Because *I'm still* acting like a twenty-three-year-old."

Neither of them made eye contact with me for a while, but shared a look with each other. Vaughn was the first one to speak after a few long seconds.

"No. You don't know what he wants yet, Sunny. Just see what happens. There's no timetable for finding the right person. I was thirty when I met Hannah. Give it a chance before you start looking for reasons it won't work."

Shit. *Give it a chance.* Wasn't that the same line my mom was feeding me a few weeks ago about Mike? That was something to think about. Everyone was telling me the same thing. I wasn't too dense to hear them.

Hannah kissed Vaughn's knee where she was leaning

and tiny Sawyer let one rip. They both laughed like it was the most hilarious fart in the world. "Not a burp, but we'll take it," Vaughn praised his baby girl.

"Maybe give it a little time," Hannah agreed. "You're not that old, and if things keep going well, then talk to him about it."

"Our first date is Friday. I'm not just going to be like *hey, are you thinking about settling down and getting married or starting a family anytime in the near future? Because some of that shit is on my recently improved and shortened to-do list.*"

She nailed me with the pillow again. "Knock it off, you lunatic. Just have fun, and if you start to feel like either he's not feeling the same way, or like it's getting serious, talk to him."

The problem was what I felt already wasn't casual. It wasn't something I was used to. It was different. It made me feel insane and wonderful at the same damn time.

I agreed that I'd take their advice considering that was exactly the reason I gave them in the text message I sent to Hannah before I came over. It had read:

ME: Halp! I need your fucking advice! 911

So, I'd asked for it and I'd gladly take it. After all, they were happy and must know what they were doing.

Vaughn made us spaghetti-something, and I hung out with them for a few hours to kill some of the time. I knew I'd be stewing all by myself.

I hadn't heard from Rhett, and on my drive home I swore every headlight was his. My stomach hit the driver's seat each time I saw a truck, and then oddly again when I realized I was wrong.

I needed to get a grip.

So when I got home and showered, after checking my phone about twenty times, I decided I'd send him a message and go to bed.

Then when nothing sounded right, I put my phone aside and considered maybe he wasn't thinking about me like I was him, and that I needed to slow my ass down.

Tuesday was just as long and I passed the time after work mowing the grass and drinking alone on my back porch steps.

"Andy, why don't guys call?"

His shaggy brown hair covered his eyes as he looked at me and crooked his head to the side like he was answering, "I don't know, bitch."

I was *his* bitch in my head.

When my phone chimed from an incoming text I nearly screamed.

Okay, I screamed, but no one was around to hear me so it didn't count.

RHETT: It's been a busy few days. Been thinking about you. I'm ready for Friday.

ME: I'm ready for Friday, too.

RHETT: I've listened to a lot of radio in the tractor. Almost like you're there sometimes.

I wished I was there. I took another drink, feeling my heart pound for the first time since Sunday.

ME: I take requests.

"Come Over" by Kenny Chesney came to mind.

RHETT: I'll have to think on it. Want to do anything special?

What wouldn't be special with him? Manual labor was even fun. I was in deep, deep shit.

ME: Anything is fine. Still picking me up at six?

RHETT: Still want to ride in the middle?

ME: Yeah.

RHETT: I'll be there at five.

My cheeks hurt from smiling like a jackass.

Wednesday sucked just as hard as Monday and Tuesday. I played even more love songs. I was annoying myself by the time Thursday rolled around. Stir-crazy, I wondered what would happen if I just showed up at his place?

He'd said he would be busy that week, and I didn't want to get in the way or anything, but I couldn't help but just want to say hi. Just to see him.

Ugh. The waiting sucked *so* bad.

I'd programmed a few more subliminal songs, hoping he'd catch my drift. All the while, aware of the odds of him listening and realizing what I was trying to convey were slim.

Stranger things had happened, though.

Thursday evening, I was bored out of my mind and had to get out of the house. So, I planned on taking an innocent little drive. Nowhere special. I'd anticipated my little venture so much that I even programmed a good road tripping playlist for that evening on WDKR.

It had rained that morning, but the clouds were finally

passing as I drove and the sun was making the sky pink and orange over the fields as I passed them. There were a few different ways out to Rhett's cabin, but the small cottage sat on a dead-end, so driving by wasn't smooth.

So, I just drove. Near-*ish*.

Chapter Eighteen

Rhett

It was the longest fucking week of my goddamned life.

Old habits die hard, and I fought like hell to not drive to her house about every other hour of the day. Man alive, I had no idea of the willpower I actually possessed.

Our talk on Sunday had replayed over and over in my head that week as I sat by myself in the cab of the sprayer I'd been working ground with. I loved when she spoke her mind, and her telling me I made her feel special—well, it stuck with me.

I wanted to call her. Wanted to send her messages. Thought of about a hundred different things I could do, but I didn't do a single one of them.

It was only a matter of time before I'd be too weak to resist doing *something*, but I tried my best to play it cool. I'd been doing an okay job of it so far, and that seemed to work. Still, it had mostly been me to text or call and I didn't want to be a pest.

I always craved her coming to me.

After I finished in the field, I grabbed a beer out of my truck bed and cracked it open for the ride home. It was only a mile to my cabin at the end of my dead-end and there was no through traffic. Honestly, the road that led to mine was just a service for the farm anyway. There wasn't much non-family traffic out there ever.

So it was odd when I was shutting the door to the shed and saw what looked like her car drive past the turn off.

Instead of heading home, I pulled to the stop sign and looked east where the car had gone, seeing the gravel still stirred up where the road curved around the corner. Cranking the radio up, I heard the tail end of an old Diamond Rio song, "Meet in the Middle."

I finished the beer and threw the can behind me, satisfied when I heard it hit the metal in my pickup's back half.

I'd only had *a* beer. I could take a little ride.

A mile down the road, I saw her car top a hill in the distance. She was heading back this way and I slowed on the shoulder and waited, knowing there was nowhere for her to go but right past me.

"Whatcha doin?" I asked when she came to a stop, even with my window.

"Just riding around," she bluffed. I called it.

Past my road? Maybe there *was* something to this less-is-more approach. There she was, and it was *something.*

"What are you doing?" she asked in return.

"Oh, I saw this little red car drive by the shed and thought I was seeing things, then I heard a song and just started driving."

There was only a certain amount of control in me. I'd managed to stay in-check all week—with nothing but my thoughts of her mouth and hands on me, and mine on hers. It was too much having her right there in front of me.

"Drive down to my house. I'm turning around," I said.

"If you're busy … or going somewhere…" she said like she was insecure of interrupting something. "I can just see you tomorrow."

Tomorrow? *No.*

"I don't have anything to do, and I'm not going anywhere but home. Come over for a while." I'd been working all day and needed a shower, but she was there. On my road. It wasn't a coincidence.

Sunny wanted to see me.

She looked at her steering wheel like she was debating whether it was a good idea or not. I was fine with either, but I *preferred* whatever decision had her pulling into my drive in about three minutes.

Even from where I sat higher than her, she was a sight for sore eyes. Tank top. Cut offs. Hair in a messy pile on her head. Sunglasses only hiding her eyes when she looked right at me. Facing forward like she was, I could see her lashes cast down.

As much as I'd wished for her to want me in the past, I couldn't resist her now that she seemed to.

Sunny was pretty when she was deep in thought, making a decision, and only grew more beautiful when she chose me. Her smile was hesitant at first, but then she said, "All right. See you there."

She pulled away in the opposite direction toward my house.

When she was out of sight I slapped the steering wheel in celebration, happy as hell the way my afternoon had changed for the better. Surely, she wouldn't have driven out my way if she hadn't wanted to run into me.

There was only one possible shitty reason, best I could figure, on my way back to the cabin. So, the second I stepped out of my truck, I aimed to clear that up.

"Were you hoping to see me so you could cancel our date for tomorrow?" Nearly any other reason was something I could tolerate.

Her face shot to mine as she answered, "No. I'm not canceling."

Good, I already had plans set up for the next night, and God, I wanted her.

I would have loved to be the kind of guy who could wait a little longer, and if it turned out she'd rather take things slow—I would.

That wasn't how it seemed, though.

When she kissed me back, I felt it, like she was where I was. The desperate little sounds she made when things turned from nice to something less wholesome. It was driving me crazy thinking about how she'd sound when we got *there*.

The issue was, I'd planned that for the next night. I understood that things change, but I'd at least wanted to take her out first. Give her the attention she deserved. Talk a little more—knowledge is power and all that.

I wasn't too naïve to think I knew everything I should. When it came to that girl, I hoped I never learned all there was to know. Every new fact, every sliver of information I was gaining about her, the better my chances were of keeping her.

It was crucial to know everything there was about her because the feelings I had, when her body was against mine, even fully clothed, made them some of the highest minutes of my life. Better than running highs. Better than wins.

Much more than that, I didn't want her on a temporary basis. There was no question about that. Pending some unexpected issue, she was my choice. The only choice. The benchmark.

I couldn't do better than Sunny Wilbanks. There was no better. She was it.

Hearing her tell me she wasn't there to cancel eased my mind.

I slid my hands into my pockets, mostly to keep my filthy paws off her until I was showered. At that moment, she was like clean linen, and I was just a greasy shop rag.

"Mind if I wash up really quick? I smell like shit." I stepped closer to her, fighting the urge to get her as dirty as me.

"No, sure. I mean, you don't..." she rambled, then stopped herself. After taking a breath, she continued, slower. "You don't smell like shit, and you don't have to clean up just because I'm here. You're fine dirty. I mean. Not that you look dirty, but you just said you thought you were."

Her words rushed out of her. She was nervous about seeing me.

Fuck that was hot, too. She was a pretty picture tripping over her tongue. I couldn't hide my grin.

"Sunny," I said before she started up again, despite how fun it was watching. I didn't want her to be too nervous. "I'm covered in shit, sweat, dirt, grease, and God knows what else, really. I *need* a shower." But no amount of scrubbing with soap would clean up the thoughts I had of her in my dirty mind.

"Well, okay then," she said.

"I'll be a few minutes, you can do whatever you want."

If that included her joining me, I was fine with that, but thought it should go unmentioned this time.

Dear God, the thought of her naked in my shower propelled my feet toward the house before I said or did something impulsive. Something stupid. Something childish.

A cold shower might help. I took the front stairs two at a time, hands finally pulling free from my pockets. My jeans were so much tighter than before.

"There's beer in the cooler in my truck and sweet tea in the fridge."

By the time I blazed through the door I'd already torn my shirt off. In my bedroom, I tossed it into the hamper, and kicked off my boots and jeans.

She walked into the house and passed the hall just as I was walking into the only bathroom I had in only my briefs. There was nowhere to hide the effect she had on me. Her eyes caught mine and a life-changing smile crossed her face, but she didn't stop. Then just as fast as she appeared, she was out of sight again.

It doesn't take men long to shower. Me? I could be in and out in about three minutes. I was torn between taking a little extra time to allow for a shave—which I'd neglected all week—and getting back to her sooner.

I chose speed.

I'd shave the next night, and compromised with myself to just trim a few scraggily areas while I brushed my teeth.

In ten minutes or so, I was finished.

When I opened the steamy bathroom's door to the cooler air in the hall, I held a towel around my waist and walked back into my room.

No Sunny.

I grabbed a pair of cargo shorts and a t-shirt, and skipped underwear altogether. Around her, briefs were too constricting. I didn't bother with socks or shoes either. I ran the towel once over my head and face, then fixed my hair in the mirror on the wall.

Through the windows in the kitchen I saw her drinking a beer on the swing, looking out over my field. The radio was on and her shoulders swayed to a song.

It was something I could easily get used to seeing.

Her, just being her.

I could watch Sunny all night, but I decided sitting with her would be better and slipped on a pair of boat shoes then ran out to grab my cooler. It wasn't there.

When I walked through the back porch door I saw it next to the wall where I'd placed it the night we came here after the bar.

She'd brought it in. What a woman.

I opened it and pulled a cold one from the icy water, then sat beside her and stretched out my legs. Just a normal afternoon after work, having a beer with Sunny on my porch. It was pretty damn good—not perfect, but my corn didn't look as bad as it should.

"Did you get a lot done this week?" she asked and sat back, letting her feet dangle as I moved the swing for us.

I popped the top on the can and answered honestly. "We did. Thank God. The river crested last night, and hopefully it will go down now." There was a chance for showers over the weekend. They weren't calling for any hefty amounts, but the river reports didn't interest me at the moment.

I asked, "What did you do all week?"

She took a drink and held her beer on top of her tan knee. Her fingernail was a slightly different shade of pink than it was the other day.

"I saw Hannah, worked, mowed the grass, that's about it. It's been the longest week of my life." She laughed.

"It did seem long," I agreed and took a drink.

"What are we doing tomorrow?" she asked. I warred with myself about telling her. There was no reason to hide anything, except I liked the hint of excitement in her voice.

I stopped swinging as I thought. She could dangle. It made it fun.

"You'll find out tomorrow."

"Well, what do I wear?" she countered, trying to get a clue.

"Whatever you want." *Nothing.*

"Are you cooking or are we going somewhere?" she asked. "I can make something, if that'll help."

Nice try, Sunshine. "You don't have to make anything. How's Andy?" I liked that dog and it was a good time to change topics. I hoped it drove her nuts.

"He's fine," she answered and tipped her head toward the ceiling as I started to move us back and forth again. I could have sworn I heard her growl under her breath, and it sparked a smile that I felt deep within in my chest.

The little hairs that had fallen out of her bun thing wisped past her cheeks as a gentle breeze filtered through the screened porch. The air smelled sweeter.

Before it registered, my hand was sliding down her leg and when it stopped above her knee, I said, "Tomorrow isn't that long to wait. You'll make it." I squeezed her skin and caught my breath when I processed the way her slender leg felt under my hand. As I studied that simple thing, my thumb moved side to side.

It could have been a dream.

I wasn't sure if what I was doing was appropriate. I was, however, sure my thoughts weren't.

How did she do that to me? Normally, I was a pretty composed dude. Not around her.

I caught her looking at my face and our eyes found each other. She swallowed and her lips puckered around a stream of air she released.

I loved that look.

She blinked away and stood, taking the few steps to get another beer, but before she bent over to get into the Coleman by my side, she paused.

"Are you going to kiss me?" The lilt in her voice was innocent, but laced with the perfect amount of need.

"Why?" I asked, wanting to hear the *words* from her lips. No room for confusion on my part. It'd been there before.

"Because I want you to."

Son of a bitch if those weren't the ones. And, oh my God, she was going to kill me.

It was fast, clumsier than I would have liked, but the result was the same.

I lifted her in my arms and found the closest surface. The washing machine. She bounced in my arms a little when the coolness of it touched the back of her legs. Her arms around my neck, fingers in my hair.

My mouth was on her, the thing I'd wanted most since the last time they paired. My lips with hers, she kissed me back just as hard. Our breaths heavy. Her legs wrapped around my waist.

I wanted to explore her, but I also wanted to try my best to wait until at least after our date. My best was failing, though. I didn't see this as some fling, and I didn't want her to think I was treating it that way, but I should have thought about that before I hoisted her up on the washer and put my hands up her shirt. Because the way she leaned into my touch only encouraged me. Cheered me on. Begged for me to keep going.

It was almost like two against one. The two of us against my better judgment.

But, oh hell, she bit my bottom lip, and I lost my mind. My fantasies didn't hold a candle to the real thing. The real *her*.

As my hands worked her shirt up, she lifted her arms when I broke the kiss long enough to look over her shoulder.

I didn't have to let it get that far. I could hold back for one more day, but I honestly hadn't planned to stop yet. That was, until I saw my sister pulling in my drive through the front room window.

Working in reverse, I pulled her shirt back down and she fought *not* to end the kiss in protest, noticing the way I was backtracking.

"Please, don't stop," she said against my mouth. What I wouldn't have given…

I pressed my forehead against hers and said, "I'm sorry. My sister is here."

She looked behind us then jumped off the washing machine like it was on fire. Before she was out of reach and we had an audience, I kissed her one more time.

Sunny's hand pressed, then pulled, then pressed my chest by the shirt away from her. She wanted more, and *fuck,* if I didn't I love it.

I turned and opened the cooler just as she sat on the swing, like nothing had been going on, and I passed her one as a consolation for what was about to happen. She offered me a smile and I offered her my can to make a toast.

"To sisters who get to the point and get the fuck out," I said.

She giggled and replied, "I'll drink to that."

"Rhett, you better have beer!" Haley called from the front porch as she made her way to us. "Your parents are driving me up the fucking wall. I swear if I hear Mom ask me one more time what I'm looking at on my phone—*one more time*—my head's going to explode."

The closer she got, the louder she was. When she got to the back porch screen door, she stopped and said, "Oh, shit. That's *your* car?"

My family was easily becoming a collective bunch of cock-blockers. My dad, acting like he did the day with Sunny's tree, and then while we were sandbagging and all of his goofy smiles and nudges. My mom at the farm. Now, my younger sister and her perfect timing. I wanted to strangle them.

"Oh, uh," Sunny said, likely not expecting Haley to react the way she was.

"What's up, Haley?" I asked to save my girl.

"Sorry," she apologized and gave me the equivalent of

don't kill me with her smile. I waved my hand and kicked out the cooler for her to get a beer and take a seat.

The moment was ruined, but everything happens for a reason and I supposed there might be a *damn* good reason the moment had decided Sunny needed her shirt on.

"How many days until you get to go back to school?" I asked.

"Forty-eight. So what are you guys doing?" she said, overlooking that it wasn't any of her business.

"Having a beer. Shooting the shit," I said. That didn't satisfy her and she looked to Sunny.

Sunny lifted her beer to her mouth and before she drank confirmed, "Having a beer. Shooting the shit." Then she chugged like she hadn't had a drink all summer.

Haley's eyes went wide and she grinned back at me. "Am I interrupting?"

"No," Sunny said with a congenial laugh.

I adamantly replied, "Yes."

They chuckled. I didn't, even though it was probably all for the best—it had most likely saved me from wrecking my original plan to wait until after I'd taken her out. The blond to my left deserved a good first date. I was only too happy to deliver one.

"You better have that house up by next summer so I can live here, or I'm not coming back. I swear, Rhett. She's nuts," Haley rattled off. "And Dad said you got the loan. Any chance you'll be done in less than forty-eight days?"

There was no way I'd be even close to pouring the foundation in forty-eight days, but I was just about as eager as she was.

"No," I answered.

"Well, shit."

Sunny sat forward and crooked one leg under the other on the bench of the swing and asked, "What year are you, Haley?"

"I'll be a sophomore, but I'm going back early because I'm an RA this year," she answered. Then mouthed, "Thank God," before she took her first drink.

"It's not that bad," I said.

She finished swallowing and pointed a finger at me. "Oh, you have no idea. I'm not going back until she's asleep tonight. So, if you two want me to move along, I can probably find something else to do. I just didn't even stick around to put on makeup so I didn't want to go to town." I remembered what it was like to be in her place, but before I could say anything, Sunny beat me to it.

"You can hang out with us. We're just killing time until Friday." I knew what she meant, but it seemed more general, therefore Haley agreed.

"I *hear* that," my sister said, whipping her head back and forth, sassy as always.

So, we drank beer and shot the shit—*with my sister.* In the end, I benefited. Haley asked her all kinds of things I wanted to know.

"Do you think you'll ever try to get a job at a bigger station? You're really funny on the radio," Haley asked a few hours and some beers later.

I found that I was just an accessory to *their* conversation. The two went back and forth like old friends.

"I don't know," Sunny almost sang like the tune was familiar, one she'd rehearsed and recited often. "I really like the freedom working here gives me. I mean, I'm pretty much my own boss. Then again, it might be nice to work with other people—well, besides Andy. *Oh, Andy*," she startled.

"What?" Haley asked. "Who's Andy?"

"My dog," Sunny answered. "I need to go. He probably wants let out. *Shit*." She stood, seeming pretty solid on her feet after having four or five beers, but they'd been spaced out and I wasn't too worried.

I stood then and so did Haley.

"Sorry to rush out," Sunny said and turned to me. "I have to go."

"I'm going to use your bathroom, Rhett," my sister said and left us alone. Maybe I wouldn't strangle her after all. She was quick.

"Five o'clock tomorrow?" Sunny asked.

"Four," I said, knowing it had originally been six, but not really caring.

She started to walk, but I grabbed her hand and went with her. We wandered through the house, and my first thought was to kiss her by the door, so I did.

But, that one didn't make me feel any better, so I followed her outside to her car.

She opened her door and stood with it between us. "I'm really looking forward to tomorrow, Rhett." Her lips looked pinker and maybe the most kissable I'd ever seen.

She leaned over and pressed them to mine and I let her kiss me. Let her lips move over mine and wet them. Let her tongue sweep across my skin. Let them close tightly before they left mine.

Four o'clock better fucking come quick.

Chapter Nineteen

Sunny

I was a dirty panther who wanted to climb him like a tree and swing from his big, thick branches. Sick with want, and I'm sure back in the day I could have been committed to a state hospital for having The Vapors.

Sweet Mother of God, I was in trouble.

He'd caught me on his road, which I was kind of hoping for. But then, he kissed the hell out of me on that washing machine, and I'm not sure I really ever came back down from it the rest of the night.

I tossed and turned, uncomfortable and restless all night long. Desperately, I needed to sleep so I didn't look even older. Soon he'd realize he was having beers and shooting the shit with someone who was ancient.

His little sister, Haley, who I could remember being small enough to push in a stroller, was a college sophomore and drinking beer.

Maybe his vision was bad, and he didn't notice. Then again, it didn't really seem like he cared. What if he just had an older woman fetish? His younger behavior backed up that theory.

He was actually going to build the house he'd talked about. I was happy for him—it was one of his goals for after he graduated.

I lay thinking in my bed, which was too hot, but I was too lazy to turn the fan on. So, instead, I just kicked the hell out of the covers so that my legs were bare. I tapped the pillow under my head to make it fluffy the way I liked.

Yep, I was wide awake.

It was two in the morning, and I wasn't any closer to falling asleep than I had been four hours before, when I went to bed.

There was one thing working in my favor. *It was Friday.*

I just had to make it a few more hours, and then I'd get to see him again.

Normally, I wasn't the *jump into bed with a guy* kind of girl—I mean, everyone has their moments—but usually I waited until I'd been out with a man a few times before I decided if I wanted to get really physical.

Then again, in college, I had sex in a stranger's bedroom with a different stranger at a party. Like I said, everyone has their moments.

What if I was *his* weak moment? Taking out the town's old maid.

No. I had to quit thinking like that. He didn't seem to think like that. I knew for a fact he was as turned on as I was. I'd felt it on more than one occasion and some I hadn't really expected it, which made me smile. Oh, and I saw it in the hall before his shower that night. He'd been wearing boxer briefs, but they didn't hide a damn thing.

It didn't matter, though. He was under my skin, and I didn't think there was anything I could do about it.

The next morning, after I finally wore out my brain thinking about ten thousand things—all starting and ending with Rhett Caraway—I stood at my sink waiting for my coffee to brew. I was up early, but it *was* Friday.

Finally.

Andy was scratching at the front door for me to let him out, and when I did I had to wipe my eyes for they were surely playing tricks.

Running up my long driveway past the station on the road was Rhett. The sun was barely up and we lived miles apart. Had he run the whole way?

"Are you crazy?" I asked. "Do you know how far apart we live?"

"Seven and a half miles," he said, winded, but he didn't look too worn out.

"Is everything okay?" I asked.

Why would he run all the way here? We had phones. He had a truck. In fact, more than one.

"I was out for my run and came this way." He'd stopped at the bottom of my front porch steps with his hands on his hips, his bright hazel eyes shining like he'd slept much better than I had. "Happy Friday, Sunny."

That made me smile everywhere. "Happy Friday," I returned. Thankful I'd already brushed my teeth, I stepped forward.

He added, "Good morning, too."

"Good morning," I replied in turn. "Do you need anything? Coffee? Water?"

He shook his head slowly and a clever grin tipped one side of his mouth. "No. Come here. I'll show you what I need."

There was *that* feeling again. The one that made me feel like my stomach was flipping inside out. The one I'd always known was out there somewhere waiting for me to find.

He stepped up the first step so that we were about eye level, cupped my cheek with one hand, and planted one on me. "You gonna be ready for me later?" he asked only a breath away from my lips, his voice heavy with a quiet masculine rasp to it, the tone just above a whisper.

I was ready for him right then, but nodded that I'd be ready for *later*.

He kissed me again then backed away after giving my ass a good swat. I yelped and remembered I was still only wearing the long tank top I'd put on for bed. His hand only briefly connecting with a small piece of my ass, the rest hitting my boy cut underwear.

"I'll be back," he said. He ran backwards for a few steps and patted Andy on the head as he passed him before turning around and running off the way he came.

At nine thirty that morning, I got flowers. White lilies with a card that said: "Wear a little dress for me."

He was good, and that mounting excitement inside me only grew throughout the day.

At two thirty, I put a little dress on for him. It had a nude, fitted inside and a lacy outer layer that made it almost look like I was only wearing lace. I hoped he liked it as I pulled out my favorite boots, deciding that even though they looked good, they'd be a practical choice, too.

Cute boots were always practical.

I took a deep lungful of air, a practice that was feeling more normal in those fading hours of the long week I'd had. I was tense with nerves, but mostly I was eager to see him and find out what he had planned.

It didn't really matter one way or the other what we did. Somehow, regardless of the circumstances, he always left me with a smile on my face. The thrill of not knowing was driving me wild, but it also kept me busy.

I decided to curl my hair into loose waves and pull half of it up into a little bun thing. I had a nice tan, and if we were going to be outside I didn't want a bunch of makeup to get all cakey and gross. So, I dusted my cheeks with a peachy color, plucked a few stray eyebrows, and put on a few patiently applied layers of mascara so my lashes wouldn't look clumpy.

Mascara was my friend.

He'd seen me without it that morning. Dammit. I bet I'd looked like Powder from that movie. Without mascara my face was freakish. I held out for hope, praying he hadn't noticed—which was unlikely, but whatever.

By three thirty, I was ready and pacing the floor in my living room as I watched the road from my window. Andy paced with me; he was a good dog. He knew what I was going through.

I looked in my refrigerator for the hundredth time, but all I had was beer, which unfortunately didn't sound all that great yet. Instead, I poured myself a glass of tea and took special care not to dribble on my white lace.

Minutes finally passed, slow as all hell, and soon I heard the rumble of a vehicle come down my road.

I quickly looked to make sure Andy had food and water. He'd be fine for a while. I gave him a scratch behind the ear. "You look handsome, Andy. How about me? Good enough?" He sneezed and I took that for a yes. "I'll be back later, okay? Be a good boy?" As always, his brown eyes looked at me somewhere between *you're leaving me forever* and *just go already so I can take a nap in peace.* I'd kept him up half the night, too.

I let him pull all the way up the drive and gave myself one last quick look and fixed a few weird hairs before I stepped out of my front door.

When I stepped outside, he was out of his truck, which looked freshly washed. Then he walked my way.

"Damn, you look so good," he said, sporting a genuine smile.

He looked fine, too. Freshly shaved, the whiskers I'd thought I liked so much the day before were easily forgotten in place of his bare, smooth skin. His tan made his hazel eyes look bright green.

Jeans, just right.

Black V-neck, just right.

Hair combed and styled, kind of off to one side, kind of messy. All of it, *just right.*

The look in his eyes was hungry and satisfied and ready for anything. I felt the same way.

"You telling me where we're going yet?"

He grinned with his mouth closed and answered, "Nope." *Cocky.*

Like I cared. He looked so good, I'd go wherever he wanted. Gladly.

"Thank you for the flowers. They're gorgeous." I kissed him on the cheek. He grabbed my hand and gave it a squeeze, then opened his door and I climbed in and sat right in the middle.

"We've got a little drive, so I brought you a sweet tea and a Twix for the road." I didn't know what to say, but again he'd surprised me into speechlessness. "You still like Twix, right?"

How did something so small like a candy bar cause such a seriously gigantic feeling inside my chest? A sensation so strong, in fact, all I could do was look at him and blink.

He searched my face, looking in one eye and then the other for what I was thinking, but even I didn't know.

It was just so thoughtful to have my favorite drink *and* my favorite candy. He'd just done it. All on his own. It made me tingle with anticipation to see what else he came up with.

"I also got back-ups just in case. They're in the glove box." He frowned a little when I still didn't say anything. "Are you okay?"

Okay? I wanted to climb on his lap and devour him. I wanted to go back in my house and show him how just his sweet treats had propelled me into wanting to please him. How already, two minutes into it, this was surely the best date I'd ever been on.

"Thank you, Rhett," I said. "I love Twix." I scooted closer so that our legs were touching.

"Good," he said. Then he shifted gears on the column

and we backed out of my drive.

After only a few minutes of driving and finally processing what he'd told me, I realized we really weren't going to Wynne. We were headed south and my mind tried to guess the different places he might be taking me in that direction. We hit blacktop, then highway, and I sipped my sweet tea and just enjoyed the ride.

When we got outside of my radio station's reach, he plugged an auxiliary jack into his radio and started playing songs off his phone. I recognized a lot of them. I'd played a few on the station—granted all later at night.

"Do you like seafood?" he asked.

What little I'd had I liked, so I said, "Yes, but I've only had a few different kinds."

His hand had been on my leg for a while and his fingers raked slow, tenderly drawn rows over my skin. "What about shrimp?"

We were almost finished with my candy bar. Instead of just giving him one of the sticks to have on his own, I'd shared both. Alternating my bites with his. I silently offered the last bit of the last stick to him and he took it. "Oh, yeah. I can eat my weight in shrimp."

I started to lick the chocolate off my fingers, when he grabbed my hand and did it for me. "Crab legs?" he asked with three of my fingers in his mouth.

I giggled. "Never had them."

He pulled them out for a quick inspection and then asked, "Oysters?" before sucking one last spot on my middle finger.

"Like *fried* oysters?"

His face grew into a perfectly wicked smile. I was

getting suspicious. He quirked an eyebrow at me and answered, "*Raw*."

Why did the word *raw* sound so sexy?

"No. I don't think so. I've never tried them, but they sound gross."

His hand found my leg again, and he gave it a gentle squeeze. "Trust me, they're good."

That was a big clue, but by the time I figured it out, we were pulling into Shank's Shells and Tails. The restaurant sat on a little lake close to a town called Knob Ferry about an hour away from home.

He parked and got out, then helped me down.

"I thought since it was still pretty early we'd take a drive and get a little snack."

I'd never been to that restaurant, but from the outside it looked safe enough, although I was still a little worried about the mention of oysters.

We walked in past buoys draped in nets and were greeted by a young girl—well, she was probably barely younger than my date. I had to start considering new ways of description. Lately, I'd been connecting age with every person I ran into.

So, the athletic looking, redheaded young woman showed us to a few seats in the back patio bar area where Rhett had asked to be taken.

It was really cool. There were large industrial doors rolled up all the way instead of walls flanking the very back wall. The bar area was open to the air and where some seats were outside of them on the large wooden patio, some were under the roof closer to the bar that was servicing that side of the restaurant.

The chairs were fun, too. Made out of old tractor seats.

The tables were smaller but hosted a variety of things. A roll of paper towels. The normal salt, pepper, mustard, and ketchup. Then a container with wet naps and about five different kinds of sauces.

"Hey guys, I'm Nick. I'm working the lake bar this afternoon on this beautifully *not* rainy day. What's your poison?" Nick wore a trimmed salt and pepper colored beard and a backwards ball cap, but he looked clean and obliging.

Rhett's eyebrows rose and he leaned toward my side of the table. "You trust me?" he asked.

But, I didn't have a chance to answer.

Nick asked, with a new level of excitement in his voice, "Oh, never been here before?"

"I have, she hasn't," Rhett answered.

"Do you guys want menus?" Nick looked around for the closest ones.

Quickly, Rhett asked again, "Do you trust me?"

I hesitated, not knowing what I was getting into, but I wanted to say yes. "I think so," was the more honest answer.

"Good enough," Rhett said decisively. "Two Bloody Mary Chapin Carpenters, a tray of Minnie Pearls with extra horseradish and sauce, and a bucket of Jimmy Dickens." I was thoroughly confused, but it was so silly that I laughed. Rhett laughed with me as Nick walked away to place our orders.

"Okay, I think I can guess what the Bloody Mary Chapin Carpenter is, but what else did you get?"

He beamed and I melted, the warmth of his smile causing me to squirm in my bright red tractor seat.

"I'll have him bring you a menu so you can read it. It's

pretty funny. All of their foods and drinks are named after country music stars. I got a tray of oysters on the half shell and a bucket of peel and eat shrimp."

I'd always dreamed of being on a date where it just felt like a ride, but if I could have held on to this one and made it last forever, even though it had just started, I would have.

When Nick came back with our drinks, which looked like meals in themselves, Rhett asked for two Crystal Gayles. I learned that was ice water.

I didn't care if oysters tasted like hell. I'd eat them. I'd eat all of them.

And, after some expertly taught lessons in how to properly dress a raw oyster from my date, I just about did. The first went down a little funny and he mocked my face several times, but I didn't care. I could see how much he was enjoying himself.

"I think it's the process that people like about eating oysters. There's a ritual to it," I commented as I doctored up my sixth one. Dabbing my preferred amount of horseradish, which was considerably less than his, I spooned on the red sauce and squeezed the second half of my last piece of lemon.

We'd fallen into a pattern of doing them at the same time, so I waited as he worked on his. Rhett didn't drink from the straw on his Bloody Whoever, but he tipped back what was left before we locked eyes, both ready to go.

We shot them back, and then we laughed. I couldn't tell you what was funny, but it just felt so good doing it that it was now part of our oyster eating routine.

"Maybe. I think they taste good," he said and dipped a shrimp in the sauce and bit off its body, discarding the tail into a bucket that was there for our disposal of shells and things.

I argued, "They just taste like whatever you put on them. I don't think they have a taste."

"Sure they do," he argued. "They taste like oysters."

He chose his next one and did his spoon-shucking trick that I'd also mastered from watching him. "Eat one plain," he challenged.

That didn't sound like a good idea, but I was feeling adventurous and so I got one ready. It looked much scarier without all of the condiments. Slimy and wet and *ew*.

I stuck my tongue out. "Okay. Okay. Okay." I chanted to prepare myself. "I can do it."

He lifted his and paused. I mirrored his actions and waited. He held his proudly for what felt like forever, I think to add to the suspense of it … and he liked watching me squirm.

What lay waiting for me in the shell was so disgusting, and I almost reached a point of retreat.

Finally, he asked, "Ready?"

"Is a frog's ass water-tight? *Yes!* Just do it already," I nagged and then chuckled. He was so much fun. Disgusting, spontaneous, adventurous fun.

His eyes squinted, which made me think of Clint Eastwood, or his son. *Whoa.* Scott Eastwood. I swallowed hard, seeing a slight resemblance.

Then he puckered his lips and sent me a kiss through the air, and our oysters went down the hatch.

I didn't know what he had planned for after our cocktails and snack stop, but I hoped he'd allowed time for me kissing his head off—because I *really* wanted to.

To hell with waiting a few dates, I wanted all of him. Whatever he wanted to give me, I'd take. Because, no matter what it was, it was all good.

If I took Hannah and Vaughn's advice, I'd need to have a conversation with Rhett *sooner* than later. I liked him a lot. A *whole fucking* lot.

Beyond his looks. Beyond his body. All the way to his personality and character. The awesomeness of the first two were just bonuses. The good stuff was *him*. The way he talked to and treated me. How easy it was for him to laugh, and for me to laugh, too.

So many times I'd been attracted to one aspect of a guy, but it never worked out because of all of the other pieces I didn't like so much.

With Rhett, I liked it all.

After we had our fill of seafood and fancy alcoholic tomato juice, we hopped back in his truck and that was when I noticed he'd covered the truck bed with a black tarp.

"What's in there?" I asked as I climbed in and looked through the back window to see if I could get a clue.

He hastily looked back there. Then he took a seat behind the wheel and slammed the door. "Nothing," he said innocently.

"Lies," I accused.

"Maybe, but you'll forgive me."

"If you kiss me real quick, I'll think about it."

It must have been an easy decision for him, because without another word his lips were on mine. I could taste the lemon from earlier and the peppermint he'd grabbed off the counter and eaten as we walked through the parking lot.

I was the liar because I didn't think about forgiveness at all. I didn't think of anything outside of how his fingers were holding my face to his at the back of my neck. How his lips never looked as big as they felt when they moved over mine. How I just wanted to let go into that kiss and see where I landed.

He said against my mouth, when the kiss was going to either turn into more or cool off, "There isn't anything like kissing you. Not a single damn thing."

Chapter Twenty

Rhett

I could tolerate holding back in the parking lot at Shank's Shells and Tails only because I knew where I was taking her we wouldn't be interrupted. Additionally, I'd had a discussion with my sister about calling before showing up in the future. To her benefit and mine, she agreed.

It was our first legit date, and I'd tried my hardest not to anticipate anything more physical than our times before, but I wanted her so damn bad. And if she wanted me back—*oh, God*—she could have me.

I meant that, too. *Whatever* she wanted was there for the taking.

It was just after seven, and she'd taken it upon herself to unplug my phone in exchange for hers to play the music on the way back toward Wynne. We passed my turn off and she looked my way, but didn't ask where we were going. I supposed she'd learned by then that she'd just have to be patient and see.

What was it about making her wait, even just a little, that was so damn gratifying? Whatever it was, she let me have it and I liked it.

Sunny was starting to trust me, and she could. I'd do anything for her. Anything to keep her sitting in the middle of my pickup's cab. Anything to keep my arm around her shoulders as she leaned into my side. Anything to ensure she always wanted to be next to me.

She'd looked like a centerfold when I picked her up. Short, lacy dress. Her hair looked pretty and messy and sexy. And her face had a smile that never really seemed to fade the whole evening. Then there were the boots. Hell, a woman in cowboy boots could set me on fire and roll me down a hill, and I'd still come back for more. The kicker was it was Sunny wearing them.

As I drove down the lane, I waited for her to ask why we were at the quarry, but she didn't. I made it to the spot I'd set up earlier and backed in, then turned off my headlights.

"Did you bring me here to park?" she guessed. I liked where her head was.

"Not exactly."

That wasn't far from my mind, but I'd had more up my sleeve than just taking her to a dark place to make out in my truck.

I hopped out, and she followed.

Pulling the rubber bungees, I unhooked the black cords that held the tarp down over my gear. When I pulled it back and revealed the stuff, she still didn't know what was going on.

I climbed up the tire and into the bed to get the other

side released.

"I am so confused," she admitted from the ground, looking up at me.

"When I was in college, I bought a projector to watch games outside at the house we rented. So, since Wynne doesn't have a theater anymore, I thought we could have our own."

"No way," she said and continued watching with rapt attention.

It was perfect and I'd already made sure it would work. I hopped out and released the tailgate so I could plug it all in like I had earlier. There was a power pole beside the truck, and before long, the large limestone wall in front of us had a blue screen shining on it.

I'd also brought every clean sleeping bag I could find, my cooler, and a speaker from the farm shed.

"It's like a drive-in, Rhett," she said. Carefully—I know because I watched—she climbed into the back and began spreading out the plush camping gear.

"What are we watching?" she asked.

"*Fifty Shades of Grey*."

Sunny's jaw dropped, then a hand slapped across her mouth. Her blush was worth it.

"Just kidding. Actually, I have a few choices." I opened the duffel bag I brought. "I grabbed a few movies I had and ordered a few online so we'd have options. I have *Blazing Saddles*, *Tombstone*, *Anchorman*, and the first seasons of *The Office* and *Dexter*."

"You brought *The Office*?" she said, her voice saturated in laughter. "I love that show. Let's watch that one."

She'd made a good choice. After I got the pilot episode

playing, I sat back where she was, leaning on a few of the extra sleeping bags she hadn't unrolled.

"Want a drink?" I asked.

Again, she looked surprised. "What did you bring?"

"Sweet tea and whiskey," I answered. It had been a long shot, so I also had beer, but I thought she'd like it. Besides, I'd made plenty of sweet tea for her that day for the truck ride.

She bit her bottom lip, releasing it when it turned into a winning smile. *Score.*

As it got darker in the quarry, we drank and laughed to the stupidity of Michael Scott and his co-workers on the TV show.

She sat a few inches away, and as the night grew longer, that wouldn't do anymore. I reached out for her leg and gave it a light tug toward me. She sipped her tea and her blue eyes met mine above the red plastic.

I'd only aimed to get her beside me, but then she kept coming and climbed right on my lap. I did *not* object.

Her small body fit well with mine. She sat her cup on the wheel well and put her hands on my shoulders. She was backlit from the projection off the quarry wall and it was stunning. Thank God I was already sitting down.

"Thank you for this date, Rhett," she said, scooting closer until her knees lay beside my hips. "I think it's the best first date—hell, best *any* date—I've ever had." She licked her lips as I ran my hands up her thighs until I met fabric, which was still pretty high.

I sat up taller and her breath caught when I moved against her.

Soon, her hands were cupping my cheeks and she was

kissing me like she meant it.

Best date ever. I had to agree. It was mine, too.

Sunny was easy to be with. She loved to laugh and have a good time. She hadn't been picky or put the brakes on my surprises, even when the not knowing became frustrating. I admitted to myself, it had taken a lot more arm-twisting to get *me* to try oysters my first time.

Yet, after all of that, she was thanking me. Over and over, between kisses.

"You're welcome, Sunshine," I whispered when she moved her mouth over my neck. My chest was as tight as the grip I had on her hips, and she rocked into me.

I wanted to touch her, wanted to find my way around her body, but that wasn't going to happen in the back of my truck. Sure, I wasn't in any hurry to stop what was happening, but I wanted her in my bed for our first time, and I wanted her there all night.

It was a wonderfully agonizing way to wait for just that. Her hands in my hair. Her mouth on my skin. The sexy moans and whimpers she made when I shifted against her when the kisses grew deeper. I couldn't get enough.

I wasn't sure how long we'd been there like that, but my needs were growing stronger and she sounded as desperate as I felt. When I broke the kiss, impulsive and spontaneously, a result of the endorphins and adrenaline coursing through me, I said, "Come home with me."

Her breath left her in a rush, and I waited for her to either accept my invitation or tell me no. She was still swaying in my arms as she sat up to gain a little space.

"I can't," she said. However, it didn't sound like she didn't want to.

"Yes, you can," I corrected. "Come home with me." I kissed the spot on her chest just above the neckline of her dress and her head fell back.

"God, that feels so good," she panted.

"See? Come home with me." I bent my knees for her to recline on as I gently persuaded her. My hand moved over the lace of her dress to cup her breast.

Still, there was only so much persuading a man should do. Knowing when no meant no wasn't something I took lightly.

"I *want* to," she admitted in one released breath.

"Then come home with me," I repeated. She leaned into my touch and I kissed her neck and jaw.

"What about Andy?"

Andy? My mind stopped to think. Who was *Andy*? My pause caused her to lean up and look into my eyes.

"My dog. *Andy*. I can't leave him overnight," she explained.

Of course. Andy *the dog.* I'd forgotten, in the heat of the moment, and the sound of another man's name on her lips almost gave me a heart attack.

This was a minor problem and one easily solved. I grinned and kissed her lips that were right in front of mine.

"Out of context this isn't something I'd ever say, but if you want to stay the night, you can bring Andy."

She laughed at my attempt at a joke, but it wasn't like my brain was firing on all cylinders. The hum of her laugh buzzed through my chest.

"You can always stay at my place," she suggested.

"I plan on it, but not tonight. *Come home with me.* I want you *there*." I didn't want to be argumentative, since decidedly we'd be spending the night together, but I wanted her in my bed. My house. My space. I didn't know why, but that's what I wanted.

"I want you, too," she confessed and her forehead fell on my shoulder. "Do you think this is stupid?"

Unexpected? Yes.

Stupid? Fuck no.

"What do you mean?" My hands rubbed down her back.

"I don't want to make this heavy or anything. I've had such a good night, but *really,* what are we doing?"

That was a very good question.

She continued. "We don't have to figure it all out right now, and it won't change anything for me." She looked into my eyes. "I still want to be with you tonight. I just might want more than that."

I'd avoided thinking into it that much, for fear of overthinking. I'd been afraid if I tried to make what was happening fit into some category, named under some label, I'd only be disappointed. I wasn't sure what she wanted. I'd resigned myself to not say anything about it until I didn't have a choice.

That still felt like the right thing to do, given my history of saying too much. I'd already told this girl I loved her three thousand times in our lifetime.

She'd been the only one I'd ever told—*and meant it.* Or maybe I hadn't meant it all those years ago, but getting to know her like I was, it rang true.

There was something about her that I instinctively went toward.

"What do you want?" I asked her. That was a safer

approach, knowing full well I could give her anything she required. *Anything.*

"I don't know yet. I'm still figuring it out," she said. "But it looks a hell of a lot like you." Her lips kissed me softer than only minutes before. The honesty in her soft, short-lived kiss reassured me.

This was right. I just needed to hang on.

"Well, just say the word and it's yours, Sunny." Her arms wrapped around me and she held on tight. Tight enough for both of us.

"Okay, let's go get Andy," she said over my shoulder.

After packing up our tailgate movie theater, we swung by her place. She told me she didn't need any help and offered to drive herself over, but I insisted they ride with me.

She needed to grab a few things for herself and Andy, and in about five minutes she came out of her garage door with a backpack and a plastic grocery bag, Andy right behind her.

She went to the passenger side door and I leaned over to open it for her.

Andy jumped in like he'd ridden in my truck all his life, and she hopped into the passenger seat. I'd already become accustomed to her sitting by me, but Andy couldn't shut a door. I'd have to figure out a better way for the next time it happened, like in the morning.

"I have to go into the station tomorrow and do programs for the weekend," she admitted.

I looked at the clock on the dash and it wasn't even ten

yet. "What time do you have to be up? I can bring you back around five or six."

"In the morning?" she exclaimed and pulled her door shut with both hands. "I'll murder you if you try to wake me up that early on a Saturday. I have to be there by nine. It'll only take me a few hours, and I have things lined up until ten."

The thought crossed my mind that it was a good thing because I planned on staying up late. "Fair enough."

It wasn't supposed to rain that night, so I was fine with leaving the stuff in the back of my truck. Even if she slept in until whatever time, I knew I'd be up with the sun. I could put the stuff away then.

I made it to my place in record time.

When I got out, Andy climbed down on my side, then immediately sniffed around the front yard. Sunny met me in front of the truck and we headed up the steps. I opened the door and held it for her, and she gave me a quick kiss as she passed.

I loved the feeling of her in my cabin. My home. My space with my girl. There was something to that, I believed.

Sunny tugged the blue bag off her shoulders and walked the plastic bag to the kitchen where only the light above the sink was on. Then she pulled out two dishes and a Ziploc of dog food. She filled the water dish from the tap and set the bowl on the floor against the wall. "Is this okay here?"

I leaned against the wide doorway and nodded. It was *perfect* right there. When Andy heard the sound of food hitting the metal bowl, he scratched at the front door. I let him in while she placed the dish next to the other on the tile beside my refrigerator.

He ran right past me, without a second thought, and tore into the bowl.

Sunny rubbed her hands together, done with her task and then looked kind of lost. There was that hint of nervousness I liked so much.

Maybe it was because I could relate to the feeling. I remembered almost puking every time I talked to her in school. How worried I'd been that I'd say or do something wrong. That's how she looked and it was endearing. The deep, uneasy breaths—meant to calm yourself, but rarely ever did. The fidgeting. What made it sexy was that *I* made *her* feel that way.

God, how had I gotten that lucky?

"Come here," I said and held my hand out to her. She didn't hesitate, but her eyes cast down as she placed her delicate hand in mine.

When she was in front of me, I tipped her chin up. "Hey, are you okay?"

I didn't want her to be uncomfortable. I didn't want her to feel unsure or have second thoughts, cheapening what I felt. I didn't want any kind of smudge on the night.

"I'm fine," she said, but fine was hardly convincing. She bit her lip, and I pulled it out with my thumb.

"Fine isn't what I want to hear," I explained.

"I'm happy," she said sincerely. "That's all. Will you kiss me?"

Of course I would, but I knew when we got started there wasn't a lot of room for discussion. I wanted to be certain there wasn't something on her mind that we needed to get ironed out first.

"Are you sure?"

She blinked once, then twice. I saw the need I felt reflecting in her eyes. "Kiss me, Rhett."

There she was saying my name again, making me abandon all rational thought to do her bidding.

I picked her up level with my lips and her feet dangled down in front of my legs as I kissed her.

"There," I said with my last ounce of self-control to make sure I wasn't missing something. It should be noted I deserved no medals of valor. I was already walking to my bedroom with her in my arms and sort of proud of my ability to multitask.

"There *is* one thing," she said, and I yielded at my door and pulled my mouth away from her neck.

"What?" I asked, looking directly at her.

"Well, I didn't want to say anything, but we have to figure out how Andy can sit by the window in your truck. He likes the window seat and doesn't mind if it's always wet." She smiled at me with the same carefree look from earlier, and whatever errant thoughts I'd had were discarded.

Andy liked the window seat? I was on to her.

It was dark in my room. As a man, the first thing that went through my mind was to turn on a light so I could see everything that was happening. But, on the basis of wanting a good chance of it happening again, I let that idea go. There was a wash of moonlight on the side of the bed I usually slept on, so I'd make do with what I had.

We kicked off our shoes, like you would at the first sight of a beach before running to the ocean. My jeans fell after I adjusted myself to allow for it.

I stood there in my briefs and waited for my eyes to adjust. I couldn't tell if she was naked or not, so I reached for her hip with my hand.

Underwear. I didn't have a preference one way or the other. Had she been naked, I would have kicked off my skivvies, but I was going to enjoy taking hers off. *Maybe with my teeth.*

Again, I reminded myself to dial it back. My hands would do.

Then, for the first time I thought about our ages, and I hoped I had enough experience to please her.

I wasn't too worried about it, mostly because there was this noise she made when I kissed her this one certain way. It always happened when my tongue found hers each time after being away from one another. She'd whimper. It was that one little thing that reminded me that maybe I could please her. Please the hell right out of her and take pride in doing it.

Age aside. There was no one *more* qualified to study her, in any capacity, than me.

Glad for not having drunk as much as I could have, I still had a fairly clear head on my shoulders. I just needed to use it. I'd go in eyes wide open and I wouldn't stop until I proved that I could do everything she needed.

I just hoped what she did back to me didn't cause too much interruption in my plan. Like a *premature* interruption.

Slow and steady, Rhett.

She grabbed my hand and stepped in the direction of my bed, the moonlight clinging to her arm and leg she propped up there. The sight of her nearly naked side, her golden hair tumbling over her shoulder as she leaned into the silver wash of light on my mattress, was almost heavenly.

Motivation to stick to my slow and steady plan was knocked down considerably. I'd say to the point where I just didn't want to fuck it up.

She lay down and pulled me to her. In the moonlight, I saw her bite her lip ever so quickly before she said, "*And* there's another thing, too."

I sat and leaned over to her, my mouth eager to claim hers in a purposeful way this time, no holding back.

"Name it," I said.

"I want to be your girlfriend."

Now wasn't that something?

"Are you sure you don't want to wait until tomorrow to decide something like that?"

She chuckled sweetly and argued, "I don't want to wait. I want it right now."

Sounded like I had an impatient little girlfriend.

"All right then. You're all mine."

It was one of those moments that hits right that second. No time needed to absorb it. It broke through all other thought.

"*Finally*," I quietly stated. A relieved breath left my chest. My lips found her shoulder. She even tasted like mine.

"And you can be mine, too," she added as her hand met my erection through my briefs between us. Her palm stroked, and my dick ached for more.

I pulled her hand away and laced her fingers with mine, then shoved them under the pillow as I rolled on top of her. Two slim legs parted around me, and I pressed into her center, our remaining clothes quickly becoming inconvenient.

Face to face, not kissing, just looking at each other

knowing something big was happening, but not sure what the hell it was.

I told her plainly, and with a very sure voice: "I've always been yours. It's about time you caught up." Her mouth went slack and I took advantage, pulling her bottom lip between mine and sucking it as I pulled away to add, "I don't want to talk anymore, Sunshine. I want you so fucking bad."

She nodded, blinked lazily looking at my lips, and whispered, "Okay, I'll shut up." Then she kissed me and made that other sound that tethered me to the moment.

I stripped her naked, then I stood as she pulled my briefs down to my knees and I kicked them away. I retrieved a condom out of my nightstand and put it on.

She inched her way further up the bed and I joined her. Again, her hand found me as I held myself above her. Her fingers wrapped around me at my base and she pulled.

"*Ah.*"

Her touch was exactly what I liked. She did it again, and I moved her left thigh so that I could get closer to her.

I licked two fingers and quickly realized that wasn't necessary at all.

"*Ah.*"

She was wet. Really wet. For me. Sweet hell, it was like a kill shot to my chest.

When my fingers swept through her she bucked and a quiet moan slipped out of her lips. Her chest rising and falling under me, her breasts parted just enough to show them move ever so gently as her shoulder hitched with her shorter breaths.

All of these things happened and just kept happening. I was merely there experiencing it, like it was my first time.

And, miraculously, like it was her first time, too.

She lined me up with her entrance then left me there. Again pairing her hand with mine, she raised them above her head. Then I pushed into her.

"*Ah*."

Her head fell back against the pillow and she sighed.

I took my time. Holding my weight against her, I waited until I felt her push back against me—when she was ready for more.

I'd like to think I went with her slow at first, but maybe I didn't. Once her mouth was on mine, and I tasted her moans instead of only hearing them, I set a pace that had her wrapping her legs around my waist.

One hand still holding tight to mine, she lifted up on her other elbow bringing our chests together.

She was trying to kill me. It was a certain sweet death for sure.

Her needy sounds became more frequent and a shiver in her body let me know she was getting close—or at least I prayed she was.

I would have chosen death over coming before her our first time. I leaned to one side and worked my hand between us, hoping to help her on her way. With my two fingers I rubbed over her until she was saying my name and few other things that wouldn't be fair to her to repeat.

I bared my teeth. It felt like the only thing I could do to help myself hold on for just a little longer. The condom helped mute things, but only just.

She kissed me hard, her tongue finding mine first, but still making that sound I liked best, regardless of who found who. Her hips rocked into me, grinding slower and slower until she relaxed in my arms. That feeling was one of the most powerful sensations that had ever run through my body.

She was satisfied. *By me.*

"I want you to come, Rhett."

Dear. God.

The seven sexiest words I'd ever heard. Wait. They were only six words, but I wasn't mentally capable of simple math at that moment. Not since we were agreeing on something so good.

"*Ah*," I moaned for more than the fifty-fifth time. Or maybe fifty-sixth. Who knew?

Why was I thinking about numbers when she was holding onto my ass like that, pushing me into her like she was?

I could have sworn I felt her tense against me for a second time, but I had my own agenda. My stomach tightened, and my hips rocked into her in long, hard thrusts.

Then I stilled my rhythm, my eyes shut hard, and my hand slapped against my headboard to hold the earth still for just a few more perfect seconds as she panted and clung to me. I think it was involuntary, but I pushed into her a few more times loving the feeling of her reflexively gripping me when I did it.

It was then I felt the cool breeze of the fan against my damp skin, and I realized I was in my room, in my bed, with my dream girl.

Then I rolled to my side off of her and my arm flew across the bed to the side that wasn't messed up like where she lay. My hand hung over the edge, and I felt a cold, wet nose brush against it.

"Andy, you're a pervert," I accused.

Hearing his name, he popped his head up and balanced with two paws on the mattress.

"Andy, you bad boy," she scolded, laughed and added, "I'm thirsty."

So was I.

"A big old glass of Crystal Gayle would be nice right about now," she added and we laughed, all the while trying to catch our breath.

I needed to get rid of the condom anyway, so I jumped up and headed to the kitchen. When I came back, she was lying on the neat side of the bed and Andy was beside her.

That wasn't happening. I could deal with her riding on the other side of my truck for a few miles, but *sleeping* on the other side of a dog wasn't in the cards. Not that night.

She was mine, and I wasn't letting go until morning.

"Scoot," I said and nudged the little brown dog. I didn't care if he slept *in* the bed, but I was getting pride of place next to Sunny. "You can lay over here." I patted the edge of the bed where I usually slept and handed her the cold bottle of water. I'd drunk my fill of orange juice at the fridge.

She opened the bottle and tipped most of it back. "He has to sleep over there, huh?"

I situated the pillows so that I could have my own and laid down somewhere close to the middle of the king-sized mattress.

"Yes. Come here," I said and she did, putting the water on the nightstand closest to her.

"That's not very hospitable," she teased.

I kissed her forehead and considered a second round, for which he'd be safer over there anyway.

She sank into the crook of my arm and I reminded her, "You said he didn't mind the wet spot."

I didn't have to think much more about round two. She made the choice for us, and climbed on top, giggling and kissing me.

Chapter Twenty-One

Sunny

I woke up a few times throughout the night, and each time I lifted my head he held me tighter. I wasn't a total novice in that situation, but at the same time it felt so different.

Not different-bad, but different-good. Different-*awesome*.

I'd always thought I didn't want to sleep that close to anyone. The few times it had happened I'd felt smothered, hot, and couldn't wait to get home and into my own bed. Lying with him in his bed, Andy having run off to somewhere quieter hours earlier, I noticed I didn't feel like I had before.

He was younger, but in his arms it was almost like he was guiding me. Like he was in control. Shouldn't I know more about this stuff? Shouldn't I be the one with the cool hand?

Older, *wiser*.

Maybe it was my age showing and that ever-growing voice in my head that over the past month had become louder and louder. The worried adult voice of caution.

Rhett was fresh out of college, surely ready to live it up after working so hard to graduate. And all of that running? Being home must have felt like a vacation.

He deserved that time to be reckless and see what was out there. I'd had my time. So that was why I'd wanted to hear him say I was his girlfriend. It felt like reassurance that we were doing the right thing.

But was it the right thing for both of us? Would he even consider what he'd be missing out on?

At whatever late or early hour it was, I eventually fell into a calm sleep, deciding I wasn't going to figure it out that night, but I needed to be careful. And, for the first time, it wasn't for my behalf. It was for his.

When I woke up, I was completely covered up by a warm quilt. The sun was out, but it still looked early. I lived in the country, but I'd never lived on a farm. The most farming I'd ever done was mowing the yard.

I heard Andy bark outside the window, and I sat up to see what was going on. Rhett was taking the sleeping bags out of the bed of his truck while my dog ran around like a lunatic, sprightly and full of energy.

He'd slept better than I had.

When they got closer to the door, I heard Rhett say to my dog, "Fine. We'll go wake her up, but if she kills me my blood is on your paws."

I laughed quietly and sank back down into the blankets where it was cozy. Then I realized I was still completely naked.

Oh, God, I was going to look a lot different in the morning. As bad as I knew it had to look, I was happy I hadn't cleaned off my makeup the night before. Most of it had probably been smudged or kissed off, but if there was someone up in the sky looking out for me, I hoped it was Tammy Faye Bakker who had the night shift after our first date.

The blanket was over my head, so I heard, but couldn't see, when they came into his bedroom.

"Sunny," he whispered and touched the end of the body burrito thing I had going on. "It's seven, do you need to get up?"

I held my breath, unsure of why I was playing opossum. Oh yeah, because I probably looked like a train wreck.

A knee dipped into the mattress next to me, then I felt his hand on my arm through the fabric. He gave me a gentle shake.

"Hey, Sunny?"

I felt Andy jump onto the bed to help him. No part of my body was showing and my dog's nose began hunting through the blanket to get to me. "Is she always like this?" Rhett whispered to my dog.

I was glad he did that. I talked to Andy all the time. It was nice that they were getting along. Andy was ride or die for me. Or whatever pet-master equivalent that kind of relationship was.

"Do you think she'll want coffee?"

My dog's nose was sniffing the covers wadded up around my neck and I nudged him.

I wanted *all* the coffee.

"Do you think she'd want some banana bread with it?"

Again, I knocked my head against the wall of blanket I was hiding under in the direction of my puppy.

His hand grabbed the top of the quilt and started to work it free from where it was tucked under my head.

What if I look like an albino?

What if I have dragon breath?

He's going to see my boobs, all morning-like and floppy.

I wasn't ready for that yet. I liked knowing—*for sure*—that he thought I was pretty. From when he was younger and told me every chance he got, to the way he looked at me now. Okay, maybe he didn't think it, but I *felt* pretty around him.

That would all be over when he saw the panther hiding in his sheets.

I braced myself for the dawn and decided to smile anyway. He laughed at me—not the best reaction, but one I'd half-ass attempted for nevertheless.

"Good morning, Sunshine," he said.

"Hi," I croaked.

"You don't look like a killer. I was expecting rage or"—he swiped at the corner of his lips—"a little foaming at the mouth, but you just look pretty." He yawned and I yawned in response, not knowing what to say anyway, still a little groggy.

"Did Andy tell you yes to the coffee and banana bread?" I inquired.

He scratched his chin, about to humor me. I loved when he did that.

"Funny enough, we were just talking about that. He didn't know if you take cream or sugar because he can't see that high."

A chuckle tumbled from my chest.

"Lots of both. When you think it's too much, add a little more." I stretched my legs and pointed my toes, holding the blankets tight up around my neck.

"Are you cold? I can shut this window. It got cool last night."

"No. I'm just really naked."

He gave me a skeptical look that told me to *get over it, we'd had sex* after all. But, what he didn't realize was there was a big difference between out for the night, drinking and feeling sexy, and how wretched I'd look that morning.

"Would you feel better if I take my clothes off?" he asked, surprising me.

I laughed again. "No," I said. "Then I'd never get coffee."

Something playful and wicked sparked in his eye. "You've got that right. I'll go make you a cup." He leaned over and stopped just before kissing my lips. "Did you change your mind?"

I swallowed and said, trying to use as little dumpster breath as I could, "About what?"

"About being mine," he replied.

Behind the light-heartedness in his bright eyes, I found a serious gaze. He wasn't kidding and looked a lot like he had when I first saw him again that summer. Serious. Thoughtful. Like he was working something difficult out in his head.

Maybe I didn't have to worry so much for the both of us. He didn't seem blind to what was going on, and it was like he saw right through me to the place where I wasn't so sure.

"I didn't change my mind."

"Good. Don't." He pressed his lips to mine, then left.

Being around him was a great workout for my abs. If it wasn't the laughing that had me doubled over, it was the way—with one look—he could make my core tighten.

How did he do that?

Alone in his room, I noticed the bag I'd brought. He must have moved it into the room that morning while I slept. Again with the thoughtfulness. I slipped on my underwear, jean shorts, a bra, and tank top, then walked to his bathroom to brush my teeth and do something with my head.

I'd seen worse, but it still wasn't that great. If we were really going to do this, then he'd wind up seeing me at my worst sooner or later. It might as well be sooner, before I got my heart broken if *he* changed *his* mind.

I walked into the kitchen barefoot, not remembering to bring a different pair of shoes. I'd been in a hurry the night before. I'm lucky I grabbed my toothbrush.

Well, he was lucky I did anyway.

He was wearing a pair of jeans and a University Track shirt with the sleeves ripped off. One of his pant legs was tucked inside one of his boots and the other laid the way it should.

I crooked my mouth to the side to hide my grin. We were a pair.

He handed me the cup, handle out for me to grasp.

Alone in my head everything felt different. Complicated. Maybe a little awkward. But, when I was there, standing in a room with him, all of the doubt felt so simple and easy to put aside.

I took a sip then committed to drinking about half the

cup. He made an excellent coffee. Damn, he was good at everything.

Rhett watched for my reaction to his maiden coffee offering. This was important first morning stuff. Getting a person's coffee right could be the difference between a return visit and an *I'm busy for the rest of my life* kind of reaction. I'd dropped guys for lesser offenses.

I held up a finger, needing another minute alone with my caffeine, then closed my eyes and let the fuel hit my veins.

"It's not that good," I lied.

He leaned on the counter and crossed his long legs, but the sight of something on the top of the refrigerator had him leaning over, behind me, to grab it.

"Good. Maybe you'll go home and get some work done."

Oh, I did not like that and I frowned, but thankfully I wasn't upset enough to stop drinking coffee. That's when it's really bad. When you're too fucked for coffee—that's a bad day.

"You don't mean that," I challenged.

"I don't?" His hands held the front and the back of a ball cap as he adjusted it on his head.

"You're going to miss me when I'm gone," I explained.

His eyebrows came together, but his eyes let me know he was just playing along. "I am?"

"Yep, you like it when I'm here."

"I do?"

I nodded as I said, "You probably want to see me later and everything." I'd become a little sassy, pretend cocky. My lips puckered in petulance.

"You got it all figured out," he assured, nodding at me and acting out the part of defensive spar.

"I *sure* do," I affirmed and set my empty coffee mug on the counter.

I liked this playing, teasing thing he did when he saw the opportunity to work me up. I saw right through it, but it was so much fun that I looked forward to the game.

He wrapped his arms around me, then spun us, pinning me against the sink. My protest was weak, but I looked him straight in the eyes. He thrilled me when I didn't know what was coming, and I loved it. Every damn second.

"I'm glad you realize all of that. Now don't forget any of it. I couldn't have said it better myself."

He was going to miss me, he liked me there, and he wanted to see me later.

Where had Rhett Caraway been all my life?

In time and through hilarious trial and error, we came up with an easy solution to Andy getting the window seat. We all got in on Rhett's side in order. It must have looked dumb and so juvenile, but no one was watching in our little bubble, which consisted of the few gravel miles from his place to mine.

Over the next few weeks, I realized he almost never thought about things the way I expected him to. In fact, he kept me on my toes.

Like, he'd use an umbrella when he picked me up, but then he wouldn't rush to get us out of the rain if we were kissing. On our third date-date, we did just that, and anyone driving by the radio station would have seen me topless, spread for him on the tailgate of his truck in my driveway. *Downpour be damned.*

We'd eventually made our way to shelter, but just barely. Only a few feet inside my garage, we finished what we'd started on the steps. Each time we were together felt like the first time. Hot, but special. Sexy and intimate. It didn't matter if we were in a bed or somewhere outside—I loved being with him.

As the weeks passed, we made it through the whole first season of *The Office*, and he helped me put in a doggy door for my roommate. Where at first we'd see each other a few times throughout the week, it was becoming a *my place or yours* situation nearly every night.

The more time I spent with him, the less time I felt like I had to spare. Time went so fast when he was around and the days peeled away.

What I felt for him grew and intensified. We were seeping into each other's lives like the wet rain had the ground at the beginning of the summer.

However, I still went to my mom and dad's on Sundays, and he still went to his. When he took me out on Friday nights, which was becoming a weekly ritual, it was always somewhere outside of Wynne. I wondered if he was feeling like I was, like our shared time was sacred, or if he just didn't want people to see us.

Like everyone had advised me to do, I was giving it a chance. So, I just went along with it when we never went to Diana's Diner or the store together.

Things like that didn't change—*not at first.*

Chapter Twenty-Two

Rhett

"We can run to town and get something. Take your time," I told Sunny over the phone.

That was becoming my motto with her. *Take your time.*

I was letting her set the pace for nearly everything, and glad to do it. I wasn't in any rush and had the sense enough to be grateful for each new thing as they came. With her, I wanted everything. *When* didn't really matter.

I'd already waited for her for so long, waited and even given up. Being at the beginning of a *real* relationship with her was something I'd never expected. I was taking it one day at a time. Thankful and feeling quite lucky.

That all said, I secretly wanted more already. I was sure she was who I wanted in my future. Still, I wouldn't push things. I could only give her the best of me when she was ready for it.

That week, WDKR was getting some pretty cool

upgrades, but Sunny made some kind of error installing the new software that morning which, unfortunately, caused her a lot of trouble. Usually, she was out of there around two, but it was close to five, and, according to her, there was still a lot to re-do before she could leave.

"You go ahead and eat. I'll keep working and just make a pizza in a while. I'm still messing with these jacked up files."

I understood how needing to get a job finished—*the right way*—felt.

Sure. I could have eaten and done my own thing, but since the rain had held off for the last few weeks, and everything was getting back to normal, all I'd had to occupy my mind all day was her.

She was always on my mind. The slight way her breasts shook when she laughed, then how they felt in my palms and mouth. The slope of her naked side as she caught her breath before a second round. I never dared complain about how she always wanted me twice. She always took control the second time anyway, and oh how I let her. The look in her eye when she kissed me first thing in the evening. That little something that sometimes flashed in her blue eyes, telling me she was thinking about what we'd done the night before. The way she rubbed my leg with her little foot to wake me up. And, with nothing more than a little motivation, she became an early bird. She'd ride me before the sun came up, often making me late for my run.

When I'd finally get to my circuits, she'd leave behind notes when she left.

R-

The second half of Dexter, Episode 4, tonight. Maybe we'll actually get through it. Maybe not. I'll cook. Okay, I'll get something from Diana's.

R-

I don't know how you run so damn early in the morning. Especially when I can barely walk. Ha! Ha!

See you later.

R-

If I get done early today, I'll let you drive me around in your tractor, and I'll bring the beer.

Then, she'd sign her name with a little sun-shaped smiley face at the bottom next to a heart.

There weren't enough hours in the day, and whatever extra time I had was spent with Sunny. I didn't want to snuff out the spark by smothering her, but when I didn't mention seeing her next, it wasn't long before she would make plans with me. The validation of that alone was powerful, and the more it happened the more I craved it.

Some days Sunny volunteered to ride along with me in the tractor or help me wash equipment. She was actually really great help and saved me a lot of time, which I made up to her in fun—*but still kind of selfish*—ways.

So since she was hard at work, I took matters into my own hands. “You just do your thing,” I said. “I’ll talk to you in a while.”

We didn’t go into town together much. Everyone’s eyes were still on us. The chatter and jokes had stopped—*at least in my presence*—but it wasn’t hard to tell we had their attention. It wasn’t that strange for me, but I could only imagine what it was like for her. So, I never pressed the issue of making appearances.

When Sunny and I hung up, I loaded a few things into the back of my truck and headed to the store for a few more.

“Two of those big New York strips,” I ordered from the meat counter. I stood there under the fluorescent lights ordering steak—like I had many times before—and browsed the other items under the glass case.

“Two, huh?” Stan, the butcher, asked. “These look okay?” He pointed to a pair of steaks near the front.

“Those are fine,” I answered and took a step down to look at the other ready-made sides they had prepared.

“I’ve got a few stuffed peppers back here, too. *She* likes them, and *she* also gets that pasta salad over there sometimes,” Stan said as he weighed and wrapped the meat. He looked me in the eye conspiratorially then cocked his head to the side waiting to see if I’d take his not-so-sneaky suggestions.

Was he butting in or just trying to move some pasta salad?

It didn’t matter. He was there to sell, and I was there to buy. I’d take the tip and stowed my pride, accepting it for what it was. If she really liked stuffed peppers and pasta salad, I’d get them for her.

"Fine. I'll take both of those, too," I relented to Stan.

It wasn't a secret who my extra steak was for—I'd been buying things for her in that store since the very first time I had my own money.

I was used to the grins and winks. Only now, they were different. They lacked the sympathy they'd once held. Their glances and gestures were more excited and contrite, as if they'd been right about something all along. They were probably just as surprised as me.

Maybe, along with trying to be patient, their reactions were why *I* hadn't suggested going to Diana's Diner or the store together very much, but why hadn't Sunny ever brought it up?

Was *she* embarrassed?

I didn't want her to get the same scrutiny I received. It wasn't that people were ever rude, but many of them lacked the skill of subtlety. We were doing well, and, in some ways, I was afraid they might remind her of all the silly things I used to do to get her attention.

For the moment, we were in our own little world, and I was sure she wanted to keep it like that since she hadn't mentioned we do anything too publicly either, *yet*.

That was the next thing I was waiting patiently for.

When the time came, and she was comfortable being in public with me—*with us*—she'd be the one to move us there. I'd be ready when she was.

The invitation to her class reunion hung on her refrigerator, and it caught my eye every time I passed it. It wasn't for another few weeks or so, but she hadn't asked me to go with her. The little card requesting a call or email with her number of guests remained plastered to the white surface of her freezer with a WDKR magnet.

Then again, maybe Sunny wasn't planning on going. Sticking to my plan of letting her set the pace, I hadn't brought it up.

The Nashville race was the same weekend anyway, but since my sister wasn't going, I wanted to invite her. Had they not been at the same time, I would have already asked her to go. But we'd only been—well, like we were—for a short while.

Although it felt like much longer for me, I was afraid to rock the boat. Not literally. Given the opportunity, I'd rock the bastard over with us both in it. *Naked.*

But—*metaphorically*—I was taking it easy.

Right?

On the way to her place, I contemplated if I was actually holding back as much as I should. I was, after all, grilling her dinner at the radio station. In hindsight, that might seem over the top.

The facts remained. *I* was still *me*, and *she* was still the *sun* I orbited around.

Carefully, I backed up my truck into the lawn of WDKR so I would be closer to the door.

After I got my grill out and set up a few other things, I poked my head inside the building and saw her sitting behind the soundboard in the booth. She didn't notice me through the glass because she was facing away, but the lights were on in the small room, and I could see her perfectly.

Her hair was long and wavy down her back, one of her slender legs propped up on the tall chair beside her as she stood at the board. Large headphones cupped her ears while she listened and swayed, in what I could only guess was off-time to the beat of the song—considering her lack of rhythm—but I couldn't hear to confirm it.

I'd never seen inside WDKR before, but I'd always imagined it differently. I'd imagined neon in the station, but there was none there. Also, I'd grown up feeling like the radio was some magic place where Sunny Wilbanks lived, bad ass and high tech, but two feet inside the door I learned my imagination as a kid was idealistic at best.

Peering behind the curtain at Oz, I hoped everything I'd been feeling and experiencing with her wasn't also just a fantasy, some twisted version of reality that I only saw how I wanted.

Regardless of how low-key and plain it appeared, it was still pretty damn cool.

Instead of what I'd conjured in my mind, there were plaques and pictures of her and her grandfather, articles from papers about the station, and some signed memorabilia from old country artists.

Actually, the more I looked around, the more I liked the real thing. Kind of like her.

"Hey, what are you doing here?" she asked from behind me where I'd wandered on the other side of the room.

I was studying a picture of her sitting on her Grandpa Sonny's lap at the soundboard. Off to the side of the frame there was a small typed-out label.

Sonny and Sunny, Summer 1993

"Just looking around," I answered. "You were a cute little thing."

"Thanks," she said. "Flattery will get you everywhere with me."

For as long as she'd been at it that day, her mood was

surprisingly chipper. My mood usually got a little sideways when I was really deep into a stubborn project.

Notably, I liked the way she looked with her headphones around her neck. That image was very similar to my nostalgic fantasies of her and WDKR.

Food, Rhett. You're here to feed her, not fuck her with her headphones on. Focus.

I scratched the back of my neck and corralled my thoughts.

"I brought my grill. How about some steak?" I asked, turning to face her head-on, which didn't help the pull she had on me.

When she had that look in her eye, my hands would itch to roam, so I put them in my pockets. I'd heard before that idle hands were the devil's workshop, and I thought it best to stow them. She still had stuff to do.

"You did?" She arched her eyebrow and added, "But I have a grill."

She obviously didn't know what she was talking about. A man's grill is an extension of himself. There's a bond there. I swear it.

I laughed. "Mine isn't just *any* grill, Sunny. It's *The Grill*. I can't just be flinging my meat around on any old burner. I know how to cook on mine."

Grills, like women, never took the same to heat up. Just like I wasn't about to start a fire with another girl, I wasn't about to waste two prime New York strips to chance on her old, dusty Weber.

"Right," she said sarcastically, but I knew the truth. "I'm almost done."

"I'll get out of your hair. You go finish up, and I'll be

listening out front."

Resisting the urge to reach out for her, I walked to the doorway, but she leaned out, pitching forward with puckered lips.

It was her move, and one I liked, so I didn't hesitate. I couldn't deny myself *and her* at the same time. I was only so strong.

She kissed me and hummed against my mouth. With her hand on my side, she pulled me closer for the moment.

"Thank you, Rhett," she said. "I shouldn't be long. I'm running a safety thing that's backing up my catalog, then I'm done."

Rocking back on my heel, lips out of range of each other, I confessed, "You look good with those headphones on."

"Oh, these old things?" She winked. "Maybe I'll give you a tour of the station after we eat."

I liked the sound of that. "Get back to work."

It was a nice evening, and there was a light breeze from the storm front that was moving in, but the weather wasn't supposed to change until around sunset. It was a good night to be outside, and I enjoyed it as I drank my beer.

With my radio on and truck windows down, I waited for the grill to warm up. The pasta salad was in the cooler, and the steaks were ready to roll. Everything was working out according to plan.

After the lawn chairs were unfolded and the card table was set up, the yard was almost redneck romantic. As I looked around at the scene I'd created on the lawn of her radio station, I began to wonder if I was *once again* going a little overboard—like I always had when it came to her.

A car came down her lane, and watching it near I was

distracted away from my apprehension.

It didn't take long for me to realize it was her dad.

I'd known Randy Wilbanks my whole life; there was no need to be nervous. However, I hadn't talked to him since his daughter's change of heart with regards to me. If fact, our last real conversation had to do with just that—nearly ten years ago.

"Hey, Mr. Wilbanks," I said, standing at their front door the week after Sunny left for college. It was yet another cloudy, rainy day.

I was starting eighth grade the next morning and it sucked that she wasn't going to be there. We would have finally been in the same half of the building at school.

"Hi, Rhett," he said with a polite smile.

"Have you heard from Sunny?" I'd wanted to come over the day after she left, or right before to tell her bye, but I didn't. I couldn't.

"You want a Coke?" he asked after glancing at his watch. "I think I need one. Peggy's got me drinking diet, but I have a few regular cold ones stashed in the garage."

"Okay," I answered. Coke sounded good, and maybe we'd talk for a while and I'd find out how she was doing.

"You hang out on the swing. I'll be right back." As I took a seat on their front porch and watched the cars splash through the huge puddle out front, he went back into the house. I heard the garage around back open, then after a minute it closed and he was soon walking out of their front door passing me an ice-cold soda.

"Sunny and I used to share a Coke out here in the afternoons, before her mother got home and she'd head to the station for work. It was kind of our thing," he admitted and opened his can.

I already knew they did that because I'd ridden by on my bike a time or two and saw them. They always waved.

"Does she like school?" I asked. "College is a lot bigger."

He took another long drink then sucked air through his teeth. "That's a good Coke. Yeah, I think she's still getting used to it, but she'll do fine. How are you holding up, bud?"

Not so good was the right answer, but I fudged it a little.

"I'm doing okay. We've got harvest coming soon, and Dad says it's a good one this year. You know I helped plant this spring, right?" I hoped he was impressed as he listened and kept drinking. "So, I've been pretty busy myself."

He crossed his legs and relaxed into the swinging bench. "Sounds like hard work."

"It is, and it isn't, but that's just what we do." Then I chugged some of my Coke, enjoying the man-to-man conversation. Luke and I talked a lot, but he was a farm kid, too. What I did wasn't all that interesting to him because he was doing pretty much the same stuff. Mr. Wilbanks was a businessman, so he probably found farming interesting.

"Got your eye on any new girls yet?"

What? That was crazy.

I leaned over and looked at him like he was losing his mind. "No." I was quick to correct him. "I still just like Sunny."

"Even though she's gone, and you can't see her all the time like before?"

He was a grown man. He should have known better. "Well, sir, you didn't stop loving her because she left, did ya?"

He smiled, probably realizing he'd been temporarily insane.

Forget about Sunny? What a dumb idea.

"You got a good point. So how's it gonna work out then? She's a lot older than you. She's going to be away at college, then you'll leave and go yourself."

I'd heard that one before—even from her—but that didn't change much for me.

"I know everyone thinks I'm crazy, but I don't care. I'm in love with Sunny. And someday, I'm going to build her a huge farm and I'm going to marry her and make her smile every day." It was a big step, asking her father for her hand in marriage at such a young age, but we were having a cold one and it seemed like the right time. "If that's okay with you, that is."

He thought, which I figured was standard procedure for that kind of thing. So I sat back and crossed my legs like he had and waited for his answer.

If he said no, I'd just have to work hard and change his mind. There was plenty of time for that.

"I don't know, Rhett. I suppose that's gonna be up to her, too. Don't you reckon?"

I couldn't argue with that.

"Yeah, well, I guess. But anything is possible."

He pulled in and parked in the two-car lot off to the side, then moseyed over to where I'd parked my truck in the yard.

"Hey there, Rhett. How's it going?"

I could have answered vaguely—beat around the bush.

That's what I would have done back in the day because Mr. Wilbanks used to seem like such an authority figure when I was a boy. He wore church clothes to work and always drove nice cars. They lived in a great house in the center of town, right on Main Street, *and* he was her dad.

I'd respected Mr. Wilbanks and always wanted him to like me. *Always.*

Quickly, I considered giving him a half-truth reply. Something honest, but not really answering the question.

Instead, a new pride spoke for me. "I'm cooking Sunny supper out here, Sir. She's been working all day, and I thought she should have a good meal. So, I'm making her one."

He nodded, accepting my answer.

"She said you two have been spending a lot of time together. I just hadn't seen you guys around town much."

How could he? We'd both been working a lot, and when we weren't, we were usually in one of our beds. That fact alone made it harder to look him in the eye.

I needed more beer.

"Want a Bud Light?" I asked, knowing it would be much more acceptable to drink if he had one, too.

"Sure, I'll take one, but I can't stay long." He walked over to one of the folding chairs and took a seat. "I just came to check on her. Peggy said she's been in the station all day trying to work out some bugs with the new software."

"I think she got it figured out. She said she's doing a back-up now, then she's done." I passed him a can. He took it and lifted it in thanks.

"I wrote that new policy for your property out west of your folks—the one on that beautiful hill. Building out there, huh?"

It would probably be winter before I had time to really dive into the project, but it would be there before I knew it. Until then, it would be mostly groundwork.

"Yep. It'll probably be a while before things start moving, but that's the plan."

His quizzical expression indicated he was at the very least on to me, but it wasn't exactly what he thought.

When I'd come back to Wynne, I had no idea Sunny and I would be like we were.

Was it always somewhere in the back of my mind? Of course. It was ingrained as deep as the roots of the oak tree I'd built my fort in. Dreams like that are *dreams*.

Still, I'd had certain goals for myself—*with Sunny or without*. It just so happened they didn't really differ much now that she was becoming a factor. I was going to build the farmhouse anyway.

"Building is a *long* process, but if anyone has the patience for it, it's you."

I took that as a compliment and flipped the steaks. I had nothing to hide. Never really did. My intentions were always honorable.

Well, what we'd done the night before was only borderline honorable, but that was between Sunny and me.

"Thanks. How's Mrs. Wilbanks?"

He grinned with the mention of his wife. "She's good. You should come with Sunny one Sunday and have lunch sometime. Peg's been begging Sunny to bring you."

She had?

Chapter Twenty-Three

Sunny

What a day it had been. Ones like that Monday were few and far between at my job, but they happened.

I was installing some new software for the studio which would better allow me to invite local musicians to play on air—something that really excited me. What I'd had would work, but the sound quality wouldn't have been as good.

So while installing the new stuff, I made a mistake and it ended up taking me twice as long. Plus, in the process of moving some of my files over, I'd accidentally changed their formats and the new program didn't like them.

I spent a long time on the phone and online, chatting with tech support. Thankfully, we eventually found a solution. I hadn't wrecked it too much, but my error added a lot of manual steps to get everything loaded properly.

After all of that work, I wasn't about to lose what I'd done. So I was backing everything up before anything else could happen. And, although it had been sunny all day, the forecast was calling for a stormy night. I wasn't sure how the new software would tolerate the power going out and didn't really want to be back at square one the next day.

Even though I was dying to see Rhett, it wasn't worth losing everything again if the power went out later. Okay, it was, but he was there and that was good enough.

When I was done, and my work triple checked, I stepped out of my studio booth to see my dad and Rhett shaking hands. I couldn't hear what they were saying, so I just watched for a minute.

Both wore smiles, and it warmed me seeing them together. I'd never been one to bring a guy around my family, but this was becoming different. Besides, Rhett and my dad kind of knew each other.

More and more, I wanted to have him around *my* people. Seeing how well he and my father interacted made me less afraid to ask him if he wanted to go to Hannah and Vaughn's barbeque that Friday night. She'd invited us a few days before, but I hadn't been sure we were ready to do *couples things* yet. It was still new territory for me.

And, he hadn't brought up doing things with anyone else yet either.

What was the worst thing that could happen? Him saying no? But I doubted he would.

No. I knew better. The ultimate worst thing that could happen would be if he said yes, then someone at the party said something stupid to him. Or if he was bored hanging out with the old people. Darrell was nearly retired, and Hannah and Vaughn were married with a baby.

Would Rhett and my people have anything in common?

Would he realize he didn't have much in common with me, too?

My friends weren't assholes, and I knew I could count on Hannah and Vaughn to be cool, but Darrell was another story. He was a jackass who meant no harm, but I could only imagine the shit he'd say.

I took a deep breath and stretched, having spent most of the day locked up in the tiny room as I stared at them through the window. Dad patted him on the shoulder and walked off as Rhett pulled the steak off *The Grill* he'd hauled all the way to my station.

My mouth watered. The cheese and peanut butter crackers stash in my drawer had been hit hard that day, but I wanted real food.

I flipped off a few light switches and headed outside.

"All done?" Rhett asked as I came to his side in front of the grill.

Yum. He had those peppers I liked. I kissed his shoulder. "I'm all done."

I was impressed. Not only had he *brought* his grill, but he'd set up a table and chairs, too.

Where did he come up with the stuff he did for me? He never disappointed.

I needed to do something for him in return, something thoughtful like he was, but I was terrible at coming up with ideas.

He candidly pointed with his tongs as he spoke. "Beer's in there. We've got steak, stuffed peppers, there's pasta salad in the cooler, and a bag with plates and stuff on the seat of my truck." He looked down at me wistfully and gave my butt a squeeze with his free hand. Ass grabbing aside, I'd never felt so cared for.

Rhett didn't expect anything from me in return; in fact, he was all about making sure I was always taken care of. And, because he never did things in a *what am I going to get out of this* way, he made me feel cherished. Sometimes it felt so one sided.

I looked up into his eyes and hoped he knew how much I appreciated how he treated me like a queen. It was special.

"Thank you," I said sincerely and wrapped my arms around him. "You didn't have to do all of this, but thank you."

"It was no trouble, Sunshine. A guy's gotta eat," he replied and kissed the top of my head.

There was one fantasy I'd had on a regular basis, and I was truly grateful for the food and his efforts. It would be the perfect night to share it with him. I hoped he ate plenty because what I had planned was going to take a lot of energy. Bearing that in mind, I knew I needed to load up, too.

As the sun went down, storm clouds blew up. Before we were done eating, lightning was flashing in the distance and a low rumble of thunder could be heard over the music coming from the radio in the cab of his truck. We ate the steaks and peppers, and I finished off the tub of pasta salad. I swore that stuff was made out of crack.

When everything was packed up, I said, "Come on. I'll show you my workbench. These mosquitos are pissing me off."

It was time for me to give him the grand tour with VIP access. All four—nowhere impressive—rooms of my small station.

"Your workbench, huh?" he queried, looking devilish.

I adored the light in his eyes. It was just for me. They were the perfect mixture of grey and blue and green—*Rhett hazel.* In all my life, no one had ever made me feel so desired and wanted, and he could do it without even saying a word. All it took was one molten look. His jaw would flex, and his focus never left my body. He was intoxicating.

But, I wanted this time to be different. Special *for him.* I wanted to seduce him. Please him. Show him what he meant to me.

I stood at the door and held it open for my boyfriend.

"Thank you," he said.

"Now, I don't want you to get too excited, but I don't do this very often." I said, trying my best at being suave. The truth was, nobody I'd ever dated before really cared about seeing inside my old radio station. "Want to come in my booth?"

If I would have thought about it earlier I would have scheduled one of my hotter playlists, but maybe the spontaneity would be better. *He could help.*

I locked the station door, unsure of whether my dad would come back or not, but it was best not to leave it up to chance. The click of the lock blew my cover, and it set Rhett into motion.

He came up behind me, moved my hair to the side and his mouth kissed a trail from my ear down to my shoulder. It felt so good and it would have been so easy to just let him do his thing.

The Lord knew how much I enjoyed when he did, but this wasn't about me. It was for him.

I turned and lifted up on my toes. "I just remembered something else I need to do." My hand grabbed his, and I led him into the small room with big glass interior windows.

Inside, I pulled out my chair and lowered it before motioning for him to sit.

His demeanor instantly changed. Usually, he looked very much in control, but at that moment I was holding the reins. The subtle shift was all it took to distract him, and he looked around the booth like he didn't want to touch anything.

I had a broadcast board, but most of my stuff was run by computer and the three screens which were centered above it. I moved the mouse across the pad to wake up the screens, then pointed to my headphones.

Silently, he read my cue and handed them to me. I pulled the cord so I'd have more slack than I usually needed. My mic was on a long gooseneck, so it could follow me wherever I was along the desk. I positioned it where I could reach, then clicked a few things to get us set up, praying I could make it work.

"See this right here?" I asked and pointed to what kind of looked like a stop light on the board. The red light was on, indicating we weren't live on the air. "When you push this green button and slide this dial up, then I'll be live. Press this red one, and I'll be off."

I turned to see his astute face beside mine. He was giving me all of his attention.

"Okay, but you could just do it," he said.

"I'll be busy." I sat on his lap as I clicked a few things and altered the playlist from what I had planned, adding a few songs that I thought fit the moment. "You can do it. You just have to be ready."

I pressed a button on the board that made the station

come through the speakers in the room and lowered the volume knob so that it wasn't too loud, knowing when he hit the green light it would override the sound to the room to avoid feedback. I learned that when I was on the line with tech support, a feature of the new system that would be awesome when I had guests in.

It was time to give my new equipment a sexy test drive.

The countdown on the song indicated I had just about enough time to give him the rest of my instructions.

I got down on the carpeted floor in front of his chair, on my knees, and slipped my headphones over my ears. Above my head, I reached for the microphone. Then I said, "When the song gets down to ten seconds, hit the green button and slide up my volume to where I showed you. I'll be on air. When I finish talking, press the red one then slide it back down."

He looked worried and completely out of his element. It was thrilling watching him be nervous.

"Are you sure about this, Sunny?"

I was damn sure.

"It's just two little buttons, and I'll do the rest."

I put my hands behind his knees, bringing him closer to the edge of the chair then started to undo the buttons on his jeans.

The lights were on and his eyes danced from what I was doing to the screen as the song hit its bridge. I could hear it through my headphones, too.

He balanced himself on the balls of his feet, his hands holding himself up on the armrests of my chair, as I pulled his pants down. I didn't bother lifting my head, but my eyes cast up at him in time to see him mouth, "*Oh my God.*"

I took him into my hand and ran my palm back and forth over his skin as he came to life even more in my touch.

The last chorus of the song sang through the speakers and adrenaline shot through me. As the last few notes played, I placed a quick kiss on the end of him. Then when I saw the on air light flash above his head, I spoke into the mic.

"Good evening, Wynne. It looks like a storm is brewing up outside here at WDKR, so I thought I'd pop on and tell everyone to be careful out there. It might be a *long* night." My hand stroked him, and as I spoke I studied the fine details of the beautiful man in front of me. "Better find someone to cuddle up with and just ride it out. I'll have *all* the new chart toppers and *all* of your favorite country gold hits playing *all* night long. Here on Wildcat Country, 98.5 FM."

When I was finished with my send off, I took him into my mouth.

The on air light went out, and then he threaded a hand through the hair at the nape of my neck as Chase Rice's "Ride" played in my booth. The piano began, and the seductive words followed as the tempo picked up.

I stayed relatively quiet as I worked him over. Rhett, on the other hand, was more confident of his engineering abilities and made sounds that would surely have me shut down by the FCC if anyone heard.

Initially, I'd planned on going back on the air for a second time, but I hadn't considered how much pleasuring him would turn me on. He tasted clean and warm and good. I couldn't pay attention to much else, so I shoved the microphone out of the way and pulled off my headphones.

I had to admit, I loved that the overhead lights were on and I could see everything I wanted to. His face and other—equally glorious—parts of his body.

I gave my jaw a small break and pulled away from him, using my hand in place of my lips and mouth. I turned my face up to his and met his eyes. He blinked slowly, struggling to remain focused. Lust filled and needy, he gazed back at me.

As his mouth fell slack and his brow bunched, I felt my face do the same, loving how he looked so vulnerable. Loving the effect I had on him.

His hand was still in my hair and as I leaned up, he pulled my lips up to his. My grip tightened, and praise spilled from his mouth into mine.

"Ah. That feels so damn good. What are you doing to me?"

"I'll do *anything* for you," I said, caught up in the moment. "Anything you want."

Then without warning, he gently tugged my mouth away from his, holding me there so we were eye to eye.

"Then take me to your parents' on Sunday."

Where the hell had that come from? I still had his dick in my hand and he wanted to talk about lunch with my mom and dad? He hadn't asked me to attend his family's stuff, so I'd held back on inviting him to mine.

My hand didn't stop, and he lifted up into it more.

My voice was weak, but I asked, "Do you *want* to go?"

"Yes," he answered.

"You can come with me anytime." Sitting higher up on my knees, I added a second hand and the speed with which I stroked him intensified.

"If you keep doing that I'm gonna," he replied out of breath, then leaned in the few inches to close the space between our mouths. Between kisses he kept talking and moaning. "I'll go anywhere with you, but that's not an invitation."

That seemed like pillow talk, considering the way we'd avoided town the past month, but I saw an opportunity. "You want an invitation, huh?" I asked rhetorically while kissing his jaw. "Will you go with me to a barbeque at Hannah's on Friday?"

"Oh, hell yes," he said and I felt him pulse inside my grip. His head fell to the side, and I kissed his neck. "Jesus, Sunny. *Ah*."

I wasn't sure if that was a real answer or just his orgasm, but I noted that he was very agreeable in that state. I could use that in the future—if I were wicked.

He chuckled and coughed, and my lips tingled from the vibration on his throat.

I grinned, feeling victorious. It was the first time he'd gotten off *before* me. Probably not a normal milestone, but a sense of total accomplishment for me, nonetheless.

"You're a naughty little girlfriend," he accused in a tone that made me go from hot to hotter.

"I thought you'd like my workbench," I challenged, peering into his hungry eyes.

He pulled his shirt over his head and said, "Oh, I liked it all right. Now it's your turn. I hope this room is soundproof."

I blushed, remembering how loud I'd been lately, but damn he knew what he was doing. "I can be quiet," I assured and probably lied.

He stood, pulled his boots and jeans off, and came at me, stroking himself back to life. Then said, "Don't you fucking dare."

I squealed as he got down on the floor with me. With one strong hand he ripped my shirt over my head, and with the other he pulled me closer to him. He pressed himself against me and I felt him growing hard against my flesh for a second time.

"Don't *ever* hold back from me, Sunshine."

When I finally had my shorts worked down my legs and off, and he'd thrown my bra somewhere in the air, we were both naked in my station.

The swift motion of him lifting me by my ass stole my breath, and my legs wrapped around him.

"Put your arms around my neck and hang on," he demanded. His voice was cool and sure.

On the contrary, I was on fire. Every muscle in me moved in his direction.

He made one adjustment, positioning himself, then leaned forward with his weight on his arms. In one powerful thrust he was inside of me deeper than he'd ever been, and he gave me everything. Hard and fast.

My back never touched the ground, I held on so tight. It was sweaty and exhilarating and more carnal than I'd ever known possible. Every time I moaned he gave me more, until colorful explosions framed my vision and he was all I could feel.

When we were finished, he kissed my breasts and my stomach as we listened to the music and storm outside.

My hands in his hair, I worried if we were going too

fast. If I wasn't getting too attached too soon because of my age and my new desire to settle down. I wondered how long I'd have to wait until he wanted the same things, and if I had that kind of time to spare.

He wasn't just the *kind* of guy I wanted in my future, he was becoming the exact one. The only one I could see there.

Chapter Twenty-Four

Rhett

"We won't be gone long, buddy," I told Andy outside on my porch as I waited for Sunny that Friday afternoon. He sat beside me on the floor. His leg tapped rapidly against the wooden floor, sounding like a Tommy Gun firing when I found that spot he liked behind his ear.

I'd teased her on the phone the day before about how long it took her to get ready. Then, when I'd gotten back to my truck, I'd heard her play Brad Paisley's "Waitin' On a Woman" and knew it had been her way of telling me to shut up.

Message received.

That afternoon was beautiful, and I enjoyed an ice cold Bay Brewing Beer—which was one of the only things I'd missed about being in the city. Don't get me wrong, I liked any beer if it was cold and in front of me, but there was something about their Honeybee Ale that I *loved.*

So, all in all, I was perfectly content—or as content as I could be.

I would have been lying if I said I wasn't the slightest bit anxious to *just get there* already. The extra time I had, sitting there with Andy, only let my imagination run and come up with all kinds of shit that might happen, but it wasn't going to stop me.

I was proud to be with her. I'd never been more proud of anything else in my life, I was certain. No first place finish. No sense of accomplishment had ever compared to how it felt every time she asked me for a kiss.

I knew what I had and didn't give a good goddamn who cared. Although, I didn't really think anyone did.

That was the mindset I'd told myself to adopt that afternoon.

I looked at my phone to check the time again. It hadn't been *that* long. Besides, it had been my idea that she came over to shower together anyway. I doubted showering with her would ever be novel for me. Selfish as it was, it was worth it.

Every day I spent with her offered something unexpected.

I learned new things I never would have guessed about her. Her hatred for mosquitos was uncanny, and the amount of bug spray I'd ingested couldn't have been good for me, but I'd sacrifice my health as long as she wanted me to.

Also, Sunny Wilbanks was part camel. Always thirsty. I believe one day she went through more than two gallons of sweet tea. She, alone, could have kept Lipton in business.

She wore makeup and fixed her hair every morning,

and usually again in the evening. I wouldn't call her high maintenance, because she never seemed to take herself too seriously. She told me looking her best gave her confidence and that she wanted to give me her best.

In my opinion, there was something so damn hot about the way she looked straight from the shower that I liked most. Just her. No artificial colors or pigments. One hundred percent pure Sunny.

And, on most days, she was a whirlwind. I was just lucky to be swept up in her sweet breeze.

She studied me, too, and I'd answered more questions about myself than ever before in my life. Hell, the bank didn't even need to know that much about me when they gave me the loan for the farmhouse.

If it wasn't why sometimes I wore underwear and sometimes I didn't, it was if my truck had a name or who was the first girl I'd kissed—which was a little later than most guys, but when I reminded her who I'd been chasing she let me off easy.

She wasn't necessarily vain about *herself*, but had *me* flexing every time she thought about it. At first it was weird, but I'll be damned if it didn't turn her on. So much so that I found myself doing it in front of her without her request. Especially when I was ready to get down to business.

Who knew the best pick up line I ever could have used was a wordless bicep flex? I wish I would have known sooner. Damn hindsight.

She had a way of making me laugh, and I think—for my benefit—she walked right into all of my lame jokes. I wasn't naturally all that funny, but her wit rubbed off. Listening to her laugh on repeat forever was damn good motivation to improve.

As she walked onto the porch, she unexpectedly stole my breath again. I was a fool to think that would ever stop.

Makeup or none.

Howling with laughter or whispering things to me before she fell asleep.

The frown in her brow before her first cup of coffee or showing off the twinkle in her eye after she'd dressed up for me.

It didn't matter. I loved every page in her book. *Even the blank ones.*

"You look *good*," I said and rubbed a hand over my mouth to wipe off my stupid grin. Sometimes they were hard to keep to myself. My poker face was becoming a thing of the past.

"You look *good*, too," she replied and came to sit on my lap in the middle of the swing where I was stretched out. "Are you sure you want to do this?"

She didn't look too worried, but there was a sweet challenge written all over her face.

"I'm ready. Are *you* ready?" I countered.

Shrugging, she asked, "What do I have to be ready for? I hang out with them all the time." Her fingers picked a dog hair off my shoulder and she blew it away, not looking me in the eyes.

I didn't believe her.

I pried, "So?"

"I mean, if I were meeting all of *your* friends, then I'd have a reason to be nervous." Her fingers played with the short, freshly cut hairs at the back of my neck. Her eyes still averting mine.

"Are your friends assholes?" I asked, dodging to catch her line of sight. She gave up and her innocent blue eyes batted my way as she gave me a phony smile. "Sometimes?"

"Sometimes?" I repeated, taken aback.

"I mean they're good people, but they have big mouths. You know Darrell O'Fallon. He says whatever the hell he wants." Her brows pinched in the middle, honest body language revealing the tension she felt.

Darrell *being* Darrell was nothing new. He was a card, but he was a decent guy, too.

Once, I was a little short some cash at the store when buying Sunny flowers, and he fronted me the money then had me mow the grass at his shop to work it off. O'Fallon was a good old boy.

"I'm not worried," I assured her. They could hit me with their best shots. I didn't care. I just hoped they didn't tease her too much for being with me.

She leaned forward and kissed my top lip, I held still and let her. When I didn't react, she doubled down, running her tongue over my bottom lip. The way she was distracting me made me wonder if she wasn't more anxious than I'd originally thought.

I also knew if I let her keep going, I'd fall prey to it and we'd never leave.

"Sunshine, I'd love nothing more than to lift that cute little skirt you're wearing and see how strong the anchor bolts are on this swing, *but* we have plans."

She exhaled and pressed her lips against me like we were saying goodbye for the night, as if it might be a while until she got to do it again.

"Fine," she gave in. "Take your panther to town." She

stood and pulled me up with her.

"Panther?"

"I'm a *panther*," she explained like it was common knowledge.

I wasn't sure what she meant, but that happened sometimes, too. So, I went along with it and took my panther to town.

From the middle of my truck, she messed with the radio as I drove us to the other side of Wynne.

We passed Stan from the store going down a side street on the way to the Renfros'. Instead of the standard few finger steering wheel wave, I received a thumbs up. I gave him one back. Those steaks made one of my all-time fantasies come to life that night at WDKR. After thinking about that, I shot both my thumbs at him.

I had to remind myself to not call *Hannah* Mutt. That nickname always seemed wrong to me anyway, but after you do things for so long it's hard to stop.

Then again, things moved on—changed—and I hoped everyone else remembered that, too.

I parked the truck on the street then lifted the cooler and chairs out of the back as a guy walked out to us.

"Hey, Vaughn," Sunny said.

"Hi. You guys need a hand?"

She looked at what we already had, and since it was everything we brought, said, "No. We're good. I don't think you guys know each other, though. Vaughn, this is..." Her eyes met mine. She took a breath then continued, "...my boyfriend, Rhett. Rhett, this is my best friend's husband, Vaughn."

She laughed though it sounded weak, and Vaughn

laughed *at* her good-naturedly. "It's good to meet you. Let me take those. Everyone is around back."

I handed him the bag chairs, even though I could manage, and said, "Thanks for having us over. I hear a lot about y'all."

Sunny walked ahead and went straight into the house. I followed Vaughn.

"We hear a lot about you, too."

Darrell and Dean were carrying a picnic table out of the garage and walking it to the backyard as we rounded the house.

"How's the baby?" I asked, knowing they were new parents and I was genuinely curious. That little girl was second only to me in the gallery on Sunny's phone.

"She's great. Finally getting into a sleeping schedule, which turns out is the biggest life goal I've ever had. She's getting fat and that's a good thing. Smiling more. She's the Queen around here." He set up the chairs and beamed as he talked about his daughter. Then he waved and added, "But you probably don't want to hear about all of that."

It didn't bother me. I was never a guy who *didn't* have plans for kids. I think it's in a farmer's DNA to want at least a few extra hands around. Besides, my family was close. Regardless of how it looked between my mom and my sister that summer, the four of us had always been tight. A family of my own was always something I'd planned for.

"I don't mind. Sunny loves her, and I see *a lot* of pictures."

"Sunny *does* love her," he agreed. "And she's good with Sawyer."

"I bet she is," I agreed.

Even though I'd never seen her with a child in her arms, it wasn't hard to imagine. She had a way with everyone. Why would a baby be any different?

I knew a bit of Vaughn and Hannah's history, so I made small talk. "I hear you got to drive the Astro Van for a while." My arm plunged into the icy water in my cooler, searching for another Honeybee Ale and waited for him to stop laughing.

"Yeah, it came in handy, but it *sucked*."

"Oh, I know. My senior year we tried to take it for a joyride, but it died in the middle of the street in front of their garage." I popped the top of the bottle and put the cap in my pocket.

Vaughn leaned against the rail of his back deck steps. "That doesn't surprise me. It's a beast."

"Who do we have here?" I heard Darrell ask behind me, and I turned to greet him.

He was wearing a t-shirt that said *World's Okayest Grandpa,* a pair of Hawaiian shorts, and his legs were as white as December snow. Honestly, I couldn't remember the last time I'd seen him in anything except bib overalls.

I chuckled, then walked out on a ledge and jumped first. "Hey, Darrell. I've never seen you in your church clothes before. You clean up nice."

The goofy smile he wore almost fell off his face as he feigned offense, clutching his chest.

"That really hurts. You're cranky, Caraway. My sweet baby granddaughter is in there taking a nap, why don't you go join her. You could use it."

I wasn't offended. I'd all but asked for it. I wanted to get the jokes out of the way before Sunny was around, or at least test the waters.

I smiled and Darrell did, too. Then he held out a hand for me to shake. I took it and he laughed.

"I just have to shake the hand of the man who can stand Sunny for more than a few hours at a time. Boy, how are you not brain-dead yet?"

Who said I wasn't? But I wouldn't have changed a thing.

"Oh, I manage."

He slapped me on the back. "I'm sure you do, Rhett. I'm sure you do. And good for you."

Sunny came out a few minutes later, but only to make sure I was okay, which I was. She didn't say anything, but she pointed a *take no shit* finger at Darrell—even though it wasn't warranted. She was looking out for me, and I kind of liked it.

All of us guys hung out in the backyard and tossed bags while the ladies hung out in the kitchen listening to a baby monitor.

I had to pee, and although Dean and Darrell didn't mind going behind the garage, I was trying to give a good impression. A public piss on my first trip to town probably wouldn't do.

As I got to the top of the porch I overheard them talking and slowed before I reached for the door.

"I just don't think I can do it," Sunny said, her voice hushed.

I froze, hating that I was eavesdropping, but needing to hear first what it was she *couldn't do.*

"Well, if it doesn't feel right, then don't," her friend advised.

Then, as much as I wanted to know, I didn't.

I walked in the screen door and wrangled the stubborn thing shut. When I turned around, I saw Sunny eating salsa by the chip full, but Hannah was gone.

"Caught ya," I said and acted like my chest wasn't hurting, but it was. I had no idea what they'd been talking about, but it felt like it was about *us*.

No matter what the topic though, I hated hearing that whatever it was, she didn't believe she could do it.

Her mouth was full, but she answered, "This is my first one."

Yeah, right.

She seemed fine as she smiled at me, but there was something inside my gut telling me something was up.

Distracted for the minute from my worrisome thoughts, and only feet inside the kitchen, I looked around the house. It hadn't looked that big from the outside.

She smiled as I checked it all out. "It's nice, isn't it?"

I remembered the old house back when it was the Robinsons' place and falling apart. It looked brand new now.

"I love this island," she said and smoothed her hand over the granite or marble. I didn't know the difference.

"Is this what you'd want?" I asked, stepping closer to her. We'd only been together for little over a month, but I couldn't help but hope when the house was done she'd think about moving into it with me. Although I'd never directly brought up the topic before, I was taking a chance.

"I don't know," she answered. Up on her toes, she wrapped her arms around my shoulders. "What do you mean?"

I pressed a hand to her back to steady her. "Well, I *am*

building a house. So guess I'll need you to help me pick stuff out this winter." That seemed like the safest way to put it. Much safer than, "I'm building us a house to grow old in. When are you moving in?"

Even with the tamed down answer I gave her, her puzzled expression kind of surprised me.

"Are you serious?" she asked.

I laughed. "Yeah. I'm dead serious. I don't even know what kind of countertop that is. I'll need help, and I want you to help me."

Her face turned serious, which didn't happen too often. I hoped I hadn't said something wrong, but it was the truth. And, honestly, it was really watered down.

"I could help you, *I guess*," she said, but something wasn't right. She wasn't looking at my face anymore.

"Spit it out."

Her arms fell from my neck, and she backed up a step. "I mean, that's kind of serious. Don't you think?"

"Well, I'm serious about you, and I'm serious about the house. Yeah, I guess it's serious all around." I kept my voice light, but the subject was anything but.

"Doesn't that freak you out?" she asked, sounding freaked out herself. "Are you ready for something like that?"

I wasn't really sure where this was coming from. She didn't seem angry, but she was getting worked up.

She reached for another chip on the counter and plunged it into the dip. "I mean, don't you want to see what's out there? Go out and party and live it up for a while?"

I tipped my head in her direction. "If you're going with me, I do. Guess I don't know what you're getting at."

If *she* had a problem, I wanted her to come out with it. I

didn't like her assuming I had one when I didn't.

She looked around, probably wanting to make sure no one was listening, and popped the chip into her mouth. We hadn't fought yet, but I expected we would eventually. Although, I never guessed it would be there and about countertops—or about some bullshit about what she thought I wanted.

I didn't want to fight with her, though. I recognized that immediately and was almost thankful Hannah came back into the room with a wide-eyed little girl.

Sunny and I both took a step away from each other and she went to take Sawyer from her mom.

"Did you have a good nap?" she asked, using a much more pleasing tone than she had with me.

The little girl looked around the room and when she found her mom's face, she kept her eyes trained on her as best she could.

Hannah kissed her daughter's forehead then loaded her arms up with plates and things.

"I can take some of that on my way back out. I'm headed to the bathroom."

"Thank God there's at least one man around here who doesn't pee on my garage," Hannah teased and tipped her head to the left toward the front of the house gesturing down the hall where I'd find the restroom. "Do you mind grabbing those buns and this when you head back out, Rhett?" She bumped into a basket of plastic silverware as she made her way out the back.

Sunny's eyes met mine before she followed, and I was glad to see they'd softened even pointed at me. I gave her a half-smile and walked down the hall.

When I got back outside, Sunny was sitting at the end of the picnic table still holding Sawyer. My chair was close to them, so I took a seat. She looked comfortable holding the little girl and I liked it.

It was way, *way* too soon to be thinking like that, but that didn't stop my brain from going there. Making note of the way she was with their little Queen. Especially, seeing how soft and loving her eyes were as she kissed the baby over and over on her nose, then how she giggled when Sawyer blinked back at her.

"Daddy said you smile now, but you need to show me," she gently coaxed. Every head bobble and movement from the baby commanded my date's attention.

Everyone began to mill around the table for plates and began piling things on. I reached my hands out for Sunny to pass off Sawyer to me, and she gave me a curious look in return.

"I'll hold her while you fix a plate for yourself."

Her forehead creased in deliberation.

I stood and moved to lift her from Sunny's arms. "I can hold a baby," I assured her. Then I looked in Sawyer's eyes and told her, too. "That's right. I've got you. I can hold you just fine." Careful to support her neck and head in one hand, I took my seat again. "We'll be just fine."

This got the attention of Hannah, who started toward me to take her little girl. Nestling her firmly along the crook of my forearm, I waved away her mother. "I'm fine. You eat. The food isn't going anywhere. I'll get something in a minute."

Sunny and Hannah shared a look, then Hannah tsked at her friend and plucked a white Styrofoam plate from the table. It was nearly like she was goading Sunny.

Darrell rounded the end of the table and nudged Sunny's arm. "Gonna make your boy a plate?"

My attention was pulled in by the little girl and how she was gripping my finger. What a sweetheart.

"What, because he's younger?" she fired back, and I took a breath.

"*No*, because he's holding Sawyer," he replied with a chuckle.

Being defensive for a good reason was one thing, but there was no need. It was clear that *she* had issues and therefore was sensitive. I wondered if it had to do with what I'd said inside earlier about the farmhouse and if I really hadn't been going as slow as I told myself I was.

Was I acting like a fool? Rushing things? Maybe it was time to pull back a little before I really fucked up. I'd put pressure on her to be around people, knowing it might be awkward at first, but I'd chosen to believe it would be fine.

I stood, walked around the table to where Vaughn was finishing a hot dog and immediately his hands went for his baby. "Come here, baby. You can sit by me," he cooed.

Sunny was watching, and our eyes met when I grabbed her hand. She set her plate back down and her shoulders slumped.

"Walk around here with me," I said into her ear. I wasn't about to make a scene, but something needed to happen.

I didn't want to fight with her, but there was something bothering her and it made me curious. It brought me back to earlier in the day when she'd called herself a panther.

Was she ashamed of our relationship? Did our age difference bother her *that* much?

"Come here." Her palm in mine, I led her to the front of the house and out of earshot. "What's going on? Why are you upset?"

"I'm not. I'm just thinking about earlier and Darrell is being a shit."

"No, he's really *not*, Sunny. You're being sensitive about it and I'm not sure why. And about earlier…"

She interrupted, "I just don't think you're thinking about things. You know. Stuff you might want to do."

I was a simple man, and I'd never been in that kind of minefield with a woman before. So I was cautious with each step.

What was she talking about? I'd never done so many things I'd wanted to in my whole fucking life. I had the girl. The job. The new house to look forward to. What more could I want? This wasn't about *me*.

"What stuff exactly?" I inquired.

"Don't you want to be wild and free, date a few more girls before you invite me to pick out countertops?"

My heart raced and I could feel the pressure of it spread throughout my chest.

"*No*." Had she lost her mind? My voice rose to a level I'd not used with her before. "Have I *ever* wanted another girl?"

Where was she getting this? She knew how much I cared about her—it was obvious. It was obvious to everyone.

Unless, it wasn't *me* she was really talking about. Maybe *she* wanted to date other guys and see what else was out there.

"Do *you* want to see other people?"

Because that was a problem. A big one. I tried my best

to remain calm, but the situation had me agitated and confused.

She put her hand on her hip and answered, "Well, no."

I was already ramped up and I rattled off, "Is that why you aren't taking me to your reunion? Are you hoping to see an old classmate or something? Wanting to keep your options open, Sunny?"

"No," she shot back. "I haven't even sent my RSVP."

My mind raced. Everything had been going so well.

Then again, we'd been on our own. Maybe *I* was getting ahead of *us*. I never intended on smothering her, but what if I was doing it anyway?

Suddenly I didn't feel like hanging out anymore. "You know what? I think I'm gonna go." She needed to think about some stuff, and so did I.

"What?" she said, wounded. Her mouth pouted, but I didn't feel like being around her friends with this tension between us.

I repeated, "I'm gonna go."

She straightened. "Did they embarrass you?"

Was she serious?

"No, but right now you are." I pointed to the back of the house. "They've all been great. You're losing your mind today. I think you need to think about some stuff." I ran a hand over the back of my neck and squeezed, feeling tightness in my muscles.

I realized if I left, and took my truck, she wouldn't have a ride.

I could use a walk. It wasn't even eight miles to my house. I'd run almost twice that many miles that morning, before the sun was even up.

"You're just leaving?" she asked.

I knew I'd pay for it, but I wasn't in the mood for burgers and hotdogs anymore. If coming with her was the mistake, and we weren't ready to deal with people, I just needed to go.

I didn't answer, but I lifted my hands into the air not knowing my way around what was happening.

Her eyes were full of hot blue flames I'd never seen. She'd never been cross with me, or me with her.

I'd much rather leave than make it any worse. That was a plain fact.

She walked away, and I walked down the road.

It's a sick feeling being in an argument with someone you care for so much. Especially when you're not exactly sure what the fight is about, and, therefore, not sure how to fix it.

As I strode along the road my temper ebbed, but my concern didn't. It took me a while to get home, and as I turned by the shed my phone buzzed in my pocket.

SUNSHINE: You didn't take your truck?

ME: The keys are in it.

SUNSHINE: Do you want me to bring it back?

Of course I did, and that was half the reason I'd left it. She'd have to drive it to my house, plus I had a plan to hold Andy hostage if it came to it. He was at my place, too.

We would need to talk, but I wasn't sure I was quite ready yet. I had some things to sort out first, but she was texting me. So that was something.

When I got home it was still pretty early and I had some thinking to do. I realized all I had was whiskey, having left my cooler with her. I thought twice about drinking it, but went ahead and did it anyway. Knowing better than tipping from the bottle, I put a few pieces of ice in a glass and poured it about half full.

That was plenty.

Then Andy and I sat in the front yard, watched a whole lot of nothing, and I really thought.

Had I overdone it?

Had my old ways just changed into adult versions of the same shit I used to pull to get her attention?

Why had I brought up her reunion? That wasn't my place.

I hoped this was just a fight, that I'd just made a mistake somehow. Or maybe that she was just freaked out by something else. Maybe in the morning, she'd want to talk about it.

I just hoped it wasn't too bad.

Chapter Twenty-Five

Sunny

I'd overreacted. In a *huge* way.

When I returned to my friends, after Rhett left alone, every last person looked at me like I was a jerk. And, I was one.

I'd warned Rhett about them being assholes sometimes, but I'd never planned on being one myself.

"What did you run him off for, dummy?" Darrell asked.

"Yeah, what the hell is wrong with you?" Dean added.

"Shut up. I know," was all I could say.

I was freaking the hell out. That's what the hell was wrong with me.

I didn't know how to do this shit, and Hannah had given me the third degree for not inviting him to the reunion yet. Apparently, she wanted to lock down a table with us before they ended up sitting with some jackasses.

I wasn't sure why I hadn't sent in the RSVP, or why I

hadn't asked him. I just wasn't too excited to go, but apparently everyone else wanted to—including Rhett.

I felt like such a bitch and only stayed a little while after we ate since they'd gone to all of the trouble. Shortly, after a few more beers, the party kind of fell apart anyway. Aaron, who briefly stopped by, got a call to go to a fire, and everyone else listened to a ball game on the radio.

I *hated* talk radio.

Regardless, it was nearly dark when I headed out, so I drove slowly. Not only was I not familiar with driving such a big truck, but I also needed the extra time to figure out what I was going to say.

When I turned into his drive, I found him sitting in a lawn chair in the front yard. He looked lonely and handsome at the same time. Andy didn't even run over to greet me when I climbed out of the cab. *Traitor*. But, I couldn't blame him.

Leisurely, I walked over, slapping at a bug trying to bite my leg on the way. *Fuckers*.

He didn't ignore me the way I deserved. Instead, he looked me in the eyes as I approached.

I bit the bullet and ate my humble pie, which tasted like a mixture of my own medicine and crow, but I choked it down as I swallowed my thick pride.

"I'm sorry, Rhett." I kicked at the grass in front of where he sat. "I don't want to fight with you. Will you go to my reunion with me?" I apologized and tried to smooth things over. Admittedly, I missed his grin and wanted it back.

Guilt sucked.

"I don't want to fight either," he said. "But I can't go to your reunion, I have a race anyway."

I'd heard him talk about it a few times, but I guess I never caught the date. I'd hoped he would ask me to go. "You do?"

"Nashville," he said and lifted a glass to his lips. It looked like tea, but the face he made indicated it had more bite.

Something inside of my chest hurt from the way he was talking. It lacked that fun side I'd gotten to know. More like when I'd first run into him earlier that summer. It was even more painful because it was my fault, so I wasn't sure what to do.

"Oh, okay," I said.

Hannah was right. I should have talked to him about my feelings before, but what guy *ever* wants to talk about that crap? Certainly not one who had recently graduated and was just starting his life.

His jaw ticked, but not in the way I liked most, and I hoped I hadn't really fucked up. Because it felt like it. He scratched Andy's head as he lay on the ground beside his chair and the small radio he normally listened to on the back porch fell over in the grass.

All I wanted to do was climb up on his lap and feel his arms around me, but I wasn't sure what he wanted.

"Should I leave?"

"You know, I want to say no. Tell you to stay. Pick you up and take you to bed. Get whatever this is straight between us—but since you brought it up, maybe that's what's best."

It stung and my heart ached.

I glanced over at my Civic, just sitting there in the good parking spot, which he always gave me when I came over so I wouldn't have to park on the dark side of the yard.

I took a few steps in that direction then paused. "Are you okay, Rhett?" I wasn't, but I hated leaving *him* mad. Hell, I just hated leaving.

"I'm fine," he said and gave me a weak smile. "I'll talk to you tomorrow."

It was the first Friday in a long time I went home alone. And I mean *alone*. Even my dog didn't come after me, and I was too ashamed to call for him when I got to my car.

I felt like shit. A big, old piece of panther shit. I'd been wrong. I wasn't even classy enough to be a panther. I was barely worthy of calling myself a mangy house cat.

So, I went to the radio station and played some sorry songs, hoping that maybe he'd hear them over the airwaves and understand how bad I felt.

After I tweaked the night's playlist, I went home and climbed into bed.

I didn't even turn on the TV. I just got under the covers and prayed that tomorrow would be better.

Instead of sleeping, I tossed and turned.

I *wanted* to pick out countertops. I wanted *all* of that, but it felt criminal swooping in on his life. He'd worked hard for what he was getting, and it didn't feel right just hopping into his dreams like they were mine to share.

To top the night off, it rained.

I was miserable lying in my bed without Rhett. I'd become used to talking to him before I fell asleep. To add insult to injury, I didn't even have Andy to cuddle up with.

My eyes blinked at the ceiling for minutes on end, restless and unsettled.

Then I decided to hell with it, hopped into my car, and drove back.

I didn't want him to go to sleep angry with me—it just didn't feel right. I drove down the road through the rain and flipped off my lights before I pulled into my empty spot in his drive.

I tiptoed up the steps and felt lucky when the door was left unlocked.

All of the lights were off, and Andy was snoring in the chair in the living room. I patted his head as I passed him on my way to Rhett's bedroom.

He was lying on his side, shirtless, the sheet only pulled up to his hip. It was dark, but he was in the moonlight and I could tell his eyes were open.

"Whatcha doin'?" he asked.

"Couldn't sleep," I admitted. "What are you doing?"

"Laying here thinking. Listening to the rain. Trying to decide whether to drive over to your place or not."

"Can I come over there with you?" I asked from the doorway. I ached to touch him, but maybe I needed him to touch me so I knew it was okay. Or at least that it would be.

Rhett scooted over and opened up the sheet for me. He had briefs on, and since I'd worn my pajamas over, I kicked off my flip-flips and climbed in facing him.

After getting comfortable, I lay my head on the pillow and looked into his heavy eyes.

"What am I going to do with you?" he asked, but his arm came around me and it felt like I was halfway back to normal. I took the first *real* breath since I'd left him earlier.

When I didn't answer he asked, "Why does not talking to you get your attention faster than just saying things?"

My hand ran its way around to his warm back. "I don't know. I'm a dumb woman," I confessed. Humility was a small price to pay.

Was that how he felt?

"What was all of that about earlier?" he quietly asked.

"Well, Hannah asked me something about us, using some stupid reference about catch and release. Then it got me thinking that maybe I was just some shiny thing you were attracted to and I should just throw you back to see if you could get the real thing. Something better than me."

He brushed hair out of my face, and I continued, "That reunion makes me feel old when I think about it, and she brought that up, too. Why would you want to go to some stupid dinner with me uptown and hang out with people I went to high school with? People I have *nothing* in common with anyway. Ones I never talk to anymore—even though they live five minutes from me. I don't even know if *I* want to go. Why would I subject you to that shit?"

God, that felt good to get off my chest.

His hand moved up and down my back over my shirt and it made me shiver. "Am I going too fast, Sunshine?"

"No," I answered. That wasn't it at all. "It feels like *I'm* going too fast for *you*, Rhett."

"There's no such thing." He leaned over and placed a kiss on my lips. "I'm sorry, too."

My fingers crept their way to his chest in the space between us.

"I just don't want to make a mistake. I don't want to lose you," he said.

There wasn't anything better he could have said because I felt the same way.

Rhett's arms tightened around me, and the space between us disappeared. His hips rolled over mine, and then

I was under him, looking up into his eyes.

"I want this mouth." He kissed my lips then moved to the crook of my neck. "And this spot right here." Then, he leaned up and pulled my shirt over my head in one easy motion. One-handed, he released my bra and tossed it to the floor.

"I want these," he added as he palmed one breast and kissed the other. My legs parted and his weight fell between them. With each kiss, my worries disappeared like fog in the morning sun.

Soon, a skillful hand slipped into my shorts and panties. His long fingers rubbed me senseless then he said, "I want *you* and *this*. All the time. Non-stop."

"I want you, too," I confessed and bucked against his masterful hand. My comprehension slowly faded as his touch paired perfectly with my need. Then he held himself away from me, his muscular shoulders hovering over my heated frame.

"None of that's worth much without *this*, though." With the pads of his fingers, he tapped on my chest, right in the middle. "That's what I'm really after because that's the *best* part. You might think I'm young, and I don't know what I'm doing, or that I don't know what I want. *You're* not ready for this. *I am*, but I'm damn good at waiting for you, Sunshine."

His hips rolled into mine. My back arched off his warm sheets.

When he spoke, his breath tickled my skin with the vibration from his low timbre. "I can assure you, if you give me *this* I won't slow down anymore. When you give me *this*, I'm gonna want it all. I know I will. I'll want you to move in. I'll want to marry you. I'll want to have babies and take vacations and have a life with you. And, you know what? It doesn't have a damn thing to do with how I felt as a kid. It's got nothing to do with how beautiful you are. Nothing to do with how you turn me on. It has everything to do with *this*." He tapped at my breastbone again, and then he patted his chest and said, "And *this*. These don't age. In here, there's no young and old. *Trust me*—it's always felt the same."

I think that's when I fell in love with him. Then again, maybe I'd already been in love with Rhett. Regardless, it was the first time I almost said it.

The words were sweet on my tongue and I lifted my head to share the way they tasted with him.

I still didn't know what to say, but I prayed he knew what I meant anyway.

We'd had a lot of sex that summer. He'd made me climb the walls with pleasure countless times, but that night was different. There was a feeling of apology and forgiveness. Fueled by tension and soothed by intimacy.

It grounded me to the Earth and things connected from my head to my heart. I wondered if Rhett could be the one.

The One.

Chapter Twenty-Six

Rhett

I had no desire to argue with her. I realized that the minute I saw her taillights fade away in the opposite direction of my house. I'd expected her to call the next morning and possibly let me have it.

So, I held back. I *did*.

It took another glass of whiskey and some serious debating between Andy and me.

I thought about it like testing a theory. If I gave her space, would she come back to me on her own? I just didn't know how long my resolve would hold out before I went to her.

I thought about how good it might feel when she did come back. Sadly, it was bittersweet and not *just* sweet. We were equally stubborn and sorry.

But, my theory held true. When I held back, she gave me more.

Until that night, I'd never had make-up sex. You hear about it and you hardly believe the hype, but there was something to it.

Sunny held on tighter than before. I pushed harder than before.

She rode me in the center of my bed while the wind slammed pecan tree limbs against my metal roof. While the thunder rolled and the rain fell in buckets, we found some sort of common ground.

There were things left unresolved, but we were together and that felt *most* important.

Later, as we lay corner to corner on the mattress, catching our breath, she fell asleep on my chest. My heavy eyes fell shut as the speed of my fingers, stroking up and down her naked back, slowed to a stop.

That weekend was kind of quiet. We watched a lot of TV and pretty much lounged around. Sunday evening, after we both skipped out on our parents, she said she needed to do some laundry and went home.

I did a few things outside until it got dark, then I ate and fell asleep in the chair in my living room.

When I woke up around three-thirty the next morning, I decided I'd just run off some energy instead of going back to bed. My feet hit the smooth lane, running down one side of the gravel as the birds started chirping.

There was something about running that cleared my head. It felt almost cleansing.

Then, over the next few weeks, I became more diligent

preparing for the race. Steadily, I added to my distance as my stamina increased back to competition strength.

Things with Sunny went back to the way they had been before the barbeque at the Renfros'. Only we weren't spending as much time together. I pulled back some, but she actually did, too.

It was strange. I craved her more than anything, but, on days when we didn't see each other, she'd begun to reach out to me in new ways. Sending me naughty texts was one of my favorites. Or she'd call me before she went to bed. Her voice would be soft at first then turn sultrier as she tired.

On my birthday, she gave me a personal shout-out on the radio and played my favorite songs the whole day. My dad called me three times. Not to say anything, but to hold his phone up to the stereo when he heard one he loved, too.

She bought me a really great pair of running shoes and brought me beer from the kitchen while she made me tacos in her underwear. We had sex in my living room, then ate strawberries and chugged Crystal Gayle naked in front of my refrigerator before we went to bed.

I mean, it was a pretty damn good day.

Even though spending so much time with her in the beginning felt good at the moment, I was seeing the merits of letting things happen on their own.

I wanted to tell her I loved her every time we spoke or saw each other, but I couldn't do it. Not when the less was more approach was working so well. Then again, holding back didn't feel exactly right either.

I'd had this great idea to take her on a trip in the fall to a cabin one of our hunters owned, but I stalled. Then the plans fell through. Additionally, after not seeing her for two long days, I found her on my bed naked when I got home from work. I decided being patient wasn't *killing* me.

I appreciated the benefits of taking things at her pace, but wanting her more, and getting her less felt foolish at times—like when we weren't together.

"So you're just going alone?" Haley asked.

The race was that weekend, and I was ready for it. She was heading back to college the next day and came to hang out with me on her last night in Wynne.

Neither Sunny nor I had mentioned *that* weekend since our squabble at the Renfros'. I supposed it wasn't worth fighting about anyway. She had her plans, and I had mine.

Although it kind of sucked that she hadn't asked me to go on her own, I had to accept that I hadn't asked her to come to Nashville either.

I stretched my legs out and took another bite of the cake our mom had sent with my sister. After swallowing, I answered, "Yeah, it's cool. I'll be focused more and probably have a great race." My times were decent and my pacing was good. But, my focus? Well, it had been elsewhere.

"You'll do fine, but why *don't* you ever bring her to the farm?" she asked.

My whole family had asked me about that, in one way or another. I was creative with my answers.

"What … and have you guys ask her a million questions?" Which was very likely, and—reality notwithstanding—a perfectly logical reason. They would totally grill her, but Sunny could handle it. She talked just about as much as they did.

The truth was I never wanted to backtrack with her again. That's what our first fight felt like.

A step back.

I didn't know if it was the farmer in me who would rather work all night rather than backtracking to work even one acre of ground twice. Or maybe it was the runner in me who never wanted to look behind at what made me stumble. Could have been both.

I always wanted to move forward. Hit my distances, finish the job. That was the goal either way. Get it done. Cross the line.

With Sunny, however, I wasn't in a hurry to do that. I never wanted to be finished. So, I had to adjust my pace, even if that meant doing something that was so far from my nature. Uncomfortable and frustrating as it was, I wasn't adding any pressure to her or us.

And we weren't moving forward very fast. We just were. So no matter how great it was, the current was weak and I missed the rush.

"We wouldn't be that bad and you know it." My sister genuinely looked hurt, her head leaning to the side, her eyes skeptical. "We know this isn't just *some* girl, Rhett. She's *Sunny*."

"I know," I admitted. Tossing the paper plate in the trash, I pulled off my cap and scratched my head.

Of all people, I was well aware of who the hell I was with.

Haley chided, "You're forgetting something, though. You're *Rhett* Caraway."

I pulled the back of my cap taut and tugged the bill over my eyes.

She kicked my boot. "Seriously, dude. Do you even remember how many girls went after you in high school?

Followed *you* around? Came to all of your track meets? I had girls coming up to me wanting to know about you. You're Rhett Fucking Caraway, the Crowned Prince of Wynne."

I looked her way, and she rolled her eyes.

"The whole damn town is pulling for you two to get together. I'm sure it's pretty obnoxious—I've been around when people have brought it up to you. But, Rhett, they can't help it. Everyone loves *both* of you. Everyone knows it's"—she paused and her eyes danced across the ceiling looking for the right word—"it's *special.* You guys might hide away for now, but we all saw you earlier this summer. You two didn't shut up the whole day at the levee when I was around you. The way she looks at you. The way you sweat so damn much when you're around her—that has to be some neanderthalic male tendency. Pheromones or something. Either way, it's totally obvious."

What was I supposed to do with all of that information?

"I get it, Hal. I do. That doesn't change anything. We're *good.*" In fact, I was about to call her before my sister commandeered my night. I was leaving in a few days and I needed to see her a little more before I left.

Haley dramatically rolled out of her chair to the ground, growling. "You *don't* get it. You two are *good*? Rhett, you two could be *great.*" She stood up and dusted herself off, pointing a stern finger at me. "You think about that, *brah.* Now, give me a hug, I need to go home."

We could be great.

That was awesome news, but apparently she wasn't going to tell me how.

I put my arm around her shoulder and smashed her

head against me. Her arm loosely wrapped around my waist.

"Stop. Hug me right," she demanded. When I let up, she spoke into my t-shirt. "Just don't let this be the first thing you really ever half-assed, Rhett."

My sister was cool. A brat, but definitely a cool one.

"Are you sure you want to go back to that old dorm so early?" I hugged her like a brother hugs a sister. Like Haley and I always had. One arm above a shoulder. One arm below.

"Oh, I'm sure. I haven't seen him in two months and I'm about to die."

Him? She'd said she was going back early to spend time with Carrie, since they were both RAs. Carrie wasn't a chick?

I pushed her an arm's length away. "So, Carrie is a *Carey*?" I clarified. She hadn't shut up about her *friend* all summer.

My jaw hung open. The little shit had pulled a fast one on all of us.

She pursed her lips together and looked pleased with herself. "It's all true *and* I didn't leave anything out. We're just friends—so far. I get taking your time better than anyone. But, I'm going back to school, and I'm making a move." As she skipped through my kitchen she hollered, "See you at Thanksgiving, pussy."

"What are you doing over there?" I asked Sunny as I held my cellphone to my ear.

She was winded when she answered the call after fumbling with the phone before saying hello. "Nothing. Just doing some stretches." She coughed and laughed. "Andy bet me I couldn't touch my toes. He lost, but I broke my ass falling over. It's a bittersweet victory."

I chuckled and thought about her lying on the floor.

"What are you doing?" she asked.

"Oh, just something I've been putting off for the last few weeks."

"Like what? I'm the biggest procrastinator in the world. If you don't want to do it you could probably wait until next week." She laughed. "You've already waited *this* long. See? That's how you procrastinate."

After my sister left, I started thinking about a conversation Sunny and I'd shared a long time ago and realized it was my move. Maybe she'd been telling me in her own way for a while now.

I said, "Open your door and find out."

Chapter Twenty-Seven

Sunny

What the what?

I scrambled off the floor and peeked out the window behind the couch. Sure as hell, he was standing on my front porch. I wondered about how much of that he'd seen. I was actually trying to do yoga, but my coordination sucked.

I even considered just taking up running after Rhett was done with his race. He'd told me that he only trains like a maniac—like he had been over the past few weeks—before a competition. If he was willing to hang back and let me stay caught up, I wanted to give it a try.

After we'd gotten into the fight at Hannah's, at first I was worried things were cooling off. They didn't really, but we weren't as attached at the hips as we'd been in the first few weeks.

Actually, it gave me a lot of time to think. Within that

time, I'd found some pretty fun ways to show him how much he meant to me. I wasn't as good as he was with the surprises, but I was improving.

The extra time had been good for me. That's all it really took for me to realize he was everything I wanted. Circumstances be damned. It was the truth.

There was a huge difference between *wanting* a guy to like and *wanting him* to like you back. It became very important to know how he felt, and while I was "stretching" I'd realized the best way to find out would be to tell him where I was.

I opened the door and he stepped aside to let the screen past his shoulder.

"Hi," I said and tried to tame down the grin on my face. He was unexpected, but always welcome.

He stood there with flowers in his hands. It was the strangest bouquet I'd ever seen. Nothing matched, and it looked more bunched than arranged like the ones from the florist at the store. Leafy and wild, he held them out to me.

"I felt like bringing you some flowers. So, I did it."

I started to leap into his arms but paused, fearful he'd fall backwards off the steps. That was the last thing he needed before a marathon. And instead of moving I spoke, impulsively.

"I love y…" I said and slapped my hand over my mouth.

He looked from me to the flowers. "Most of these are weeds, but I thought … wait. What did you say?" He shook his head and then peeled my fingers off my mouth. His face changed from sweet to dead serious.

"…*them*. I love them." I laughed like a maniac and bit my bottom lip, unsure if it was about to *almost* pop out again. I straightened, and the only thing I could think to do was blink.

So I blinked over and over like it might clear away my clumsy tongue. Then again, I'd been biting the words back for weeks, afraid it was too soon.

"You almost threw me there," he confessed as he took a step back, then another in my direction after his balance wavered.

I'd nearly thrown myself, too. Right off an embarrassing cliff.

My hand moved out to steady him.

"They're beautiful," I said.

"Did you almost say...?" He squinted and licked the corner of his mouth.

My heart raced. I was busted. Kind of. I mean, I hadn't *actually* said it all the way.

I smiled brightly and nodded my head noncommittally. My ability to control speech was all messed up and suddenly words jammed up in my throat.

"Are you trying to tell me I could have saved hundreds of dollars by giving you stolen flowers all of these years?"

He let me off the hook, but I supposed it was true. It never was about *what* he gave me, only that he *had*.

I stepped back and let him in the door; as vulnerable as I felt, I had the urge to move around. I took the flowers into the kitchen and retrieved a vase from under the sink as he said hello to Andy.

They really were kind of pretty. Yellow, orange, blue, and red. All randomly mixed up. While I arranged them in the water, I pretended that what I damn near said hadn't really happened. That seemed like the best move. Ignore and move on.

"Are you ready to hit the road tomorrow?" I asked. The race felt like a safe topic.

Rhett's chest pressed against my back and my eyes fell shut having missed him the whole day. "Yeah, I'm all set." His hands wrapped around me, and he pressed a kiss into my hair.

When there wasn't anything left to do with the stolen bouquet, I turned in his arms. His legs parted and flanked mine as I leaned back against the sink.

"So you *love* the flowers, huh?" he asked.

With my head tipped up to look into his eyes, I found his smile first and stopped there to appreciate it. His full lips were kissable, looking warm and soft.

"I think I do," I answered, but I knew what he was getting at. He didn't make a meal of it by toying with me though.

He asked, "You gonna miss me when I'm gone this weekend?"

More than I would have ever guessed.

He was leaving to go to Nashville, and I was planning on going to the bar for the alumni "night out." It didn't sound all that fun, but Hannah and Vaughn would be there. At least I could hang with them.

"I always miss you when you're not around," I confessed. Apparently, I'd hit my head on the ground or something when I fell because I was all about letting whatever I wanted fall out of my mouth. "You're my boyfriend, Rhett. I want you around all the time."

His smiled widened. "I'm glad to hear it," he said. "Are you ready for your big weekend?"

If by *ready* he meant *dreading*, then yeah. I was as ready as I'd ever be.

"Actually, I'll be glad when it's over."

I left off the fact that I really wished he was going with me—I knew I could behave better than the last time we'd been around people. I was sure of it, but now I didn't want him to miss his race. I knew how hard he'd been training, and I was excited for him.

"Come on. You'll have a good time." He rocked us back and forth gently.

The truth was, I didn't give a shit what anyone thought anymore. I loved him. I only hoped figuring it out hadn't taken too long.

I'd never find another Rhett. No matter how long I looked. No matter where I went to find him. There was only one *him*.

Over the past few weeks I'd gone out of my way to show him that. Honestly, I'd had a really good time doing it, too. Finding things he'd like. Surprising him when I could. I wanted things to move forward, but I didn't know what that was.

I relented. "It'll *probably* be fun. But, hey, I was about to get a bowl of ice cream and watch TV in my bed. Can you stay the night? I have chocolate."

Since he was there, it was a good opportunity to do another thing I'd fantasized about.

"I can stay, but I think I'll skip the ice cream tonight."

It was his favorite, and far be it from me to tempt an athlete before a big race, but I couldn't help myself. I reached into the freezer, but he didn't let me go. Luckily, I was just able to grab the tub of Chocolate Fudge Brownie.

Then I got into the drawer beside us and pulled out a spoon.

"Come on. I'll let you lick it off of me," I taunted.

My sexy man closed his eyes and bit his lip. "Okay, maybe just a bite or two."

He had exactly three before he pulled the ice cream from my hands and put it on the nightstand. We didn't even turn the TV on. There wasn't anything on television that could have even come close to rivaling the things he was doing to me.

"When I get back from Nashville, I don't want to sleep without you anymore, Sunshine." Rhett kissed his way back up my stomach. His cheeks red and his lips wet, he looked better than any dream I'd ever had.

"I don't want to sleep without you anymore either," I agreed as I pulled his mouth to mine. He tucked his hands and arms under my head beneath the pillow as he slowly pushed inside me.

His signature, "Ah," rumbled through our kiss.

"I just want you, Sunny. That's all I ever want. Okay?" His voice grew deeper and it was as sweet as the chocolate on our lips.

"Okay, Rhett. I'm ready, too." I was ready for him to take me over the edge in my small bedroom. I was ready to take our relationship wherever it felt like going. Mostly, I was finally ready for *all* of Rhett Caraway's love.

He didn't almost say the words like I nearly had that night, but he didn't have to. I felt them.

If he was leaving town on schedule as planned, I knew he'd be heading down his road toward the highway and still well within my little radio station's range.

"It's finally Friday, everyone. That last song was one of my new favorites. It's a track I recorded here last week with the up-and-coming Wind Through Wichita." I pulled down the volume at the end of the song and spoke to the airwaves. "I got a call from the guys yesterday and heard they booked a big show down in Austin, TX after they uploaded their LIVE at WDKR recording to their website. We wish them lots of good luck.

"Also, we've got another local doing some pretty awesome things, Wynne. Every Sunday we run the All-American Country Countdown *LIVE* from Nashville. Well, they're sponsoring a marathon this weekend and our very own track star is competing. Local farmer and all around great guy, my handsome boyfriend. Do your best, Rhett. You *always* do."

I slid the music volume back up and clicked the mouse for the next song to begin.

"Here's a hot one from Maren Morris—"I Could Use a Love Song" on Wildcat Country, 98.5 FM."

I went ahead and did the programming for the weekend, since I wasn't rushing off to see Rhett that afternoon. Then I realized I could probably build a little every day and start skipping Saturdays altogether.

I tipped back the last of my sweet tea and saw the light flash on my phone, having put it on silent for work.

RHETT: I just you. Thank you.

ME: You're welcome. Good luck. Be careful and DON'T TEXT AND DRIVE. Let me know when you get

there.

It was only a few hours, six if he hit the traffic just right. I'd Googled the route the other day. It made me nervous, him being on the road. So I was happy for the extra work to keep me busy.

He sent me a text hours later as I was walking back into the house to get ready for the bar.

RHETT: I'm here. Have fun tonight. I hate that I'm missing your stellar dance moves.

He was very funny. *Not.*

ME: I hate that I'm missing you running in those shorty shorts. I saw them the other day. I might want to borrow them sometime.

RHETT: lol I'll wear them for you.

ME: Good enough. When will you be home on Sunday?

RHETT: Early. I plan on leaving before the sun comes up.

I liked the sound of that.

ME: Don't go looking for any girls.

RHETT: I only ever look for one and she's a pain in my ass.

ME: Talk. Talk. Talk. You love it.

RHETT: You're right.

I felt a knotting in my stomach, the good kind. I knew we'd say it eventually, and I only felt positive excitement waiting. It was unmistakable: he made me *feel* loved.

I could wait for the words.

I sat my phone on the counter in the bathroom, turned on the shower, and ran the water up to the right temperature. Tossing my clothes in the basket—or at least close to it—I checked my phone one last time before I got under the water.

HANNAH: I'll be riding solo with you tonight, but I'm running a little late. Sawyer isn't feeling so good. Vaughn is staying home.

ME: Okay. Meet me there.

Instantly, I was excited. *Girls' night.* I smiled as I threw my towel over the hook near the shower.

Then, as I washed, I started to feel kind of bad for her—for them. They hadn't been out in a long time. They adored Sawyer, and although she was healthy and growing, I think they were still paranoid about something going wrong.

I blew out my hair and jammed out to the station. In the nostalgic spirit of the reunion, I'd made playlists for the weekend from songs when we were in school. It hit me again how fast the time had gone.

Would I blink and miss all of these first years with Rhett?

Would they go by before I knew it?

I didn't want to waste any more time. I wanted to be with him, and I was even surer about talking to Rhett about the future when he got home. Our future.

It was something that we sort of avoided, but I think we'd both been a little naïve. Turns out, when you're finally sure of what you want, you're not as afraid to go for it.

The thought that he'd been so sure so much earlier in life sometimes boggled my mind. Who else on the planet could say the man they loved had only ever loved them?

My heart swelled, and as I put my makeup on and ran the curling iron through my hair, something strange happened. It was like a floodgate opened and so many other visions floated so vividly through my head for the first time.

Thoughts of marrying Rhett.

I stopped what I was doing and just stood and stared at myself.

Why hadn't I thought about that?

Oh, and the farmhouse. That *was* going to be our home. He wanted to pick countertops out. Suddenly, that felt so meaningful.

He was everything I'd ever really wanted in a man. Equal parts responsible and reckless. Smart and sexy. A good man. The best.

He was all *mine.*

Who knew I'd have my first real-life epiphany the first night of my ten-year high school reunion weekend?

I had a future with Rhett. A *great* one.

I passed the packed parking lot at the bar and kept going. When I finally came to a stop, I knew it was probably going to be a long night.

One bottle.

Two bottles.

The hours passed kind of slowly, but I enjoyed the company and let a lot of my old doubts fade away.

RHETT: Are you having fun? Let me know when you get home.

I swayed my hips and read the message.

ME: If you thought you were too young, then you

should see my date.

RHETT: WHAT?

I sent him a quick picture of Sawyer and me.

Hannah had been excited about the reunion, and she had every right to be. She was happy and had so much to be proud of. She'd always been someone everyone liked, but she'd changed a lot. Besides, after everything they went through with their little girl, they deserved a break.

Vaughn was her *one*, and she was his. That's what they had—each other's future.

I put the baby in her crib and walked out to the hall, closing the door all but a crack.

I dialed Rhett's number.

"What are you doing?" he asked when he answered the phone.

"Babysitting," I admitted and chuckled quietly, careful not to wake up the Queen. She'd had a fever earlier, but she was just hungry and tired at that point. She'd eaten, but crashed out halfway through her bottles. "They were going to skip out and stay home because Sawyer didn't feel great today, but I pretty much kicked them out. Hannah really wanted to go, and they haven't had a few hours to themselves in a long time. So, I'm just chilling with Queen Sawyer. Thinking about stuff."

I heard a dinging sound on the other end of the line. "I'm just headed up to my room. Tell me what you've been thinking about," he softly requested.

It would have been so much easier to say over the phone all of the things I'd thought about, but I didn't want to go easy on myself. I wanted to work for it a little. I'd wait and tell him in person—face to face. He deserved that, and I knew just what to do.

"I'm thinking about you and *us*."

"That sounds perfect, Sunshine. Just perfect," he said.

It totally was.

Chapter Twenty-Eight

Rhett

After a huge dinner in the hotel restaurant, I talked on the phone with her for a while. As many trips as I'd been on, that one was the loneliest. I was never the type of guy who needed a girl on his arm, but I missed Sunny and wished she'd been there with me.

I was done being safe. I knew what I wanted.

Something had changed with her from just the night before, and I only prayed it was for the better. Maybe she'd finally want to start making plans. Maybe she'd want to share some ideas for the future. Topics we'd both danced around.

I didn't really give a shit when the future happened, I only cared that she was in it. That she saw me in hers.

It didn't even matter if we still went back and forth between houses, but, when it came time to move into the new place, I was sure I wanted her there. She needed to know that.

I woke up early the next morning, stretched, had some eggs, and headed down the block where the race was scheduled to start. The streets were littered with people from all walks of life, all there for the same reason.

To race. To win, or at the very least, make it to the finish line.

Winning wasn't necessarily my goal anymore. I was happy with a solid finish. After I registered, I worked my way to a good starting spot. I looked at the course again on my phone and concentrated on my pacing.

As I was setting up my music for the twenty-six miles I had before me, I received a few messages all at once.

MOM: Have a good run today. Do your best. Dad says good luck, too.

HAYLEY: Drink a lot of water and kick ass. Love you.

SUNSHINE: Have a great race. I miss you. Call me later.

I'd have to see how the race went, but if I wasn't too tired I was already considering driving home that night—instead of the next morning. I had another goal in mind, and I was going to start chasing that one like I should have been.

A familiar quiet fell over the crowd as we waited for the shotgun start.

The first few miles were mostly spent making my way to the front, then finding my stride. The music helped me keep a good pace, and even when I hit the hills I was pleased with how I was doing. My feet met the pavement with purpose, knowing I was headed toward more than just a finish line.

I was in love with Sunny and tired of denying it.

Overall, I was satisfied with my twelfth place finish. I actually beat my personal time goal, which was probably more important to me anyway. After the race, I mingled around for a little while, walking down my pulse. When I got to the hotel, I showered and checked out early, deciding home sounded better than another lonely night in Nashville.

When I got out of the city, I stopped at a restaurant for a quick burger. After going through the drive-thru, I pulled into a parking spot to eat and let everyone know how I did. I sent a group message to my mom and my sister.

ME: Finished twelfth. Heading home tonight.

Then without waiting for their reply, I called Sunny.

"Hey, how'd you do?" she asked brightly as soon as she answered.

"I got twelfth, and I beat my own time. So, that's good." I took a sip of the sweet tea I'd ordered. Lately, I'd been drinking about as much as she did.

"That's awesome. Congratulations. You gonna go out and party? Celebrate?"

I would have if she was with me, but it didn't sound that great without her. Terrible dancing and all, she was what made doing most things fun.

"No. Actually, I'm headed home." I looked at the clock on the dash of my truck and did a quick calculation. "I'll probably be rolling into town around eight."

"Really?" she squeaked, and I liked how cheerful she sounded about my change of plans.

"Really," I said. "I know you have plans, but maybe when the reunion is over you could come out to my place, or I can meet you at yours?"

"Well … actually … um…" she stuttered. "*Shit.*"

Sunny never stalled when she spoke. *Ever.* Regardless, whether it came from her time on the radio or just that she had a talent for saying things, her words rarely tripped over each other.

And shit? I wanted to see her and she said *shit*? Something was up.

"Is everything all right?" I crumpled up the sandwich wrapper and half of the uneaten burger as I held the phone against my ear with my shoulder.

"Yeah, Rhett. Everything is fine. Everything is cool," she insisted. "We just need to talk about some stuff, and I'd planned to do it tomorrow."

The words *I love you* raced up my throat. I'd waited too damn long.

"I know you're busy tonight—"

"No. That's not it. I just … I need to go."

"Wait."

"I'll text you in a little while. I've gotta go. Bye." Then, she hung up.

I pounded my hand against the steering wheel and my chest rose and fell as I tried not to freak the fuck out. Sunny had never been so dismissive, so rushed to get off the phone.

Was this it? Was she done? The other night I'd thought she was about to tell me she loved me. What if I'd only heard what I'd wanted to again.

The miles and hours peeled away as I got closer to Wynne. Closer to home.

I was ready to do whatever was necessary to keep her.

Not just keep her, but make her happy. Give her everything.

All along I'd been thinking if she'd just give me her heart, then I'd give her mine, which was total bullshit. Love doesn't work like that.

I'd been naïve for the last time with her. And, by the grace of God, if she gave me a chance to tell her—*show her*—how much I wanted and cared about her, then maybe I could change her mind.

I hoped I wasn't too late.

After I turned off the interstate and hit the county line highway, I turned my radio dial back to 98.5 FM, just as I'd always done when I was coming home. It would be static for another few miles then I'd hear the familiar voice I always listened for.

It started to sprinkle, which was surprisingly a good thing, and by the time the country sounds were streaming through my speakers clearly, it was all out pouring down.

My phone chimed, and I flipped it over on my lap.

SUNSHINE: I hope you're close and listening to the radio.

Even though I normally didn't text and drive, I carefully replied.

ME: I'm about 20 minutes from Wynne and listening.

SUNSHINE: <3

That makeshift heart was everything. Every damn thing. It was exactly what I needed. God, that woman made me crazy.

I sped closer to town, my tires humming down the highway through the rain.

"That was "Are You Gonna Kiss Me Or Not" by Thompson Square, and I tell you what, Wynne, I've been there. Waiting for that first kiss from Rhett just about killed this country girl. All I have to say is thank the *sweet* Lord for fallen limbs, sandbags, and Mrs. Caraway's meatloaf." She laughed and her electric tone had me sliding my hand over the spot where she usually sat in my truck beside me.

"Here's a big shout out to the Class of 2006 and an even bigger shout out to Rhett for getting twelfth place in the All-American Country Countdown Marathon in Nashville this weekend. Not too bad for a small town guy. I'm so proud of you. We all are."

The dread I'd felt when I first started toward home was washing away as I got closer to her. Hearing her talk on the radio again, for all of Wynne to hear, had pride swelling in my chest.

"And, Rhett, when you roll into Wynne, you should just head uptown. I'll see you there. I remember when we were younger you'd call the station and dedicate songs to me. I know *you're* the runner, but this one is from me to you. Here's "I Run To You" by WDKR favorite, Lady Antebellum. "

My chest filled with warmth, and another message flashed across my phone's screen.

SUNSHINE: I'm uptown. Come see me.

I topped the hill and saw my hometown. As I drove, people honked and waved at me, probably hearing what I had. I waved back and I made my way to the center of our little city.

The square park in the heart of Wynne was packed, but I found a spot across from the Shirley Banquet Hall where her reunion was. Just as my headlights turned into the empty space, they washed across a flash of yellow ahead.

I turned my wipers up on high then clicked my lights onto bright.

There she was standing on the ladder to the water tower wearing a dress in the pouring rain.

I had firsthand knowledge of what that ladder was like, and I jumped out of my truck as it sat running.

"What the hell are you doing?" I hollered as I ran the hundred or so yards to her. My legs burned from sheer exhaustion followed by sitting in my truck for hours. So I wasn't fast by any means.

She climbed as I ran and when I saw what she'd done, I froze.

Sunny loves Rhett was written in yellow.

She leaned over the edge of the small town's tower.

I looked up at her, and the rain pelted my face. "Sunny, please come down. You're going to get hit by lightning."

"Can you see it?" she shouted. The fabric of her dress flapped as the breeze picked up. "I did it for you, Rhett. Do you remember?"

How could I forget? Nobody in a thirty-mile radius would let me. Mine had read somewhat different from hers, but it was no less life-changing. Still, it was raining like hell and all I wanted was her feet on the ground.

"I see it. I love it. *Please*, come down."

"Okay. Okay," she said and started to descend. I neared the ladder and watched her from below as rung by rung she made her way to the sweet, wet earth.

When she was at a safe height—and I could breathe again—I allowed myself a good long look up her shirt. I was just a man, after all.

She hopped to the ground when the ladder stopped

and spun into my arms.

"I think I need to build you a tree house at the new place. Not afraid of heights, huh?"

I felt her chuckle against me, her arms around my neck.

"Nope," she said, smiling.

"Good, then you can help." Her blue eyes blinked away the rain as it dripped down her face. She was stunning, even sopping wet. "Listen, I need to tell you something and I should have said it before."

"Me first. Rhett, I love you." She leaned up and kissed my lips. "I love you."

Just like that, my life went from good to great.

"I love you, Sunshine. I've loved you for as long as I can—"

"Excuse me?" Three swift pats struck my back. "Which one of you wants to tell me what's going on up here?"

Officer Long.

My hold on Sunny weakened, and she slid down my body, as I pivoted to face the cop who'd busted me in the same park all those years ago.

"Hey, Marv. I did it," Sunny confessed.

"You know that's vandalism on government property, Sunny? You're gonna have to come with me," he said.

By that time, a crowd had formed under the awning at Sally's across the street, everyone watching while the red and blue lights flashed. Additionally, all of her classmates at the party were now looking out of the open door of the banquet hall, too.

"Are you serious? *Marv—*" she exclaimed. "I'll paint over it."

That's what I'd had to do. Of course, I also got grounded

for the rest of the summer.

Before I knew it, Marv Long had ahold of one of Sunny's wrists, putting her in handcuffs. While she studied the new bracelets connecting her hands, Marv winked at me.

"You can't be serious," she argued, still laughing and hardly believing she was going to jail. "Rhett," she said, waiting for me to come to her defense, but I didn't have a chance to answer as Marv gave her a slight nudge in the direction of his flashing squad car.

"Come on," he said.

She stomped off with him, barefoot through the grass.

"Rhett, come and get me."

I was going to do just that.

Chapter Twenty-Nine

Sunny

After we were in the car and out of the rain, I listened to my Miranda Rights for the first time in my life—totally shocked that I was actually in trouble.

"I cannot *believe* you're arresting me," I droned from the back of Marvin Long's cop car.

"Oh, Sunny, calm down," he scolded, but his shoulders shook like he was laughing as he sat in front of me. "Now, how could I *not* arrest you? I arrested him for doing the same daggone thing. Fair is fair."

He had a point, but I wasn't a criminal. We both knew it. I grumbled and nearly fell over as the car went over the curb when he pulled into the new Wynne Police and Fire Station building only two blocks from the damn water tower.

He flashed the lights and turned on the siren before he put the car in park. Five or six heads peeked out the window of the great big garage door.

How embarrassing.

Marv stepped out and opened my door, and then we walked inside the building. My cousin Aaron met us in the shared corridor and asked, "What the hell did you do?"

"Sunny can't talk right now. She'll get a call in a while." Marv held his hand up to Aaron.

Maybe I *was* in trouble. Times had changed, and I wasn't a kid like Rhett had been.

Shit. The panther made me do it!

He led me through an area that looked like a waiting room at a doctor's office then through another door. "You can sit right there," he said and pointed to a bench opposite a desk. The stocky older man took a seat behind it and pulled out a pad from one of the drawers. "I'm writing you a warning for vandalism."

A warning? That was good news.

I leaned forward and my dress squished water onto the floor. "Thank you. And I'll clean up the paint."

He walked to a cabinet, unlocked it, and pulled out something orange. Then came over to me, his keys still in his hand. As he unlocked my handcuffs he said, "Oh, I *know* you'll clean it up. It actually works out perfect, because the tower hasn't been painted for over ten years. The town board was just talking about you two. Funny enough, they hoped one of you would do something like this." He chuckled. "It took you long enough. Maybe your boyfriend will help ya. He *does* have experience."

I smiled from the mention of Rhett and the relief that I wasn't going up the river. "I guess he does."

"You can use that bathroom over there. Change into

these so you don't have to sit there and get soggy." He put the orange thing in my hands and pointed to the door on the other side of the big office.

I changed into the hideous, yet oddly comfortable, prisoner get-up. It was a little big, but it was nice and dry.

When I came back out, Marv was hanging up the phone. "We could make a lot of money arresting you every now and then. I've had three calls from people trying to bail you out," he teased.

I took a seat on the bench and placed the wad of wet dress at my feet. "When can I go?"

"Well, I'm holding you for a little while. I can't just let you paint the water tower and then off the hook too easy. Makes me look bad. I'll let you go in an hour or so."

My phone, along with my purse and my keys, were all still uptown in my car.

Both of his phones rang non-stop, and each time he answered them the same way. "She's still filling out paperwork." Which wasn't true, but I didn't say anything and I never asked who it was. I could only imagine because he never let on.

"Sunny, I'm gonna have to put you in a holding room for a few minutes," he said and shuffled around a few papers on his desk.

"Uh, okay." I'd never been in jail, so I wasn't sure what a holding room meant, but I knew it probably wasn't as cushy as the office.

And, I was right.

It was pretty much a tiny room divided into two sections by a half wall. One side had a bed and a small desk thing and the other section, the side behind the wall, had a toilet and a tiny sink. The holding room *was* a jail cell.

"You won't be in here long," he said at the doorway behind me. "Just relax and I'll be right back."

I was officially scared straight. Even though the room was clean and not all that frightening or anything, I wouldn't be back. My career as a lawbreaker was decidedly short-lived as I sat on the thin mattress against the tan cinderblock wall.

Nevertheless, even being in jail couldn't get me too down. Rhett had said he loved me, too. So, since I had nothing but my mind to occupy me, I thought of our future and all the things to come.

It felt like a long time, but it was probably only twenty minutes or so before I saw Marv's head through the small glass window on the door.

"Someone's here for you. You ready?"

I was ready as hell to get out of there, but mostly I was ready to start my life for what felt like the first time.

Marv stepped back and I saw Rhett down on one knee a few feet behind him.

"I'll give you guys a few minutes," the old police officer said and left us alone.

I was smiling so wide that my cheeks ached. My heart pounded like the bass line of a fast song, and my blood tingled like there were tiny champagne bubbles fizzing through my veins.

"You look funny," Rhett said and chuckled, which was one of the best sounds I'd ever heard. Then he nodded for me to come closer and held out his hand. I took a few steps and laced my fingers with his.

"A long time ago I told a girl I loved her, and she told

me she knew, but couldn't love me back." When he paused, he grinned and cleared his throat. "She gave me some advice that night in this very jail. Well, not this one—the old one—but you know what I mean. Things have changed a little." He winked and my breath caught in my chest remembering what I'd told him all that time ago.

"I followed that advice, Sunshine. She's written me a lot of notes. Some of them were pretty dirty, actually. She's given me some of the best gifts. Many of them priceless, but the biggest one was her heart. She calls me and spends time with me and makes me smile and laugh. She's heard songs that made her think of me and played them for all to hear."

Warm tears fell from my eyes as he kissed my hand, then he reached into his pocket.

"I'll be damned, if she didn't even paint the water tower for me. And you want to know what? I'm dying to marry her. I need her to be my wife so I can spend a lifetime showing her how she's *always* been the one for me."

I bent and kissed him, my free hand cupping his cheek. "I love you," I whispered against his lips. "Thanks for waiting on me."

"Marry me, Sunshine. That's all the thanks I need."

He let my hand go to open the box, and immediately I recognized the ring.

"Where did you get that?" I asked in awe.

"Well, I asked your dad a long time ago if I could marry you, but I went back again tonight to see what your parents thought. I told them I couldn't wait anymore. I only want you—now and forever. They gave me this ring."

I stared at my grandmother's engagement ring. The one Grandpa Sonny had given her. She hadn't worn it since he passed, saying her wedding band was more important. Rhett slipped the precious jewelry onto my left hand.

"Will you *finally* put me out of my misery and marry me, please? Sit in the middle of my truck seat, drink all of my beer, pick out my countertops, and make me happy?"

How could a girl say no to that?

"Yes, but…" I paused and leaned in to kiss him again, and he pulled away.

"No. No *buts*."

"*I was going to say:* Yes, but only if you help me paint the water tower."

He stood laughing and wrapped his arms around my waist. "Okay, that's a deal."

Then his mouth claimed mine, *really* claimed mine. No holding back. No apologies. Rhett kissed me with authority and purpose.

All I could do was just hold on.

Epilogue

Rhett

We were going to have our rough spots, just like every other couple in history, but I believed those times would only make the good times better. Like that perfect summer of *Sunshine and rain.*

We'd take the good with the *less* good—because, let's face it, it wouldn't ever really be *that* bad.

I moved into her place not long after her arrest, which worked out great for my parents because they were then able to lease out the cabin to hunters.

That next spring, after all of the countertops and paint colors were chosen, Sunny, Andy, and I moved into the new farmhouse. *Our house.*

While I'd helped my contractor where I could, I knew it would go faster with a professional, and the construction quality was much better than what I was capable of. We even built a handful of extra rooms in the basement of our huge garage where Sunny moved WDKR and finished work on her studio. As it turned out, the signal was even stronger at our new home on the hill, and she had lots of extra space for musicians to come and record—something they'd normally have to drive hundreds of miles away to do.

Watertower Records already had two bands planned for summer sessions. I was so proud of her.

I ran two marathons that spring and had another planned for the fall, in which Sunny was actually running half. She'd started training with me every morning after Nashville. She sprayed herself down with a lethal dose of bug spray and swore at me the whole time, but she did it until it got easier.

Those were the things that rushed through my mind as she came out of our bathroom wearing a white lacy dress, very similar to the one she wore on our first date, only longer and fancier. She looked gorgeous, and I felt underdressed in my trousers, even with the button up shirt and tie.

"Are you sure this is okay?" I asked, looking down at myself. She stepped up to me and ran her hand over my stomach.

"We're getting married under a tree house. You don't need a tuxedo to stand in a field, Rhett."

She was right. After all, she usually was.

"You just look so damn *good*, Sunshine," I said against her lips as my eyes darted to the clock on the nightstand checking the time. Then, I closed my eyes and took in the moment.

She was the first to pull back. "If you keep kissing me like that we're going to be late for our own wedding. The whole town of Wynne is waiting for us." Her words said one thing, but her mouth was proving them wrong as she then kissed me back in earnest.

"To hell with it. They've waited this long, what's a few more minutes…"

She smiled against my lips.

"Come on," she coaxed. "It's about damn time we go become Rhett and Sunny Wilbanks."

Acknowledgments

As always and above all else, thank you to every beautiful reader!

Beyond that, it feels like these acknowledgements are becoming a little repetitive. My teams, my support system, doesn't change much—which is something I take pride in. Maybe we're on to something?

To the beta readers, launch team members, my editor, cover designer, formatter, proofreaders, and all of the bloggers who support me and this community—thank you.

To the writer's groups who act as sounding boards and provide me with so much entertainment, friendship, and resources—thank you.

To my Take the Bait honeybees—thank you will never be enough.

To my family, friends and my husband, I love you.

For more on M. Mabie, please visit mmabie.com